Stiff Hearts

A Novel

by Jo Deniau

DORRANCE
PUBLISHING CO
EST. 1920
PITTSBURGH, PENNSYLVANIA 15238

The contents of this work, including, but not limited to, the accuracy of events, people, and places depicted; opinions expressed; permission to use previously published materials included; and any advice given or actions advocated are solely the responsibility of the author, who assumes all liability for said work and indemnifies the publisher against any claims stemming from publication of the work.

Excerpt from "Burnt Norton" from COLLECTED POEMS 1909-1962 by T.S. Eliot. Copyright © 1952 by Houghton Mifflin Harcourt Publishing Company, renewed 1980 by Esme Valerie Eliot. Reprinted by permission of Houghton Mifflin Harcourt Publishing Company. All rights reserved.

Dorrance Publishing Co
585 Alpha Drive
Pittsburgh, PA 15238
Visit our website at *www.dorrancebookstore.com*

ISBN: 978-1-6376-4153-8
eISBN: 978-1-6376-4790-5

To my late mother, Floralee,
for whose most precious secrets
I have been the guardian.

Stiff Hearts was inspired by my mother's adventures, and mishaps, in mid-1950s Greenwich Village. This book is the culmination of a long journey my friends and mentors have shared with me at critical milestones along the way. I want to express profound gratitude to my beloved niece, Kim Palmer, for her astute editorial contributions to this labor of love. Deepest appreciation to New York actor and friend Marylou DiFilippo for hosting me so I could explore Greenwich Village and find the bar where my mother worked. Hearty thanks to my college pals Virginia Hacker and Christine Carlson for not only being beta readers but also for exploring the Indianapolis Union Station with me. To gifted artist Deborah Madigan, who has believed in my novel from its beginnings at Ohio University, I am wishing "the sun, the moon, and the stars." To my dear Boulder-years soul sisters Patricia Peluso and Karen Anderson, and to my Philadelphia cohort Genevieve Judge, I extend thanks for your valuable insights. Fond regards to Latvian American documentary filmmaker Egija Hartmane-Salem ("Kokle") for providing the traditional song "Jauns un Traks" ("Young and Crazy") for my book. I am indebted to the late novelist Daniel Keyes, my instructor in Graduate writing classes, who championed my initial short story, "In Gillian's Room," and to novelist Mary Robison for her assistance as my thesis director with the novella my story became. Finally, I offer warmest praise to every sentient being who has managed to melt a stiff heart.

Time present and time past
Are both perhaps present in time future,
And time future contained in time past.
If all time is eternally present
All time is unredeemable.
What might have been is an abstraction
Remaining a perpetual possibility
Only in a world of speculation.
What might have been and what has been
Point to one end, which is always present.
Footfalls echo in the memory
Down the passage which we did not take
Towards the door we never opened
Into the rose-garden... .

Chapter 1

Gillian Jeanne Rysert stood with her suitcase at the bottom of the front porch. She wore a simple white cotton dress, hemmed almost to mid-calf, which she had made on her mother's old Singer sewing machine. Her voice seemed to come from far back in her throat. "Did you ever love me?" Gillian asked her mother Hannah. It hadn't come out the way she planned: "Love me?"

After spending twenty years without her inner power emerging, she had felt a little force break through her inertia. She could chart her life in moments when she had failed to *will* such strength. She could also weigh her failure by the look in her mother's eyes.

Gillian's mother was no longer a beauty, especially when she wore no makeup, as now. Yet the cadences of her alto voice were strangely hypnotic. Hannah was still a "perfect thirty-six" but in a five foot tall body. Gillian couldn't help contrasting her own longer limbs, her slim body, her smaller breasts, with her mother's compact ampleness. And she wondered if her face powder covered the freckles that had embarrassed her since early childhood.

Hannah twisted one lock of her fervid red hair. For a moment, her face softened, and she looked like she might say something kind for a change. In an instant, however, something tamped out whatever warmth might have tried to escape from the prison of her heart.

1

Hannah patted a spit curl coiled at her temple while she stared at Gillian. As if rendering the finale of some other conversation, she sneered: "The apple doesn't fall far from the tree." Her mouth bent up in an ugly, pinched little squiggle. Hannah grasped the back of Gillian's neck briefly before releasing her to scuffle toward the curb in her worn flat shoes. The weight of Gillian's dilapidated suitcase made her list to one side.

Gillian hadn't bothered to protest her mother's mean reference to Gillian's late father. She was proud to be like him. She looked back at her mother. If only Hannah had come down from that porch, stood beside her, wished her luck, asked her to write. Gillian searched Hannah's face for some trace of regret, or even *regard*, that might be hidden behind those light repelling eyes. This scorn, this control, darkened further now. It reached Gillian's most vulnerable self. The one who felt worthless.

The lilting call of a male cardinal filtered through Gillian's congested brain. "**Suh**-weet. **Suh**-weet. **Suh**-weet. **Suh**-weet. **Suh**-weet." There was no answering call. *Like me*, Gillian thought, *he is alone. No matter how beautiful he is. No matter how sweetly he sings.*

Hannah noted Gillian's absorption in the cardinal's song. Her seaweed-green eyes glittered. Gillian observed that her mother's eyes shot out little slivers of ... *envy*?

A taxi pulled up to the curb, where Gillian now stood. "Miss Jillian Rysert?" the cabbie inquired.

"It's 'Gillian', with a hard 'G'," she said.

In the back seat of the cab, Gillian took off her jacket. She had sewn into the lining of her handbag some crisp hundred-dollar bills. These funds were the remainder of her inheritance and what she had managed to save from her earnings at Woolworth's. When the taxi reached the end of her street, Gillian felt her limbs no longer belonged to her. She imagined herself falling in a downward spiral. The last thing she saw before she *died* was her mother's ossified visage.

ST. LOUIS UNION STATION: 1936

One Saturday morning, when Gillian was seven, her father Chester took her to the St. Louis Union Station. She had expected wall to wall people, but Chester told her that since the second war ended and so many drove cars now, the numbers of train passengers had diminished. He guided his daughter through the station's grand hall, which was the main waiting room. Gillian found the sixty five foot, barrel vaulted ceiling remarkable. In contrast, she was disappointed that there was no wrought iron chandelier. According to her brochure, the once glorious chandelier had housed three hundred and fifty light bulbs.

"In the last war," Pop said, "they took out the chandelier for its iron. In the midway they also scavenged the wrought-iron gates from the platform." He clenched his right hand. "Iron is like a man's fist," he said. "That's what a man can depend on, no matter what."

Gillian knew her Pop's statement required no response. She was again thinking about the vacant spot where the chandelier once hung. Still, she was glad its beautiful glass prisms and ornamental wrought iron were captured forever in her brochure. On the brochure's back panel was a color photo of the imposing, triptych like Allegorical Window. It was made of Tiffany glass.

Chester rubbed his sore leg. "In the midway, you can still watch trains come and go," he said. "I want you to see something."

Gillian pointed at the color photo of the Allegorical Window. "And this?"

"In a minute. I promise," Chester said. "Close your eyes." He led his daughter past the oyster bar within a majestic, vaulted archway made of Guastavino tile. "Just stand here and listen."

Gillian loved every adventure her Pop shared with her, and so she happily waited for today's surprise.

His back to Gillian, Chester stood more than a dozen feet away, by the other side of the arch. When he spoke in a whisper, his words echoed back to Gillian.

Chester was up to mischief: "Your mama has a rod up her ass," he said.

"Pop! Hush! Gillian whispered fiercely. "Someone might hear you." But no one did, for this was the famous Whispering Arch. Gillian surveyed the Whispering Arch and felt satisfied that it was safe to play this telephone game with her Pop. "Mama's heart is a chunk of ice," she said.

"Aw, come on," Chester replied. His voice travelled neatly to his daughter from across the arch. "You can do better than that."

"Her heart is a headstone," Gillian said, expecting to laugh. Instead, she started to cry, noisily. As usual, she had no hanky, so she wiped her nose on her forearm.

No one except Chester heard her voice, and he rushed to take her hand. "Here's my handkerchief," he said. "Now I want you to see something wonderful."

"Okay, Pop."

"Why do you look down so much?" Chester asked. He piloted his daughter back to the station's entryway and pointed at the Allegorical Window. "Look up," he said.

The Allegorical Window rose above them. It was adorned with more stained glass than Gillian had ever seen in one place. This was a thousand times better than church windows. "What does it mean: 'Allegorical Window'?"

"What does it say in the brochure?"

"It says the window 'depicts the three main train stations in the U.S. during the 1890s'."

Father and daughter stepped back to get a better look.

"That Tiffany glass is hand cut," Pop said. "I've never seen such sublime craftsmanship!"

Gillian let her eyes absorb the color of each section.

"See how serene 'St. Louis' looks in the middle?" Chester said. "And see how 'New York' and 'San Francisco' are turned toward 'St. Louis'? That means our station is the best."

"Which one's New York, Pop?"

"The one on the right. That's the East," Pop said.

"They're all women! How can women be cities?"

"Aren't ships she's?" Pop said. "Why can't train terminals be she's too?"

"Maybe someday I'll take a train from here to New York City," Gillian said.

"I don't see why not," Chester said.

"Could I get there without changing trains?"

"Most of the time in life you can't just jump from A to Z. First you have to go from A to B," Chester said. He hugged his daughter. "Take it one step at a time, Darlin', and you can't go wrong."

ST. LOUIS UNION STATION: 1949

Gillian entered the St. Louis terminal and set her suitcase down. Exhausted by the residue of her mother's venomous presence, she took a deep breath. She was running late, and so she would not have time to stop and admire the Allegorical Window. Because she and her Pop had not toured the entire passenger concourse those many years ago, Gillian was disoriented. She squinted at the other passengers, who were checking baggage, and buying cigarettes, newspapers, and sandwiches. She raced through the terminal elbows-in and made herself as small as possible until she could proceed along the midway. She noticed details that had escaped her when she and her father were last here—like the wooden, church-pew-like seats that stretched the length of a huge waiting area. Gillian headed toward an unoccupied seat in front of the Pennsylvania Railroad gate for Train 319. Soon after, passengers swiftly queued up, and so she joined them. It was 12:30 p.m. Her train was late.

At last a man in uniform opened the restraining gate, and all the other passengers streamed around Gillian. It felt as if they were going *through* her. She decided to match their pace or she would get trampled and never make it to New York. Per the timetable, the whole trip would take twenty hours, twenty-five minutes.

It was the first time Gillian had seen a train this close-up. The matte black undercarriage of mechanical parts and the bulky steel girders that loomed above her seemed all of one piece. The collected achievements of America's best mechanical engineers concentrated here in sheer mass. Almost every outside component of the train was metal: corrugated steps, handrails, door frame, and carriage couplings.

In contrast to all the metal, there were delicate ivory colored roller shades, pulled down at each small passenger window. After passengers had settled in their seats, however, the shades slid up one by one. From inside, people looked out at the station, at Gillian and at the few others still waiting to board. Most of them looked happy.

A little tug tractor with pudgy wheels pulled along an old baggage cart that looked to Gillian like a miniature parade float. Its wheels and high push-bars at either end were made of iron. Piles of luggage were secured by thick ropes to the small, rectangular flatbed.

A dark skinned porter jumped down from the train and approached Gillian. He looked resplendent in his deep gray trousers, matching military-style hat, and white coat. He asked Gillian where she was bound.

"New York City," Gillian said.

He smiled. "Just that one bag? If you show me your ticket, I'll take you right to your coach."

"Miss Jillian Rysert," he said.

"It's Gillian. With a hard 'G', she said.

"Better come aboard now, Miss. We're about to depart," the porter said. "Remember to change trains in Indianapolis."

"So I can go from A to B?" she joked. No one heard. She decided not to take her seat just yet.

Gillian's train lurched and then slowly, noisily, began to move forward. Gillian clutched her handbag to her side. When the train had scarcely rolled a city block out of the station, Gillian found the observation car at the end. She pressed its heavy metal door open, grasped the stout brass handrail and looked at the complex spaghetti-strand tracks that converged here. The feeling of all this metal fortified her and bolstered her resolve to transform her life. Gillian's train headed out of town. The engine cried a haunting WHOOO-WHOOO. Scenery flew by like the life Gillian was leaving behind.

Chapter 2

ST. LOUIS: 1934 – GILLIAN'S FATHER

Chester Rysert was the first American born male of three generations of German glass blowers, glass flatteners, and glaziers. He loved all glass, any kind. Colorful or plain, decorative or household. He had not pursued glass making, for after he was honorably discharged from command of his unit during The Great War, his heart pumped too little juice to support such a dream. Nevertheless, knowledge of the trade flowed in his veins.

Every morning Gillian watched her Pop work up a lather in a little crucible-like ceramic bowl with his Fuller anthrax-free badger hair shaving brush. He would dab generous amounts of foam all over his face, upper lip, and neck. This made him look like Santa Claus. The even, gliding strokes of his straight razor mesmerized Gillian. Her father clearly had mastered this daily ritual. Still, Gillian feared that he would cut himself. When he finished shaving, he smelled of Lifebuoy. He would say: "I have to sit down now. My leg. The shrapnel."

Even if it was morning, he would go to the icebox, take out a bottle of Old Grand-Dad Kentucky bourbon whiskey and pour his first drink of the day. Long ago, Gillian had forgiven her father for drinking away the pain of his war wounds. Her mother had not. All her life, Gillian would see Chester through her child eyes. Unlike Gillian's mother, her father treated her like an equal, he showed her how proud he was of her. Most important, he had always been kind.

Every time Chester spoke of the last war, Gillian was too young to share either his horror or his pain. And yet, she felt a little guilty when he told his stories, without understanding why. She allowed herself only slight awareness of her own physical body, and this general somatic oblivion felt safer. Any passion she let arise from her came mostly through her eyes, her vision. Like the penetrating colors of stained glass she remembered from the rare times they attended church as a family. On Easter and on Christmas Eve.

In the daytime, Chester hung out at the American Legion Post, where he sat and drank with his friends. Those other survivors were the only souls who understood what Chester had endured. Most evenings, Gillian sat beside Chester on the couch while he read the St. Louis Dispatch or shared wildlife photos printed in National Geographic. Hannah hissed that Chester looked at National Geographic only for the photos of "bare breasted 'Ubangi' females," but Gillian didn't care if her Pop did look at those pictures. It was more important that, every night, Chester tucked her in bed and kissed her forehead. She knew he loved her.

When Gillian was eight years old, a cataclysmic family event occurred. Her baby sister Letitia was five months old when she died of the croup. Instead of taking Letitia to the doctor again, Chester insisted that they use an old back country remedy: half a teaspoon of kerosene to break up the mucous in the baby's throat. "Ninety percent of the time," Chester said, "it works." But it didn't work. Gillian heard her mother scream, "The ax has fallen at the root of the tree!" The entire aftermath blurred.

After Lettie's burial in 1937, Gillian's parents separated. Chester moved to a small one bedroom apartment downtown, and Hannah let Chester see Gillian once a week. Every Friday afternoon, Gillian perched on the window seat and peered out the living room bay window of their rental house. She waited for Chester to drive up to the curb in his 1934 dark blue Chevy three window coupe. The car had cost him nine hundred and ninety one dollars. A fortune in those days. Gillian often wondered if her Pop had funds hidden in his mattress or in some faraway bank account, because even with paying maintenance for Gillian and Hannah, he did quite well financially. On the surface it looked like Chester lived on half his monthly disability payments and proceeds from the sale of some ancestral land in Pennsylvania his father had left him.

Finally, Gillian's parents divorced in 1941, and Hannah began to work full-time at Kline's. There, Hannah was one of the garment workers who sewed the new "junior" size clothing for women who were "just past the age of indiscretion." Having graduated high school herself, Hannah insisted that Gillian focus on her studies. In addition, Gillian learned how to sew her own clothes. Now a pre-teen, she took note that fashion for the hip young woman meant a higher bust pocket, and a smaller and shorter waist.

By the time Gillian was fifteen, she and her father had the same routine each visit. They started with an early dinner at Pope's Cafeteria, topped off with a chunk of apple cobbler. Next they took in a movie at the glitzy Fox Theatre. So many flashy white bulbs, with lights running and down in a series. They lit up, then dimmed, one by one.

"St. Louis Woman" was one of Gillian's top-three favorite movies. Chester had wanted to go because of the film's football theme, but he promised his daughter that it was also a musical. From then on, Gillian dreamed of being as glamorous as the film's blonde soprano, Jeanette Loff. She envisioned herself singing for a nightclub full of men in tuxedos. She was truly her father's child: good in school and at exploring the world through magazines and the cinema.

Until late at night, Gillian and her father listened to such programs as "The Lone Ranger" on Chester's Crosley cathedral tube radio. All the while, Chester would sip his whiskey. Several rounds. When it was time to turn in, Chester slept on the couch and gave Gillian his bed.

After one of those movie nights had ended, Gillian wakened to what sounded like a hound dog moaning low. She crept out to Chester's living room, where he sat on the couch. He held his face in his hands and sobbed. Gillian had never heard a man cry. She felt the modulating timbre of his weeping would cut her in half.

"God took my Lettie," he said. "My baby girl."

"I know, Pop."

Another night, out of the blue, Chester asked Gillian to tell him about her high school friends. Even though she knew he was not criticizing her, she felt reluctant to tell him the truth: She had no friends.

"Not even girlfriends?"

"Nope."

Chester asked her why.

"The girls are all so mean," Gillian said. "And I guess I stink at small talk."

Chester chucked his daughter under the chin and said, "They're just jealous 'cause you're so pretty."

I am pretty, Gillian thought. *At least I have that.*

"And what about ... the boys?"

Gillian didn't want to tell her Pop that often she faded into the woodwork on purpose. The truth was that she was afraid of all her classmates. However, she had a crush on her math teacher. "There's no one special," she said to her father.

Chester looked concerned, but he didn't push Gillian further. "What are your plans after graduation?" he asked.

"I'll probably try to get a job at Woolworth's."

"Ever think of going to college?"

"Never," Gillian said.

"I would help with the money ..."

"It's not that," Gillian said.

Chapter 3

INDIANAPOLIS UNION STATION: 1949

On her train ride from St. Louis, Gillian had managed to sleep through four station stops, but the slower, louder chugging of the engine woke her. The train's brakes screeched as they approached their next stop: Indianapolis Union Station. It was 4:50 p.m. and Gillian had successfully progressed from "The Gateway to the West" to "The Crossroads of America." Gillian's train glided smoothly into the Indianapolis Union Station's elevated platform outside the terminal.

Gillian was eager to stretch her legs, get a newspaper and use a real ladies room. She entered the grand hall. When she reached the high, arched entryway, she could see smaller, ornate arches on her right. The grand hall was two blocks long, eclipsing that of the station in St. Louis. Three stories up, its vaulted ceiling curved like the inside of a huge, upside-down Viking ship, and inlaid in its entire length was dramatic stained glass. Gillian sighed, for the long center strip of hundreds of yellow-ochre and yellow-gold squares of glass in the ceiling made her long to share it with her father. The glass squares let sunshine flow across the ribbing of the massive red brick arches, down the tapered stone walls and onto the inlaid terrazzo floor.

Mysterious energy drew Gillian's attention to a mammoth circular window high up on the north end of the grand hall. The late-afternoon light emanating from the window was muted, but she would still be able to make out the symmetrical tracery that radiated from the center. She wanted to get a closer look at the stained glass accenting its geometric details. *Pop would be thrilled with this*, she thought.

Gillian was so jazzed that she decided to buy her first pack of cigarettes. She found a vender, whom she asked, "What's your mildest cigarettes?" She checked out the round window again. From here she could see more of the colors ornamenting the designs.

"Just starting?" the vendor asked. "Chesterfields. I saw Bing Crosby in an ad for these, so they must be okay. Just one pack? And take some matches too."

Gillian liked the little gold coronet in the Chesterfield logo.

"Need any magazines for your trip?"

Gillian looked over the array of magazines and selected *Vogue*. She pointed to the iron railed balconies that flanked the round window. "Could you please tell me how you get up there?" she asked.

"To the Rose Window? By the way, there ain't no roses in it. 'Rose window' is a style." The vendor swept his arm across Gillian's view of closed doors on a landing to the right of the rose window. "Those are railroad offices, and they don't like passengers being up there." Then he grinned. "But take these stairs behind me," he said. "Good luck!"

Gillian couldn't believe how nice these people were. Such a contrast to her mother and others she knew in St. Louis. She grabbed a brochure about the Indianapolis terminal and climbed to the second, and then third floor. She tried to make herself invisible when she moved past the offices of railroad personnel. Their privacy was secured by white pencil pleated curtains, shirred to café rods at the top and bottom of their windows.

Gillian sneaked by the PRR Sales Office and Penn Central Indiana Division Office. She felt triumphant when she rounded the corner, for now she could stand in front of the rose window and view it up close. This window dwarfed her. As the newsstand vendor had said, no stained glass roses adorned this window. Instead, intricate *art deco* patterns in a series of concentric circles brought Gillian's gaze quickly to the center. There were orange rust, light blue, and pale yellow stained glass designs.

She lit her first cigarette and inhaled way too much smoke. Her resulting coughing fit drew the attention of someone in Office 207. The man who came out smiled but said, "You really can't be up here, Miss. It's just the rules."

"Just one more minute. Please?"

"Okay, but I'll be back to make sure you're gone. And, by the way, the colors change. It depends on the time of day and the season."

This detail made the rose window even more magical to Gillian. She felt happy and surprisingly complete. *"Look up," her Pop had said.* She closed her eyes so she could feel the colors on her face and body. She immersed herself in them. The colors meant something, but she wasn't sure what. Again, she longed for her father.

Gillian was jolted back to Earth by an ear-piercing, echoing announcement that the Spirit of St. Louis train to New York had arrived at the station. She looked over her shoes on each granite step so she wouldn't trip. She vaulted down two flights and ran along the passenger concourse. She wasn't even winded when she got to the gate for Train 30. Other passengers already had crowded in front of it. En masse they climbed the stairway that led to their waiting train.

When passengers reached the platform, porters took their bags and the passengers prepared to board "The Spirit." The caption for the train photo in Gillian's brochure touted the sleek and streamlined Spirit of St. Louis as Tuscan red with yellow "whisker" pinstripes and a black roof. To Gillian, Tuscan red looked a lot like cocoa brown. The logo of this Pennsy Railroad diesel locomotive was red and yellow.

Gillian found a porter, who said, "Your compartment is right behind the dining car. That can be good or bad."

"I'm sorry. What?"

"It'll be convenient, but it gets loud at night sometimes. You know, people get tipsy and the volume goes up."

Gillian relaxed and smiled. "I sleep like the dead."

The porter continued, "You're gonna love our twin-unit Pullman dining car. It's air conditioned. Can you believe it? And, along with our regular crew, we have a barber, electrician, stenographer and a lady's waiting maid."

Gillian grasped a steel handle at the right of the steps. "Oh, I don't think I'll need any of those people, but thanks anyway." She pulled herself up by the thin handrail and onto the corrugated platform between two cars. She followed the porter, who made a sharp left turn in the narrow entryway.

"The Spirit is part of our famous Blue-Ribbon Fleet, Miss. We'll take good care of you."

This train was so luxurious that it had no coach seats. It was all-Pullman, which meant Gillian could sit comfortably and read her magazine and sleep in a bed. She thought she might be able to get some rest after the stop in Newark, Ohio, because her train was not scheduled to arrive in New York until just after 9:00 a.m. the next morning.

Now in her own Pullman car, Gillian took off her shoes and sat near the window. She thought: *I am on a train. I have left Miz-zur-ah. I will be in New York City tomorrow. I must be nuts*! Because she could not relax, sleeping was out of the question.

Well out of Indianapolis, the flat terrain seemed to zoom past Gillian. There would be many more stops throughout the night. She smoothed out her rumpled train ticket and reaffirmed the date stamped on it: Friday, April 15, 1949. The numbers wrinkled and blurred and swam. Already fatigued, Gillian had no idea she was crying with relief.

The next morning in Manhattan, Gillian asked her taxi driver to take her to the YWCA on Lexington and 53rd. The cab's seat covers smelled musty, even with spring air blowing in through the half-cracked windows. Gillian's eyes felt scratchy after her long train journey from St. Louis. Traffic noises sounded distant and lulled her while she listened to the meter click off dimes. She let herself go with the motion of the cab, which passed banks, department stores, bars, and food markets.

Gillian got out at the Y, a neo-Roman building. After her long train ride, her dress stuck to her body. Her feet were sweaty. Dampness had spread under her arms, staining her slip. *No one sees my underwear anyway*, Gillian thought. When she got a decent job she would buy a new slip. No. She would buy two: a new white one and maybe a pink one. No. A black slip. Something made of the new nylon, lacy and black.

The widowed matron, Mrs. Stewart, led Gillian down a long hallway, past a common bathroom that had three shower heads and two stalls. She showed Gillian to her tiny room. "You are lucky," Mrs. Stewart said. "Most girls share a room with three others. We don't serve meals here," she said. "You'll have to eat out or order-in Chinese," she added over her shoulder.

Gillian's new quarters included a small, chipped chest of drawers, a narrow cot-like bed, and a writing table with desk lamp. There was no window. She squealed when a cockroach the size of a cigarillo stub darted from under the drab woodwork and leapt onto her bed. A familiar depression crept in. She felt she had no home, and this convent-like cell was no home away from home.

I must be nuts, she thought. She had hated most of the years with her mother, and yet she suddenly was afraid she had made a huge mistake. She was thinking this escape from Hannah was actually too much too soon. But there was no going back now.

Chapter 4

In her bones, Gillian believed that some young man would be her salvation. So had her mother Hannah and Hannah's mother before her. Some, as yet faceless, man would prize them as rare birds, feed them and coo over them. This magical he would love them superbly, forever. Perhaps he would even restore them to wholeness. No ancestor in Gillian's maternal line held this belief as a hope in her heart; rather, it was a need imprinted in their brains like an addiction. However, after they had married, their longing turned to gall. A gnawing lack began to starve their speech and harden, oak-like, their more feminine instincts.

Gillian's own love void could have been filled if she had seen love-light in Hannah's eyes. Or if Hannah had held her so close Gillian could absorb the scent of her mother's freshly washed hair. Or if Gillian could have felt herself sinking into the comfort of Hannah's soft bosom. But Hannah could not bestow upon her daughter the love she herself had not had. And so it was, back through Gillian's entire maternal line.

Gillian was nearly breech born, and Hannah had periodically reminded her of this: "I remember how painful your birth was," or "The midwife had to reach inside me to save you. Can you imagine my agony?" The truth was that when Gillian's head crested and proceeded out of her mother's body, the midwife noticed the umbilical cord partially encircled baby Gillian's neck. As the birth progressed, the midwife successfully turned Gillian's upper body away from the cord.

Gillian once responded to her mother's familiar barrage by asserting, "Maybe I wasn't supposed to live." In the background of her mother's life, Gillian often wished she hadn't been born. Since the day Gillian began to talk, she also wished Hannah had not named her Gillian, with a hard "G". It was as if Hannah could not bestow softness, in any form, on her daughter. Throughout her twenty years, Gillian had done everything she could think of to please Hannah. Nothing worked.

Whenever Hannah spoke of her own childhood near Poplar Bluff, Missouri, Gillian suspected that her mother's people lived a peculiar, kinesthetic existence. They obeyed some extreme physical code or language of survival transmitted by the blow of a fist on someone's jaw or by the boom of a gun firing far away in the woods.

The distress of knife-edge survival had molded each previous generation of Hannah's female bloodline. They rarely spoke but struck out often. Physical harm deposed honest family talk. Early on, Gillian had learned it was reckless to counter her mother with spoken words, for Hanna had answered such "insolence" with a brisk slap across her daughter's cheek.

As if to excuse her temper, Hannah regularly chanted her credo: "There's been a lot of violence in our family. You can tell yourself, 'I'm not going to lash out at my kin', but you do." Gillian believed herself to be a mutant who had inherited nothing from her mother.

Gillian's emotional poverty was as cruel to her as was the physical violence her mother had endured during her own childhood in the Ozarks. What they both lacked was a mother's nurturing. What each sought was escape from that deprivation. They were convinced that marrying and changing locations would somehow make them whole. This was Hannah's legacy, and this she passed on to her daughter: making sure nothing but anger moved them.

When Gillian turned five, she wanted to be "a big girl." She and Hannah stood at the corner of a busy St. Louis crossing, and Gillian refused to take her mother's hand. It had turned out to be a fatal breach of their already shaky bonding process. Gillian was punished for this act of independence only by her mother's look of contempt when they reached the other side of the street. Hannah had worn the same expression every day since then. The woman seemed to believe Gillian had chosen not to be her daughter.

Also at five years old, Gillian had almost drowned, and this memory made her know she couldn't count on her mother to protect her. It was summer. Gillian had slipped off the third step of someone's swimming pool in St. Louis. Bubbles sprayed upwards in the water. She felt blanketed and sleepy. She sank to the bottom. Suddenly someone pulled her up by her hair, like a water lily by its roots. Pain stabbed fast-fierce in the tiny places inside her lungs. Whoever dragged her out of the water now laid her on a baby blue bath towel. The outside world finally came into focus, including several people Gillian didn't know. They looked profoundly concerned. Where was her mother?

Gillian had been too young to realize what happened to her. She had perceived only bubbles and green water. It felt soothing to float and then sink down, down in the water surrounding her. There was no fear, no pain. Afterwards she lay on that blue towel beside the teenage girl who had saved her. Hannah stood next to Gillian just long enough to see she was okay and left immediately with some man. This so chilled Gillian that her heart dropped like a stone.

Early on, Gillian began to think of Hannah as her wicked stepmother and herself as Cinderella. Gillian was so small that she had to stand on a chair to wash the dishes in the evening. Because the light over the kitchen sink had a low-watt bulb to save money on electricity, Gillian couldn't see the dishes very well. As a result, she missed a few spots, and Hannah spanked her once for each dirty dish she found in the rack. Gillian also had to take the garbage can out to the curb every Monday night for trash pickup the next day. In the summertime she was covered with mosquito bites by the time she dragged the can out and ran back into the Ryserts' rented house.

Neither Gillian nor Hannah consciously chose this chasm between them. The death of Gillian's baby sister, "Lettie," had stolen what was left of Gillian's hope. It had convinced Gillian of the world's unfairness.

Gillian never saw her sister dead, but what she imagined haunted her. An image of a small, glowing, stiff body, suspended in a black sky. The most horrible part was the baby's face. Crystal drops lined her closed eyes and her old-woman smile was set hard into her features. The baby' smile could paralyze. Hannah had worshipped "Lettie," whom she considered to be her real daughter. Gillian knew she could never have Lettie's magical ability to be loved.

19

Gillian often imagined how if she had a child she would be kind to her. She wouldn't hit her, no matter what. She would praise her, gently brush her hair and ... love her. Most of all she would talk to her. It would be like she was her own mother, loving herself and watching herself grow up. This other new Gillian would be her own resurrected Self.

And yet when mothers dragged their unruly children into Woolworth's, scolded them for touching "things" and for other acts of disobedience, the fine hairs on Gillian's arms stood up. On edge, she knew those mothers would slap their children and make them scream. When children made those sounds, it was like rusty weathervanes screeching in shifting high winds. Whether emitted from tantrum or gaping need, those shrill cries made Gillian go emotionally fetal, to collapse inward, to protect her nerves.

Gillian rarely cried after her eighteenth birthday. It was the last time her mother could call her a crybaby. She forbade herself all painful feelings and gave full permission for her brain to control her behavior in every upcoming situation. Gillian had ceased to allow herself the "self-indulgence" of feeling sad, for she perceived that grief weakened her. If she showed Hannah how she felt she would hand her mother another victory. Gillian had long since decided to give her mother the same nothing her mother gave her.

Gillian had escaped from her mother before it was too late, before St. Louis could imprison her for the rest of her life. She resolved not only to make the best of her decision to come to New York but also to thrive here. More importantly, she would find someone to love her. She thought, *Here in New York I can drink a whole bottle of wine if I want to. I'll meet a kind young man, have dinner with him, sneak him to my room. We'll talk about life. He'll come to know me inside and out. He'll love me for who I am.*

Chapter 5

Gillian sat at a table in the corner of a crowded cafeteria. With the hope of changing her luck, she had just had a stylist cut her hair. It was now chin length and capped around her head and face. She was only drinking coffee. Her eyes were puffy red from crying for the first time in years. She had exhausted herself with fretting about whether she had been rash in coming here. So far, Gillian had failed to find work because she couldn't type or write in shorthand. She was keenly aware that her savings were dwindling, and sleeping in that sterile, claustrophobic room at the Y made her feel even more alone and afraid.

Across the room, Dolores Valencia was enjoying a grilled cheese sandwich and cream of tomato soup. A back slidden Catholic, Dolores Valencia was warm and generous. Emotionally astute. Dolores' short, curly black hair was styled in the latest fashion: a "fringe coiffure." Her mild facial features made her look boyish. As now, when she was intensely interested, her sable colored eyes looked huge.

When she noticed Gillian, she crossed the room to her. Dolores' outfit was Greenwich Village stylish, assembled mostly from current fashion and touches of thrift store classic. She wore a thin, short sleeved white cotton top. The high waist of her cocoa colored, wide legged rayon pants was nipped in, accentuating Dolores' hourglass figure. "I hope I'm not intruding," she said, "but are you all right?"

"I'm so em-bare-ussed," Gillian said in her Midwestern twang. Her chin and lower lip began to quiver, and she put her hand over her mouth. She was about to throw up.

"Oh, God," Dolores said. "Okay. Tell me your name. Mine's Dolores. I love your haircut, by the way."

Gillian told Dolores her name, that she was from "Saint Louie," and blurted, "I'm living at the Y until I can find a job."

"Come on. Nobody really lives at the Y!"

Stunned, Gillian just stared at Dolores.

"Don't mind me," Dolores quickly added. "I meant why not the Barbizon? It's classier."

"It was easier to set this up through the Y in St. Louis," Gillian said. "And it's way cheaper than the Bar-bi-zon."

"I see. That does make sense. So you're from Missouri."

Gillian nodded. Dolores' manner, even her appearance, soothed Gillian and calmed the emptiness inside.

Dolores had the least "baggage" of anyone else in New York whom Gillian would meet. If Dolores sensed discord in a relationship, she questioned *herself* first. She pondered whether *she* had blundered. Had she made the other person uncomfortable? Because of her keen emotional intelligence, the only feeling that disempowered Dolores was temporary confusion. "By the way," she said to Gillian, "you'll get used to New Yorkers. The way we talk. When my mother Lorna wants me to really listen, she starts with 'Dolores'. That's a statement. In New York, *everything* is a statement. **Cottage** cheese. **Green** beans."

Gillian cheered up. "Where I'm from, everything is a question," she said. Cottage **cheese**. Green **beans**."

"I heard that," Dolores said. "Anyway, Lorna says, 'Never trust anyone west of Weehawken or south of Coney Island'. She thinks home is a stretch of eight blocks on the Lower East Side because she can buy or see anything she wants there. Once, when a friend of hers moved *ten* blocks away, Lorna cried, 'I'll never see her again!'"

Gillian tried not to look at the remaining half of Dolores' sandwich.

"Have you had lunch?" Dolores asked. Without pausing, she handed Gillian her plate and said, "I shouldn't eat that much cheese anyway. Want it? It's okay."

Gillian gratefully took the delicious toasted cheese sandwich half and ate it slowly, so she would not appear too greedy.

Dolores took out a round powder compact and looked at her nose in the mirror. "Got too much sun on my rooftop last weekend," she said. "I think my nose is molting. If my nose sheds one more time, I'm afraid I'll find a nude lobster under there. Or maybe a bare crayfish."

"In Miz-zur-ah we call them 'crawdads'," Gillian said. "Did you know you can eat them?

"I didn't know," Dolores said. She refrained from commenting on Gillian's pronunciation of "Missouri."

"You can only eat the tails because even the big ones don't have much meat on them."

"Do 'crawdads' live in caves?" Dolores retorted.

"No," Gillian replied, sincerely. "They live in creeks." She pronounced this *cricks*. "In streams with rocks and rushes. They hide where it's gooky. You get a deep-fry basket—."

"Hideous creatures," Dolores said.

"If you put the basket in front of them," Gillian continued, "they go backwards, lickety-split. So you have to put the basket behind them and then get their attention by moving a big stick in front of them. That scares them and they jump backwards, into the basket. You have to lift them out of the water fast, or they can hop out."

"Not very sporting," Dolores said.

"Oh, a lot get away. Sometimes when you poke around in their nests, in the rushes, a whole half dozen big fat ones take off backwards and get downstream half a mile before you can even blink."

Dolores took a big drink of water. "I want to get this over with," she said. "How do you ... kill them?"

Gillian brushed her bangs out of her eyes. "You throw them *live*, head-first into boiling water. *Live*. That kills the feeling in their antennas right off so they don't feel anything."

"Oh," Dolores said. "I heard lobsters scream when you boil them. I can't eat lobsters anymore because I keep seeing their eyes. You know. How they're at the ends of those skinny little tubes. When you are about to toss them in, they beg you to spare them. Did you ever see a live lobster up-close? They look like enormous insects." Dolores put her compact away. When she leaned toward Gillian, a gold pendant and chain swung out from the top of her blouse.

Gillian asked to see the pendant.

"It's Saint Anthony," Dolores said. "A gift from my boyfriend before—."

Gillian's face held a question. It was not the one Dolores answered.

"You must be a Protestant. He's the Saint of lost causes. Or even lost people. But to continue, I moved to the Village in 1944, before the last war ended. Because of Lorna's maternal brainwashing, I felt like I had moved half-way around the world. I was eighteen when I made my break. 'Dolores,' I said to myself one afternoon, 'You must say goodbye to your childhood. See the world.' Lorna called me daily to make sure she still had a daughter. 'Come back home. You are not eating,' she said. I told her of course I wasn't eating. But the truth is, Lorna knows how much I love food. In my fifth floor walkup I also live on port wine and my six thousand books of literature, but there *is* a deli at street level, below my flat. Luckily, I work at Brentano's. It's a wonderful book-store on Fifth Avenue. I get a discount."

Her voice timid, Gillian asked Dolores why she called her own mother "Lorna."

"Because that's her name."

Not used to repartee, Gillian said, "Oh."

"Really it's because I like her. I don't call her Lorna to her face though. I think of her as a person, not just as my mother."

"I wish …" Gillian blurted, "I'd rather not tell you about *my* mother, though."

"Why not?"

Gillian leaned forward a little in her chair. "Well, I wish my mother was a real mother. Instead of such a person."

Dolores nodded.

"No. I mean it. Obviously Lorna loved you as *your mother* first. I needed my mother to be my mother. She never was, so I don't like her as a person." Gillian looked confused about what she had just said.

"I thought you didn't want to talk about her."

"I didn't. I guess I did. My mother is the whole reason I left Miz-zur-ah two weeks ago," Gillian said, and she recounted her last morning in St. Louis.

Dolores paused before asking whether Gillian wanted to talk about her father.

"Maybe. If we get to know each other better."

Dolores touched Gillian's forearm. "I hope we'll meet again," she said. "I know where to find you. At the Y. But I must get back to work now. I'm glad to have met you."

"You too," Gillian said. She had never had a close female friend. Now Gillian hoped she would see Dolores again. She felt better than she had before her Pop died.

THE YWCA: A WEEK LATER

It was Saturday night, and Gillian sat in a sewing classroom inside the YWCA. She and other residents occupied a row of Singer electric sewing machines. Little golden lights illuminated the threaded foot of each machine. Gillian was loop stitching the hem of a cobalt blue, high-waisted, gathered skirt.

A dark-skinned woman to Gillian's right blurted, "I can't even thread it! I'll never be able to sew."

"Here. I'll help you," Gillian said. "It just takes practice." She talked the woman through the process and watched her every step of the way. "Now try it again," she said.

"You a teacher?"

"I just know how to sew," Gillian said.

"Thank you kindly."

"Sometimes you just need a friend to help you out," Gillian said. She went back to her machine.

The front desk matron came in. "You have a visitor," she said to Gillian. "A 'Dolores'."

"Could she come in here?"

"I'll get her," the matron said.

Apparently, Dolores had been waiting right outside the door. She came in straightway. She looked a little sheepish, in contrast to how Gillian remembered their first meeting. "I would've called you first, but I came over on a whim," Dolores said. "I see you're keeping busy." About Gillian's skirt she said, "That is beautiful."

"Sewing's about the only thing I have in common with my mother," Gillian said.

"Did your mother teach you?"

"Yes." Gillian said. "I'm glad to see you!"

"May I sit with you a while? You can keep sewing."

"That's okay. I can finish it tomorrow." Gillian switched off her machine light and smiled at the dark-skinned woman, who was happily sewing her own skirt. "Let's go to the lobby and talk. It's comfy out there. Much better than my room."

Dolores asked Gillian to join her for brunch the next weekend.

Chapter 6

EAST VILLAGE: SATURDAY, MID-MAY 1949

Dolores stood up and waved Gillian over to her table at the Minetta Tavern. Today she wore black gaucho pants, a pale lavender blouse and cutout T-strap heels. With her figure, Dolores could wear just about anything and look fabulous. However, Gillian had yet to see her friend in dungarees or saddle oxfords. "Have any trouble getting here on the subway?" Dolores asked.

"It was kinda scary," Gillian said, "but I was really looking forward to seeing you again."

A waiter approached and asked for their orders. Gillian stared at the brunch menu.

"I recommend the Minetta French Dip," Dolores said. "And two side salads," she said to the waiter. "Mine with French Roquefort. And yours, Gillian?"

"Just oil and vinegar But this is way more than I can afford right now," Gillian whispered to Dolores.

"My treat," Dolores said. She asked the waiter to bring coffee, "right away, please."

Tears formed in Gillian's eyes.

"Don't be sad, Gillian."

"I'm not. It's your kindness."

Dolores looked away. "I've been trying to get my psychiatrist to believe I have not one drop of maternal blood in my veins," she said. "Meeting you has forced me to overcome four years of analysis!"

For a moment, Gillian questioned Dolores' motives. She then wondered how she could repay her new friend.

"You're talking to someone who has read *Jane Eyre* three times," Dolores said. And *Ivanhoe*. You know: books about heroines and heroes."

"But I can't let you pay. I'll call the waiter back and order an appetizer instead."

"Maybe you could sew a Patrón De Costura Bolero shrug for me."

"That should be easy," Gillian said. She took a sip of water. "Is it expensive? Seeing a psychiatrist?"

"Way-too. And, if you're wondering why I see a shrink, maybe someday I'll tell you."

After brunch at Minetta's, Gillian followed Dolores up the third of five flights and panted. "How do you do this every day?"

"I used to be afraid," Dolores said. She phrased her words with each step she achieved: "that the authorities … would knock on my door. Shout 'Nuyorican!' and ask for my papers. 'Nuyorican' means 'New York Puerto Rican'."

On the fourth floor landing, Gillian stopped to rest.

They headed up the last flight, and Dolores continued: "I like it that people don't just drop in to a fifth floor walkup, which guarantees that they'll call first."

Both women entered Dolores' apartment. "Please. Make yourself at home," Dolores said. She gestured toward her long, maroon couch, then went into her tiny kitchen. Gillian could see all the way through to a small room with a loft bed that had a steep wooden ladder affixed to the front. It reminded her of the top half of a bunk bed. Clothes hung underneath the bed on the back side, and Dolores had placed a small writing table and folding chair under the ladder on the near-side.

Gillian continued to survey Dolores' apartment, which was filled with books. Several on the coffee table beside Gillian were open, with little strips of paper that marked specific pages. Each book lay on top of another.

From the kitchen, Dolores said, "Want some wine? I keep only port. Those expensive dry wines taste like mouthwash."

"That would be fine," Gillian said. "You've read all these books?"

Dolores came in with the port and two small wine glasses. She offered Gillian a cigarette from a black enameled box full of filter-tipped Viceroys and took one herself. She lit them both from a heavy cut-glass table lighter and took a deep drag.

Dolores decanted the port and said, "When I moved to the East Village, it was just before the Allies drew up the Armistice." She took a sip and sat down next to Gillian. "I didn't want a boyfriend, and I wasn't seeking a big career. I wanted solitude."

"You don't want a boyfriend? Why not?"

Tears filled Dolores' eyes and she looked away. She composed herself and said, "Let's just say that the wars took a toll on all of us."

"I'm sorry if that was too personal," Gillian said. "Maybe, when you get to know me better, you will feel like telling me more." Gillian felt worn out, but she was also fascinated. Besides her Pop, no one had ever talked to her like this. Conversing in an interesting way. She accepted more port from Dolores. "I think maybe I'm looking for—."

"True love."

Gillian wondered how Dolores could know this about her so soon. It made her uncomfortable. "You were telling me about when you moved here," she said.

Dolores continued: "I spent whole evenings reading books like *Middlemarch*. Pages of endless paragraphs, where you must track … They're called subordinate clauses."

Clearly, Gillian didn't understand.

"Okay, so reading all those clauses is like movement. To move forward, each depends on the one that precedes it. It's like what I believe dancing would be like, though I'm not sure. By the age of six I was an outcast from the Latin community because I couldn't dance!" Dolores started her own second glass of port. "My classmates at St. Michael's danced on hot summer nights to Victrola music. I told them I dance in my head. They weren't impressed. They stuck their tongues out at me and winked at each other. Now, just out of spite I think, I don't dance."

"I only like slow dancing," Gillian said. "You just follow the guy."

Dolores took her shoes off, stretched her legs out and put her feet on the coffee table in front of her. "I've been wondering … how's your job hunting going?"

"I've broken in a new pair of shoes," Gillian said, "while interviewing for jobs I know I'll never get."

"Like what?"

"They only want secretaries or office girls or stenographers. I don't type, and I don't like people ordering me around."

Dolores' laugh was rich, earthy. "I'm with you on that," she said. "Just tell me what you want, and then let me do it myself."

Gillian was sleepy now. She placed her empty glass on the only part of the coffee table where there were no overlapping books and half-lay back on the couch. In a poster on the wall above Gillian's head, Carmen Miranda grinned from a daffodil yellow background. Carmen's lips were outlined in deep, glossy red. A complex woven necklace spread downward from her chin to her collarbone.

Dolores got up. "Why don't you stay over? Sleep off the port? Tomorrow's Sunday. I'll let you get a word in edgewise. I promise."

The next morning Gillian quietly found what she needed to make coffee. She tried to see if Dolores was awake, but her new friend was out of sight at the back of the loft bed. As the percolator started bubbling on Dolores' two-burner stove, Dolores turned over and looked at Gillian as if she had never seen her before. "I am just remembering that I asked a veritable stranger to stay overnight," she said, her morning voice a little gritty. "But maybe you aren't a stranger anymore."

Gillian looked down. "I guess I had too much wine. I'm sorry."

Dolores climbed down the loft bed ladder and came to Gillian. "Don't ever say that again. The moment I smelled coffee, I knew I'd made the right decision to adopt you. It's positively endearing, seeing you there."

Gillian felt better now. "Should we have our coffee on the couch?" she asked.

"Perfect," Dolores said. She cleared her books off the coffee table and put them on the floor beside an already overflowing bookcase.

Gillian asked, "What did you do with the lamp?"

"Oh, it's still plugged in, just back there," Dolores said. She indicated the floor beside the bookcase. "Aren't we lucky? It's cooler today than usual. Usually I have to vent the hot air out of here just to get to eighty-five degrees. This coffee is delicious!"

"Do you work on Sundays, Dolores?"

"No, thank God."

"Can I wash my blouse? It's the best I brought with me."

Dolores smiled. "I'm fighting a maternal urge to wash it for you myself," she said. "It's silk?"

"Yes, which means it'll wrinkle."

"An iron, my friend. No problem."

Gillian turned on the cold water in Dolores bathroom sink and added some Lux Liquid. "This is the cleanest, whitest rubber sink stopper I have ever seen," she said.

Dolores told her the stopper was new.

Without really looking at her blouse Gillian rinsed it repeatedly. "I feel much better now," she said.

"For what?"

Gillian giggled like a child and shook her sun streaked hair out of her face. "I am too stupid," she said, "and you are so kind."

Dolores looked at Gillian now with special fondness. "Picking my cheap cafeteria was very bright of you. Crying openly in an eatery full of callous New Yorkers was very brave," she said.

"In Miz-zur-ah people are like sleepwalkers," Gillian said. For a moment, she became distracted by the thread of a cobweb that intersected with a dart of sunshine in the corner of Dolores' living room. "I knew that in New York everything would be alive," she continued. "And it is! Light, color, sound. Millions of people; the noise of traffic, shoppers and street vendors."

"You talk like a painter I know," Dolores said.

"I want to keep learning all I can until the day I die," Gillian said.

Dolores took Gillian's blouse and said, "I'll hang that out to dry for you. Then I'll go downstairs to the deli and get us toasted bagels and cream cheese."

Gillian looked perplexed.

Dolores was now dressing. "You've never had a bagel and cream cheese." It was a statement.

Gillian poured herself more coffee. "Dolores? Sometimes I wish I could just speak from my heart. You know? I mean, I don't talk the way I feel."

"I understand. After breakfast I'll walk you to the IRT."

Chapter 7

It was Friday night. Another of half a dozen overnights for Gillian at Dolores' apartment. This time, however, Gillian had been gone the entire evening. She tried to be quiet, but she woke Dolores up at 2:30 a.m. by stumbling over a settee that was a little too close to the door. "Nuts!" she whispered.

From her tiny back room, Dolores groaned and leaned over the side of her loft bed. "How was your first night as a bar maid?"

"Swell," Gillian said.

"Gee whiz," Dolores replied, with only slight sarcasm. "I can't believe you found a job. In the Village, no less."

"Thank you for letting me stay here again."

"You should ditch the Y and move in with me," Dolores said.

"I need to use their sewing machines a while longer," Gillian said. "Go back to sleep." She brushed her teeth, stripped to her underwear, and lay down on Dolores' couch. In minutes, she was asleep.

The next day, Gillian and Dolores headed down Christopher Street. Gillian said, "It's friendly here, don't you think?"

Dolores looked up at the sky. "Everyone's an optimist when the sun's shining," she said.

When Gillian turned right on Seventh Avenue, she stopped.

Dolores bumped into her friend. "Why are we walking this way?"

"I want you to see Harry's Bar."

Dolores looked offended. "For God sake, why? It's Saturday. Remember? It's your day off. We should go back to Washington Square and see some art exhibits. Then we can go down to MacDougal Alley."

"For just a few minutes, Dolores. I need to get my pay from Harry."

"But we haven't had lunch yet!"

Gillian walked so fast now that Dolores had to skip beside her. "We're almost there anyhow," Gillian insisted.

Dolores stopped abruptly in front of Levitsky's Treasure Trove, where sunlight glittered in the display window. "Look at that pin," Dolores said. "It's a 'D', like 'Dolores'. Bet it's not real gold, though. Let's go in here, just for a few minutes."

A little sign read "Ring Bell," but when Dolores pushed the black button, the bell made no sound. The two women could see inside the store through a small window in the middle of the door.

There were cameos, costume jewels supported by heavy prongs, a three-strand pearl necklace, a gold and black enameled cigarette case, and hand painted porcelain thimbles. At one side, peacock feathers protruded from the top of a tall clay urn. At the other, a variety of wooden canes stood in a painted ceramic umbrella stand: an ivory walking stick, crowned with a carved fist, and a mahogany one sculpted to look like a dragon's head. A third was wrought in metal and topped with a woman's naked glass torso. Its head had either been severed by accident or never was part of the original design. A set of art deco frosted glass nymphs, arms uplifted, formed two candlesticks. In the marbling of an ebony cigarette holder, inlaid with mother-of pearl, the sun made minute rainbows.

A middle-aged woman stared at Gillian from among mounds of old clothing piled on the counter. Her name was Mabel Levitsky. She had swept back her long, wavy hair, which had a wide, perfect white stripe, zigzagging up and back from each temple, like Elsa Lanchester's in "The Bride of Frankenstein." Mabel's wavy hair was secured with thick tortoise shell combs that barely kept the strands under control.

A large ashtray on the countertop overflowed with cigarette butts. From one pile of clothing Mabel picked out a pair of black dress trousers with a red satin stripe down the outside of each leg. She pushed these under another stack.

34

Then she looked up at Gillian and Dolores, who remained outside the store. Mabel wove through the used treasures that lay all over the floor and yelled through the window: "You want something specific?"

Dolores pointed at the cigarette holder in the window. "Look, Gillian. Isn't that just the cat's meow?"

"You can come in," Mabel said through the closed door. She pressed a button by the door frame and the lock clicked open. "People usually just want to browse," she said. "You can see that's impossible. I got to do inventory and there's no one to help me. No one appreciates what a job this is. Look at all these things! People think they can walk in and pick around until they find something. I have no *tshatshkes* in *my* store! I got lovely things from all over the world and I don't want them pawed over." Behind the counter on the wall was a certificate that proved Mabel had the right to conduct business here.

Mabel's bearish black eyes rolled sideways and then came back to Gillian's left hand. "You're not married," she said. "My husband Viktor came back from the first war an amputee. All he does now is watch WJZ-TV, from Roller Derby to The Life of Riley." Mabel riffled her fingers along a piece of curtain lace. "And he smokes those stinky cigars like there's no tomorrow." She glanced at a curtained doorway at the rear of the shop. "Don't get married," she said.

Dolores suppressed a laugh. "Why?" she asked.

"Why *do* girls get married? Because they think it makes them somebody. Before the first world war I was 'Mrs. Viktor Levitsky, wife of the Acme Ball Bearings plant manager', only he ain't no plant manager no more. And, see? His disability compensation only goes so far."

"Didn't you and your husband get married because you were in love?" Gillian offered.

"Oh sure. But 'being in love', that's all in the mind. I did what every girl dreams of. Listen, Honey. Romance makes you an addict. When you're in love, you're wonderful and he's wonderful, and together you're something the world's never seen before." She peered into Gillian's face. "You don't have a boyfriend right now, eh?"

Gillian paused. "Well …"

Mabel just kept going. "When things change, you are both stuck with who you really are. But a woman can't do without men *all* the time because they can make you feel so good. When you're young and pretty you can have a lot of fun. Yeah. They're real romantic at first, but that ends as soon as the babies come along."

Dolores had edged back near the door.

"You have children?" Gillian asked Mabel.

Mabel flung a long piece of lace over her shoulder. "Of course not," she added. She folded the lace in thirds.

"Then how——."

"You think you have to go through something to know if it's true? I could've got into some nasty scrapes at your age if I had tried all the *shtopn* that crossed my mind."

"How else can you learn?" Gillian asked.

Mabel grabbed Gillian's arm. "Don't step on those beads!" She sighed. "Okay. You wanted to see what?"

"The cigarette holder."

"A gift for someone," Mabel stated.

Gillian hadn't thought of that.

Mabel frowned. "Because it's not really right for your face. But you smoke. Listen, that piece is worth a lot. If you can't use it, it's too expensive. You know what I mean? You got to know what you're gonna do with things before you own them. Take for instance, I got bolts of fine laces. Only *I* know exactly what kinds I have in here and how many yards they are. I know in this stack I got four eighteen inches and in that stack I got lengths of thirty four and a quarter inches. People have actually asked me to cut pieces off!"

Gillian wondered how anyone could know what was in the Treasure Trove without excavating it. There were fine antiques as well as pure junk. Gillian assumed Mabel had found today's outfit inside her shop: a black-feathered boa over a tight black dress. And red house slippers. These, and her manner, showed Mabel could be unyielding. "I admire your window every afternoon on my way to work," Gillian lied.

"I do put a lot of my best things out there," Mabel said. She noticed Dolores standing by the door. "You want something from the window too?"

Someone knocked on the door.

"Why *can't* they ring the bell?" Mabel shouted. "This is not a browsing shop," she told the young woman who wanted to come inside. "If you don't know what you want, you can't come in," Mabel yelled. The girl quickly changed her mind and disappeared.

Gillian told Mabel she tended bar at Harry's.

Grunting, Mabel sat down on a low step stool. "Not on weekends," she said. She picked up a square glass table lighter that looked like a saltshaker. "When you're old enough to look back on your life," she said, "you will see you made a lot of your mistakes on purpose."

Gillian nodded as if she understood.

"You'll see you're exactly where you planned to be. Oh, none of that's clear in your head when you're young. You just sort of turn into the person you made up all along the way." She asked Gillian how long she had lived in the Village.

"Not very long," Gillian answered.

Mabel continued: "Then *you* don't know it's one of the few places where it's safe to be yourself. But you can't say just anything to just anybody around here. The Village is full of secrets. If you don't have any, you're not really a local."

Dolores looked bored out of her mind, leaned against the door.

A little man wearing a gray Fedora knocked twice, and Mabel pressed a button under the display countertop. Dolores had to jump back when the man burst right in and made a beeline to the back of the shop. Mabel told him she would be with him "in a minute," and he went through the curtain. "That's not my husband," she said.

Mabel took Gillian by the wrist. She said, "Look at this Belgian lace over here. Do you know how many *years* it took someone to make one square foot of this? Why, *I* wouldn't have time to repair one square inch of it. That's how long it would take. And people want to buy some pretty lace to hang in their window! But here's something that gave me hope. A woman came in here a couple months ago and ordered this for her daughter's wedding dress. Do you have any idea how much lace that took or how much it cost?"

Gillian just wanted to get away from Mabel. "Well, I guess——."

"No, you do not have any idea," Mabel said. "They don't make this anymore. It's a miracle there's any this fine left."

Gillian shot a look of "help me!" at Dolores.

Dolores said, "Won't you be late for work?" (She emphasized every word.)

Mabel looked toward the curtain that separated the shop from the Levitskys' small flat, consisting of back rooms of the Treasure Trove. "You don't work today," she said to Gillian.

"I still want the cigarette holder, please," Gillian said.

"I'll give it to you for the price of a decent lunch: seventy-five cents."

"Seventy five cents," Gillian said. She gave Mabel three quarters.

"Make a nice gift for someone," Mabel said.

Gillian joined Dolores out on the sidewalk. "Wow," Gillian said. "What a character."

"You'll learn that the Village is the safest place to be a character," Dolores said.

Chapter 8

HARRY'S BAR

The bar where Gillian worked looked deceptively small from the outside. It was summer. However, the door to Harry's Bar, painted dark green on both sides, was closed. This lent a little mystery to the place. The room itself was a long skinny rectangle, and the walls were paneled in real wood. Against the outside wall, there was room for only half a dozen square tables. Harry, the owner, had covered these with green-and-white-checked oil cloths. Through a high window, morning sunlight poured down on two tables nearest the door. Suspended along the outside wall above each table was a light with a Hunter green shade made of fiber glass and resin parchment.

Facing outward from the corner of the bar's inside wall there was a deep-rose colored cigarette vending machine. Since over the counter cigarettes cost only twenty three cents, some tobacco companies put two pennies in each machine vended pack. Old Gold came with little coupons smokers could collect like "green stamps" and turn in for merchandise. When customers put in a quarter for most brands, however, they got a pack of twenty cigarettes and a full book of matches worth a penny.

Catty-corner to the cigarette machine at the open end of the bar was a Wurlitzer jukebox, which played both sides of twelve 78 rpm records. The bulging legs of its "Mae West" stand and housing were made of ornately carved wood that matched the hue of Harry's bar top. Gracing the rest of the Wurlitzer were colorful etched glass panels: a male harlequin on the left side and a pinup posing female on the right. Silk-screened mirrors of Asian art deco motif sectioned the top. All were illuminated by fluorescent lighting from inside the Wurlitzer.

Harry kept some older hits like "Blue Skies" on his jukebox, but he also made sure to keep his other selections up-to-date. Once a month, a record distributer checked twenty four tally boxes inside the jukebox to see which records people selected the most. When he updated the song selection, he made sure that Harry's five favorite oldies were included in the twenty four vinyl records on the Wurlitzer.

Light shone through a stained glass window behind the expanse of a heavily varnished oak bar. Just below this window there was a high, backlit cabinet with glass doors. On the shelving stood tall, thin shot glasses, brandy snifters, and glassware for aperitifs, wine, champagne, and beer. Unquestionably, this bar was both impressive and cozy.

Harry had hired painters to layer the bar with varnish, both to beautify it and to preserve its past. To Gillian, scratches on the wood in the middle of the bar formed a design. A slightly curved and cross hatched line inside two large, severely bent lines were dug hardest. When Gillian was in a good mood, the lines looked like two people kissing through a screen door.

Dozens of indentations pitted the front of the bar as well. Legend had it that underworld thugs had riddled the bar with bullets during their hit job on the owner. This episode resulted in an abrupt change of management. After that, the bar was dubbed "a bucket of blood," but no violence had occurred there once the perpetrators were sent up the Hudson River to Sing-Sing Prison.

Here, Gillian worked five days a week, from five p.m. to two a.m.

Gillian half sat on, half leaned against, a bar stool and gazed up dreamily at the stained glass window behind the bar. "Look up there, Dolores," she said. Inlaid in blue opaline glass were the words In Memory of Olive E. Nichols. "Olive's name makes the colors more intense, don't you think?"

Dolores looked both confused and annoyed. "Why?" she asked. "The woman's obviously dead. And I bet she wasn't even a drinker. Gillian, why *are* we here on your day off?"

Gillian pointed. "Those colors are alive when the light shines through them. I can feel them." Gillian was affected by more than the colors themselves. It was the way they moved and changed and whirled, as if they were alive. The colors meant something to Gillian that she could translate only through the feeling at the top of her head, and on her skin. The colors lifted her out of the density of her body and allied her with her father's passion for glasswork.

Dolores sighed and perched herself on a bar stool beside Gillian. "Okay. So, what *do* the colors mean?"

"They mean," Gillian said, "everything."

Dolores rolled her eyes up at the name Olive E. Nichols. "Oh, that does explain it. Yes, I think the colors are pretty, and I realize I must be crass to not understand the allure. But it's a church window. In a bar for God sake." She looked hungrily into her shopping bag.

Intense blue, yellow, red, and green made soft geometric shapes on Gillian's face. "It doesn't matter where this stained glass window came from. It's the colors that are important. What I feel. This stained glass window reminds me of someone dear to me." Gillian turned back to Dolores and gently removed her friend's hand from the shopping bag. "I promise we can go in a minute."

But then the door opened, and a man in his early thirties came into Harry's Bar. He was only of average height, about five foot nine, but quite attractive. Jānis Dieviņš had emigrated from Rīga, Latvia, nine years before. A university graduate, he was like other such Eastern Europeans: cultured, well-mannered, and charming. Only his intimates knew Jānis' inner feelings, which he hid beneath his impeccable demeanor. Even his own compatriots found him to be a bit of a cipher. They had witnessed Jānis' more than occasional, sometimes unexpected, eruptions of passionate discourse. When he felt no respect for someone, he let him know it, for he did not suffer fools gladly. If someone made the mistake of *pretending* he knew a lot, Jānis could go volcanic, quickly dispatching that fool with a piercing glance or word.

Something about the way Jānis moved made Gillian forget Dolores and Harry's Bar. It even made her forget the pleasure of the stained glass window's colors on her face. Upon entering, Jānis had looked immediately at Gillian. He sat down at a table across the room and continued to stare at her.

Gillian wondered how he could be so bold and yet not offensive. How a man could have such black hair and such light skin. His tan slacks and soft yellow shirt emphasized his pallor. She thought, *He isn't poor*. Neither did he look

41

like a businessman or a tourist. The man was still appraising Gillian, and she observed him just as boldly. Why didn't he ask for a drink? Where was Harry? Gillian could not stop looking at his hands. *Not the hands of a laborer*, she thought. He had hands like a sculptor's, with strong, graceful fingers.

Jānis took a cigarette from a thin gold case. Fascinated, Gillian watched him put tender pressure on one side of the case with just his thumb. The case sprang quietly open. Then he lifted out a cigarette, tapped it lightly three times on the case and put it between his lips. He lit up with a match from the gilded green "Harry's Bar" matchbook on his table. Gillian hoped Jānis wouldn't notice her staring at his mouth. She measured the texture of his lips, felt a pleasant shock inside.

Jānis missed nothing. "I have no lighter," he said, "because I do not like the smell of lighter fluid." In the empty bar, Jānis' voice carried across the room and went straight to Gillian.

There, Gillian thought. That this man was repelled by lighter fluid made perfect sense to her.

Now she felt Dolores' elbow dig rudely into her side, which abruptly ripped her attention from the most delicious feelings she had ever experienced.

"Svengali," Dolores said, her voice accusing, unpleasant. She was a bookworm. She had a quip for every occasion.

Gillian did not get the reference. She stared at Dolores. "What?"

"Nothing," Dolores said. A new expression creased the corners of her mouth.

Gillian was unaware of the effect she had on these New Yorkers. Back in St. Louis, her mother had instilled in her a distorted projection of who she really was. For a moment, this innocence rendered Gillian guileless regarding Dolores' motives. Then Gillian reacted from some level of rebellion, even with slight malice, for the timbre of Dolores' voice held an echo of past criticism. She couldn't decide if her friend's Svengali statement bore a hint of jealousy.

Gillian could feel Jānis still *inspecting* her. She said to Dolores, "I'm getting him a drink."

Dolores' face flushed. She turned away and looked straight ahead at the liquor bottles that lined the top of the long console behind the bar. "It's your day off, Gillian."

"We can go in a few minutes," Gillian said. Then she addressed Jānis: "Would you like a drink?"

Jānis seemed as if he were deciding something. Then he glanced around the empty bar. "Do you work here? Am I too early? I can wait." His voice landed pleasantly between tenor and baritone, nuanced with a foreign, slightly nasal inflection.

Gillian couldn't place his accent. "As a matter of fact," she said, "I do work here."

When Jānis smiled, Gillian somehow knew this was as rare for him as it was for her. She could sense he was quite serious. Embarrassed, she said, "Actually, it's my day off. I don't mind, though." *Now* this *is a magnetic man*, she thought. Gillian loved his voice. She loved the way he held his cigarette like it was a woman's fingers.

Jānis smiled again.

Focused on Jānis' mouth, Gillian could see that his teeth were perfectly aligned, very white. It reminded her of Pepsodent commercials.

Harry, the bar's proprietor, came in from a back room. About five feet seven, Harry was middle-aged, pudgy, and bald, except for a few long strands, fortified with hair oil, which he had combed across his shiny pate. He looked like a man who had grown comfortable with being "an average Joe." His hands were also ordinary. Not coarse, not exactly refined. He wore slightly scuffed, size nine brown shoes. Harry was a beer drinking bar owner who could talk to almost anyone about almost anything. He was a rolled up shirtsleeves, white socks man: good-natured, generous enough, unheroic, and completely dependable. "Here to pick up your wages early?" he asked Gillian. Harry handed Gillian her money in cash.

"Thanks," Gillian said. She gave Harry her own scarce smile. "I wondered where you were."

"It's been slow this morning," Harry said, "so I was catching up on some paperwork."

Dolores introduced herself and extended her hand to Harry while Gillian appraised Jānis.

Harry wiped the bar down for a minute. Then he asked Jānis if he wanted a drink.

Jānis left his table and came up to the bar. He moved smoothly, with a masculine grace, like a leading man in a slow motion film sequence.

Harry winked at Gillian and said, "We could use a little extra excitement around here today."

Dolores looked away, said nothing.

"And so young and pretty," the foreign newcomer said. "Your girlfriend is very smart, I'd say."

Dolores colored.

Harry scrutinized Dolores' face. "You okay?"

Now Jānis stood so close to Gillian that she could smell his skin. No cologne. Just light musk with an herbal trace. No. Maybe his scent was of light musk with a trace of fresh cut pine. Normally she would have recoiled when a stranger, especially a man, came this close to her, but he seemed familiar. It was as if they had known each other for a long time, perhaps even as children. However, it was obvious to Gillian that this man was born far from St. Louis.

"I have not come here before," Jānis said. "I almost walked past this green door. Something made me hear 'Try this'. Maybe I do not want to drink. But to be here makes me feel happy." Though he included Harry and Dolores in his speech, his gaze held only Gillian's.

Gillian felt stupid, suspended. She could think of nothing to say. Absorbed in his sensuous aroma, she merely looked back at him. His voice affected her like the colors. She was also intensely conscious of the way he looked at her now, his eyes the color of gunmetal. They glinted, silvery, under the soft curves of his eyebrows. She decided he could *feel* her when he appraised her. That was the effect of his look.

"My name is Jānis Dieviņš," he said.

"**Yah**-niss **Dee**-uh-veensh," Gillian repeated.

With a broad grin now, Jānis pressed his hands together: "Bravo. You have a good ear, Miss. Miss—."

Dolores had slid down her bar stool as if she were dismounting from a dressage horse. She stood, shopping bag in hand, and waited impatiently for Gillian.

Gillian heard herself give Jānis her first name and thought how odd and far away her own voice sounded. She continued to show her regard for Jānis. "And this is my friend Dolores."

"God," Dolores commented under her breath. "'Some Enchanted Evening'," she added. Her sarcasm apparently had been wasted on Gillian. However, the tilt of Jānis' mouth revealed that *he* got Dolores' reference to the love song in the new Broadway show, "South Pacific."

44

Because Gillian had seen no Broadway plays, she missed Dolores' sarcasm. Gillian said to Jānis, "We have to go now," but she didn't move. It was as if she now stood a few inches above the floor. Gillian was sure Jānis would look away before she did. He didn't.

Still behind the long bar, Harry was masterfully developing an Italian hoagie. He piled on ham, capicola, provolone, shredded iceberg lettuce, pepperoncini, thin tomato slices and Italian dressing.

The ever hungry Dolores fixed on Harry's hoagie like she was going in for a kiss.

With his mouth full, Harry said. "The window's nice today, eh?"

Jānis smiled again and pointed at the stained glass. "All those colors are *moving*. I can feel them on my skin," he said to Gillian. As if he had just that moment thought of something, he added: "Please excuse me if I am being, as you say, forward. Friends tell me I am too honest. Is that bad?" He opened the beautiful cigarette case in the same elegant way as before and offered Gillian a cigarette. Below the short filter, encircling the cigarette, was its brand: *Gitánes.*

Imported, Gillian thought.

Jānis said, "Do you smoke?"

"Only for show," Dolores chimed in. She stood behind Gillian now, had her friend by the elbow.

Gillian asked whether Jānis' cigarette case was gold. When she realized she might have been rude, she said, "Oh. I'm sorry I asked that."

"Yes gold," Jānis said. "I wish gold is what *I* am. But I am not yet gold. My *māte*, my mother, gave this to me before I got on the ship from Rīga nine years ago. This is in *Latvija*."

Gillian let Jānis' voice go all the way through her. She boldly admired his long fingers. *I bet you* are *the same as gold*, she thought. He felt to her as warm as a bath, as rich as liqueur. "Yes. I'd like one of your cigarettes," she said. But she didn't want him to light it and was surprised that he seemed to sense it. It was silly, but she wanted just to hold it. Maybe sneak away with it and keep it in a box in her room at the Y, where she could take out the elegant cigarette and look at it whenever she pleased.

Jānis put the gold case back in his pants pocket. "I would like to see you again," he said to Gillian. "May I call you?"

Gillian needed no time to decide. She noticed Harry's attention on her and felt Dolores grip her elbow even harder. "Yes," she said.

Jānis felt his shirt pocket for a pen.

"Here." Gillian said. "I'll write my number on this cocktail napkin." Without asking Dolores, she wrote down the number of the payphone outside Dolores' flat. But the phone's outside in the hallway, " she said. " Someone else might answer."

Jānis smiled and said, "I'll send you a *thought* telegram before I ring you."

Gillian just stared

Now downright sullen, Dolores peered into Gillian's face.

Harry noted, "We have a special on Mai Tais today."

Jānis bowed slightly, took his hands out of his pockets, and left Harry's Bar without looking back.

Dolores pulled Gillian toward the door. "Art exhibits," she said. "MacDougal Alley. Your day off."

Chapter 9

The bright light outside Harry's Bar dazed Gillian. If she hadn't felt the cigarette in her hand she would have thought she had hallucinated her encounter with Jānis. She wanted to open the green door behind her to see if that classy man, textured in light from the stained glass window, was still there. But Dolores gripped Gillian's arm the way men do when they aim women's bodies where they want them to walk.

Gillian shook off Dolores' grasp. "What's wrong with you?!"

"I get grouchy when I'm hungry," Dolores said.

This lame excuse did not fool Gillian, who was both vexed with her friend and excited about the young man.

"You don't have a phone," Dolores said, "and the number you gave that guy just made me your answering service."

Gillian felt only a little guilty. Jānis might be her salvation, and she would let nothing stop her from meeting her destiny. "What other choice did I have?"

"You could have said to call you at the bar," Dolores said, pouting. "Anytime during your work hours."

Gillian could see that connecting with Jānis might jeopardize her friendship with Dolores. In fact, she believed Dolores was jealous of him. She admitted to herself that she did want to keep the love of this smart, passionate woman. Dolores had rescued her from loneliness and from an alien city that threatened to turn Gillian back out in the cold. For the time being, Gillian couldn't see that her friend was just being protective. She said nothing.

They now headed for MacDougal Alley. Dolores clutched her shopping bag close to her side and Gillian looked up between the buildings at the sky. They passed the IRT station near the corner of Christopher Street and waited to cross in front of a shop called Village Cigars. One story high, vertical signs along either side of the doorway advertised: CANDY & SODA and CIGARS & CIG-ARETTES.

The door opened inward and a lanky, repugnant man darted out. To Gillian at this moment, the man's skin and clothing seemed all of one piece: His hands, neck and face were a sort of transparent yellow. Beige stripes ran vertically down his brown shirt like wires. His cream colored pants wrinkled heavily at the knees. He moved lizard like. He spoke in another language and leaped into a Yellow Cab.

"What a lowlife," Dolores said. "Looks like he's been too long on the oolong."

"What?"

"That means he smokes marijuana," Dolores retorted.

Gillian *had* felt an unpleasant prickle on her forearms, where danger always registered like little electric shocks. Of course, it was absurd in this case. That man had nothing to do with her. Normally, one on one, Gillian could tolerate those she thought of as the un-beautiful: unshaven derelicts who reached their hands up for coins, maybe for something else. The ungraceful feebleminded, whose half-perceived realities bounced and flickered on their faces. The insane, whose slights and failings etched terror in, or took life from, their gaze. The re-pulsive man Gillian had just seen made her think of all these unfortunates at once. She also sensed that his ugliness ran deep. She decided that what could be seen of him on the surface was a projection of his entire being. That the *source* of his pockmarked skin, and his reptilian movements, was some grotesque spirituality.

LOWER EAST SIDE ...

Dolores sat in her mother's kitchen. A wooden crucifix hung on the wall above the sink. Displayed on the small dinette table was a cut glass salt and pepper set, which had been a wedding gift in Puerto Rico. The shakers' gold plated tops were slightly tarnished. Dolores' mother Lorna and Dolores were just finishing breakfast.

A more petite version of Dolores, Lorna Valencia had the same ebony eyes as her daughter's, but age and loss had made her eyes appear to have shrunk. Her light olive skin was supple, and her nails perfectly manicured. Lorna's and her late husband, Dolores' father, already lived in this small one bedroom apartment when he was drafted into the service a second time. He was killed in the Battle of Kasserine Pass in February 1943. With her widow's pension, Lorna could live comfortably in her rent controlled apartment.

"Are you loco?" Lorna said to her daughter.

"What's so loco about wanting to help a sweet young woman who's new to the city?"

"Because you know so little about her. And because there are so many like her who are trying to make their way here. Have another quesito."

"Too much pineapple sours my stomach," Dolores said. "She's different, Ma. I don't know. She's not a moocher, if that's what you think."

Lorna covered Dolores' hand with her own. "You know what the Orientals say."

"What?"

"If you save someone's life, you are responsible for them for the rest of *their* life. Did you tell her about Antonio?"

"Not yet."

Lorna held her daughter's hand. "You think maybe you can save *her*, even if you couldn't save him?"

Dolores leaned forward and touched her mother's hair. "After I get off work tomorrow, I'll do your roots."

Chapter 10

YWCA: MANHATTAN

Gillian awakened from a nightmare about the ugly "lizard man" she and Dolores encountered outside the cigar shop. It annoyed her that this creep should invade her blessed sleep and take over her dreams. Why could she not have enjoyed, instead, a rerun of her encounter with the exotic foreigner she met yesterday at Harry's?

It was Sunday and Gillian looked forward to reading her bodice ripping Harlequin romance. She heated coffee in a small pot on a portable plug in hot plate. She opened a white paper bag of croissants she had bought at the end of her day with Dolores. Now that Gillian had met Jānis Dieviņš, the juicy paperback of *Close to My Heart* eclipsed her accustomed reading of the *Sunday Times*. On its back cover the book teased: "There was every reason why Lydia shouldn't have married Chris Stark. She had known him only a few days before they eloped—and the few things she learned about him held no promise for an easy future. A tender and unusual story about a woman who wagers the power of her love against disillusionment."

The texture of the croissant Gillian tasted now was waxy from the cold butter fat that saturated its once crispy layers. Still, she ate it hungrily and began to read *Close to My Heart*:

> *She had seen him first when he came into the dining room to lunch.*
> *He was tall and fair with strong shoulders and a face not handsome,*

but arresting. "I don't want anyone to help me," he said. But she knew that she wanted to help him in every possible way; that she loved him and that he loved her, but that helping was a different matter from just loving someone. He had to learn to believe in himself, to trust her. There was another man who loved her and being married to him would have been easy and pleasant. Only she simply could not do it; she had to find out if her love, in peace, was stronger than what the war had done.

Two more days passed, during which Gillian finished a new outfit she had been fashioning for two weeks. The sailor pants were high waisted, aqua green with flared legs trimmed across the bottom in white stripes. White stripes also ran diagonally down the edges of the large pockets. Gillian had also sewn an overblouse of white cotton with a sailor collar trimmed in middy braids of deeper aqua green. Both the narrow three quarter sleeves and blouse were hemmed wide.

Gillian hung the outfit on a clothes rack in the corner of her room and wondered why she had not heard from Dolores. She really cared more that *Jānis* apparently had not called the payphone outside Dolores' flat. Gillian was revved up further by finishing *Close to My Heart*, and so she called Dolores to ask if she could stay overnight after work. Surely Jānis would call the next day. She wanted to be there if he did call.

Instead, Jānis showed up outside the bar, just as Gillian and Harry were locking up. Jānis hesitated, then said to Gillian, "I know it's late, but are you hungry?"

Harry looked apprehensive. He said to Gillian, "Do you need me to come with you on the subway?"

Gillian heard nothing but Jānis' voice. He spoke of a neighborhood diner, seafood *crêpes* and mimosas.

Jānis unfolded from his wallet the top sheet of his naturalization papers and gave it to Harry. "I risk much in not having this with me," he said. "But I want you to keep it, as you say, 'for ransom'." He looked serious. I will come here late tonight, while she is working, to get it back from you.."

"It'll be all right, Harry," Gillian finally said.

Harry studied what Jānis had just given him. "Okay, then," he said. "Goodnight, young lady. Good night, young man."

Chapter 11

CONEY ISLAND

It was hot and humid. Gillian wore her new outfit, whose large pockets would be perfect for holding any seashells she might find on the beach. When she and Jānis had boarded their train to Coney Island she was surprised at how colorful he looked because, so far, he had been rather solemn. Today he wore a light straw Panama hat with a tri-color band of red, yellow, and blue. His button looped suspenders were barred with navy-red-navy. Immediately after they stepped off the train now, Gillian wished she had worn Bermuda shorts instead of her tent like apparel. She was already sweating from the train ride. She walked with Janis, still feeling the thrill of what he had said at the all night diner a week ago: "I can't get you out of my mind."

A close fitting white tee shirt with a black band around the neck, pocket, and short sleeves, showed off Jānis' fine biceps—especially when he crossed his arms over his chest. This he did every time the two stopped walking. Jānis seemed out of place here. Singular, foreign.

They drifted along the river of beachgoers on the boardwalk. Gillian enjoyed watching the men in straw hats and beach wear. Jānis appraised the women wearing only bathing suits and sandals. They passed a small shop where people got their photo taken and tourists bought postcards to prove they had been to Coney Island.

"Let's take our photograph," Jānis said with an enthusiasm that startled Gillian.

The photo booth was tiny and the couple already inside it were crammed together. The girl sat on the boy's lap. "Not today, okay?" Gillian said. "I don't think I look that great …"

After the other couple had left the booth, Jānis grabbed Gillian's wrist and slipped a quarter in the slot. He pulled Gillian into the booth and closed the curtain. "It will take four pictures," Jānis said. "Ready?"

They looked through a slanted pane of glass, into the mechanism that was about to take their photo.

The first flash caught Gillian totally off guard. She wasn't about to let the machine take another awful photo of her, so she immediately posed like a sexy pinup girl. This made them both laugh just when the third flash occurred. As if on cue, both of them looked serious and sincere for the last photo. Parts inside the processing mechanisms began to swish and grind. Uncomfortable with being crammed in this little booth with a virtual stranger, Gillian squirmed.

Jānis pulled the curtain back. Then he lifted Gillian by her waist and placed her outside the photo booth. When the slightly overexposed, sepia colored strip of four prints dropped into the external receiving slot, Gillian let out a little squeal.

"This is what I was afraid of," she said. She pointed to the first photo of the series.

"But look at the other three," Jānis said. "We can throw the first one away. Then you can choose two. I'll keep the other."

"Which one do you want?" Gillian asked.

"The third one," he said. "Where we are laughing."

"I'm surprised," Gillian said.

"Why?"

"Because you seem more like a serious guy. I think it's the first time I've heard you laugh."

Jānis said, "But that is why this photograph is perfect."

Gillian looked at each photo again. "The one of us laughing. It is a good one," she said. "We both look happy, don't you think? You don't want my pinup photo?"

"I think this is not really you," Jānis said. "But I do like this serious one too, at the end. Here we look like a couple." He then blushed.

Though Gillian found Jānis' embarrassment refreshing, she also needed to set some boundaries for now. She had let this man in with her imagination. She was not yet ready to open her heart to him.

They walked past more shops and eateries. Jānis was especially charmed by kids who sat in miniature red fire engines that circled around a central hub. "Do you like children?" he asked Gillian.

Jānis' question dropped through the middle of Gillian's chest like a great falling icicle. She knew Jānis hadn't meant to accuse her. Yet, she felt ambushed. In fact, Gillian usually kept her distance from children, finding them noisy and … alien. Having been neglected and unloved by her mother, and feeling abandoned by her father, every child had become "other." She had little empathy for, or connection with, them. "Yes," she said to Jānis now. "I do like children." She had just lied. The truth was that she felt indifference to all children, except for the child within *herself.*

However, Jānis appeared to believe Gillian. "That is good," he said.

They stopped in front of a stand that advertised "Hawaiian tropical drinks: 5 cents." Hanging from the thatched roof of the shack like structure were clusters of bananas and pineapples, and coconuts with bright colored, leering faces both carved and painted on them. The place also advertised frozen custard.

Gillian accepted a frozen custard from Jānis and said, "I'm glad you told me not to bother wearing a bathing suit." Prudishly, she hid her mouth behind the piled custard and took small licks while the custard began to snake down several sides of the cone. "By the way, I like your straw hat," she said to Jānis.

In contrast, Jānis freely took bites of his custard and dabbed it off his chin. "I would like to see you in such attire," he said. "However, I knew it will be crowded on the beach. More crowded than this boardwalk. Only inches between a thousand beach towels and a wall of people in the shallow water."

"I'd be afraid to go in the ocean anyway," Gillian said. She felt a little exposed.

Jānis teased her: "No sharks out there … I *think.*" This levity seemed a departure from Jānis' usual formality.

"No," Gillian said. "That's not it. I almost drowned once." In the years since that episode, Gillian had come to see bodies of water as death traps. If she and Jānis walked by the ocean, would huge waves engulf her? Would she disappear, sucked down by riptides? Would she lose this freedom she had fought so hard for?

Jānis waited for Gillian to tell her story. He lit one of his *Gitánes* cigarettes. When Gillian fell silent, he offered her the ignited cigarette and asked: "Are you ready to be completely swallowed by humanity?"

"I guess," she said. But Gillian felt overwhelmed with sensations: people's loud voices, noises of beach buggies and vendors. Even laughing gulls, who relished the occasional tossed bread crusts and French fries. The tinny organ grinder's tune broke through when his red cart passed them in slow motion. While the organ grinder's little white faced monkey held out a tin cup, the spokes of his cart's bicycle style wheels moved counterclockwise.

When Jānis plunked some loose change in the monkey's tin cup, the creature tipped his red fez cap. "I come here," Jānis said to Gillian, "to remind myself of how full of people the world is. I come here to remember it is not just myself, with my past, my worries."

Gillian tried to take in what this man was saying. Still, she felt overwhelmed, and she pressed one of her arms over her stomach. Her entire body seemed to contract in on itself like a clam closing its shell.

Without talking, Gillian and Jānis moved through the midway, past Hyman's Bar & Grill. Soon after, they heard the razor voiced carnival barker: "Freaks from the four corners of the world," he yelled. "Only one thin dime, one tenth of a dollar. See Madame Zenda. Hurry, hurry. Look them over. Marian, the Headless Girl from London."

Gillian looked away, walked faster. "I don't want to see them."

Jānis piloted Gillian behind the crowd that had begun to gather. "Why not?"

"I can't bear to see how hideous they are," Gillian said. "Do *you* want to go in there?"

Jānis looked sad. "No."

"Why not?"

"Because I don't want them to see how much I pity them," Jānis said. "They show how cruel God can be. Let them keep the little pride they still have. I won't take that from them."

"Then I won't either," she said. She pronounced it "eether." "Uh oh!" she said. "Dolores keeps making me say 'I-ther' so I'll sound 'mid-Atlantic'."

"You do not need to change," Jānis said.

Gillian was grateful for this man's sensitivity. Yet she also sensed an edginess in him. Maybe he was nervous because this was their first date. Did he like her? She knew she liked him. Still, she held back.

The carnival barker's pitches faded now. The gusting *fffff*-sound of the wind and the rhythmic *eeesh-haaah* of cascading ocean waves almost muffled the barker's harangue: "There are thin ones. There are fat ones. They're all inside. Tom Thumb and his brother. 'Nip' and 'Pip', the pinheaded people."

Gillian and Jānis let themselves drift into the crowd that moved further along the midway. When they had to shout to hear each other above the din, Gillian's apprehension gave way to the exquisite hilarity of her surroundings. She laughed. "So life's like a carnival?"

Jānis looked relieved, grinned. "You understand," he said. "Sometimes chaos can make you feel more alive."

"*If* you can hear yourself think," Gillian said.

"Did you ever ride on a … you know: a roller coaster?"

Gillian laughed. "There you go. Right away!"

Jānis' smile tightened.

"Okay, so I'm afraid of the roller coaster," Gillian admitted.

"What *does* feel safe to you?" Jānis asked.

"The Ferris wheel. I may be scared of water and roller coasters, but I'm not scared of heights."

"I will give in," Jānis said, "if you will give in too?"

"You mean if I ride the roller coaster with you? I'll think about it," Gillian said, "but I won't promise."

Now Gillian and Jānis stood before a big gleaming sign: "Wonder." There was a huge right pointing arrow, "Thrills," also illuminated. Jānis bought their tickets at a blue teller's booth, and together the two climbed into one of the odd, dipping seats of the Wonder Wheel. The seat looked flimsy. However, Gillian felt comfortable leaning into the flexible seatback.

There was room only for two normal size people. The couple's hips touched. The sides of their bodies pressed together. When the Wonder Wheel began to revolve, the cars did not "sit." They tilted and slid. Below, on the left was the famous Steeplechase; on the right, an expanse of beach front and thousands of sun worshippers. Above them a web of cables crisscrossed a blue, cloudless sky.

LATER …

"I admit it. I enjoyed the Ferris wheel," Jānis said. "Are you hungry?"

"I'm ravenous!"

"This tame ride we just did … I need some excitement," Jānis said. "If you get on the Cyclone with me, I will buy you a Coney Island dinner after." For emphasis, he added: "I will *really* respect you if you do this with me."

"Respect?"

"For me, respect is big," Jānis said.

Gillian looked deflated. "I did kind of promise," she said. "I want you to respect me, but I'm terrified."

Just then, Jānis looked like a little kid who wanted something so much that he couldn't stand still. "Do not worry. I will protect you."

"When you look like that, how can a girl say no?"

"On we go then!" Jānis shouted.

The Cyclone sprawled out from the corner of Surf Avenue and 10th Street. This roller coaster had six "fan" turns and twelve "drops" in its more than six thousand feet of wooden tracks.

At her first glimpse of the highest of the Cyclone's several sweeping wooden curves, Gillian felt her stomach lurch. *I must be nuts*, she thought. *Risking life and limb for a guy I hardly know.* And yet, she admitted to herself that she too longed for excitement, for adventure. However, when Jānis helped Gillian into the front car of eight car strand, he had to restrain her from hopping back out.

Suspense built during the long, steep climb up ninety feet of track. At the top, at the moment of truth, the string of cars made a crazy vertical drop. At hairpin turns, the cars bumped violently. Then there was the roar, rumble, and *whoosh* of the cars on the steep, curved tracks. Gillian tried to look at the people in the cars behind theirs. Through half closed eyes, Gillian could see guys turn and grin as their lady friends screamed. She loved the climbing up part of the tracks but her whole body tensed up each time their car free fell down. Gillian clamped her eyes shut but stifled her own inner scream. Her eyes closed, Gillian yelled: "How fast do you think we're going?"

"I heard sixty miles an hour," Jānis shouted. "Is this not wonderful?!"

"I'll tell you later," Gillian shouted with her eyes still closed.

Gillian and Jānis continued this one minute, fifty second ride. It seemed endless to Gillian. Jānis grinned at the expressions on Gillian's face as the couple took drop after drop, twists, and turns, until the strings of cars stopped on the flat landing,

The safety bars released, and Gillian and Jānis stumbled straight out of the car.

"I feel like I just got off a runaway horse," Gillian said. "My legs are wobbly."

"Still hungry?" Jānis asked.

"I can't believe it, but I am!"

"Come," Jānis said. "I will introduce to you to a famous treat."

They came to Nathan's at the corner of Surf and Stillwell avenues. "Hot frankfurters. Hamburgers. Roast Beef. 5¢."

"Miss Gillian Rysert," Jānis said, "please meet the famous Coney Island frankfurter! Today, for you, it is only a nickel."

Gillian surveyed the hundreds of hot dogs revolving on a grill that extended the whole front length of Nathan's huge corner stand.

Jānis motioned toward the boardwalk and said, "If you find a table, I'll bring our food."

Gillian found a table and sat down. She panicked when she lost sight of Jānis. Aloud, she said, "Oh!" She felt like a single ant in a hill of thousands, and yet she ached with how alone she also felt.

Jānis returned in a jiffy with two Coney Island frankfurters and two draft beers in paper cups. He also juggled two paper boats of hot corn on the cob, salted and smothered in butter. "Here," he said. "Sweetest corn on earth. I promise."

Gillian did not let on that she disliked the bitter taste of beer. At least it was chilled, and it cooled her off. Jānis drank his beer with such gusto that foam coated his upper lip.

Gillian smiled and reached toward Jānis' mouth with a paper napkin. "Let me get that beer mustache for you," she said. The gesture felt intimate, and Jānis clearly took note of this. Self-conscious, Gillian focused on her Coney Island frankfurter. She felt a little snap when she bit through its skin. She enjoyed the cascade of flavors: onions, mustard, relish, and juicy beef hot dog that protruded out one end of a soft, steamed bun. She sampled the corn on the cob, which dripped with golden butter. "I think I got butter in my hair," she shouted over the din of the crowd.

Jānis laughed. "I too," he yelled back. He handed Gillian a wad of napkins. "It is a part of the experience," he added

"I wish I had a picture of us here, with butter all over us," Gillian said.

"You look too serious," Jānis said.

"Just tired," Gillian answered.

"Time to go then."

ON THE SUBWAY HOME ...

"I hope you don't mind me asking," Gillian said, "but when we were on the Ferris wheel, why didn't you try to hold my hand?"

"When you meet someone new," Jānis said, "you must not go too fast. You must go to A, switch trains, then go to B."

"That's what Pop used to say!"

"Pop?"

"My father," Gillian said.

"Oh. Like *Papa*."

"Pop told me once: 'You can't just jump from A to Z'. You have to go one step at a time."

"Your 'Pop' sounds like a smart man," Jānis said.

Gillian did not want to ruin the mood by telling Jānis her father was dead. "We were talking about trains," Gillian said. "And meeting new people. The first train I ever took was from St. Louis to Indianapolis. That was on the way here. Then I met Dolores. She's been good to me. My first friend here."

"Dolores is pretty," Jānis said, "but not as pretty as you are."

Because Gillian had not learned how to embrace compliments, she returned to her talk about trains: "My brochure talks about 'the Whispering Arch' in the St. Louis Station.," she said. "We tried it out. If you speak in a low voice to someone on the other side of the arch, they can hear you loud and clear. The Indianapolis Union Station was even better. There was a huge, round window high up in one end of the station. It was full of beautiful stained glass."

But they had reached the cavernous Chambers Station, where the IRT Lexington Avenue Line and Manhattan Elevated 3rd Avenue *el* met the BMT.

Jānis guided Gillian out of the subway car. "There is a place much like that in Grand Central Terminal," he said.

"What?"

"It's called 'The Whispering Wall'," Jānis answered. "Maybe someday you can try it out with me." For a moment, Jānis looked distracted. Then he asked Gillian if she had enjoyed their day together.

Gillian peered into Jānis' quicksilver eyes with gratitude for his coming back to her so soon with their dinner, for riding with her on the subway, and for giving her the most exciting day of her life. "I feel great!" she said.

Jānis laughed. "I too!" He offered Gillian another cigarette. "I'll walk you home."

At Dolores' apartment building, Gillian decided not to tell Jānis she lived at the YWCA. "This is where my friend lives. I'm staying with her until I can get my own place." She couldn't tell what Jānis was thinking.

"May I see you again?" he asked. "Where can I reach you?"

"Every weekday at Harry's Bar. From five to two," Gillian said.

Jānis hesitated. He didn't try to kiss Gillian goodnight.

Gillian thought she should be disappointed. Actually, she felt relief.

Chapter 12

The next morning, Gillian spread the *Sunday Times* over Dolores' coffee table. She pored over the "Apartments – Rent" section. "On Friday night, a gal in Harry's Bar told me about an apartment for rent," she said, "but I thought I'd check the Times first."

"What's your hurry? You are such an easy guest."

"You've been great, Dolores, but now I need my own place."

"Don't get your hopes up. It's harder than you think to find a good apartment, especially in the Village."

Gillian circled a small ad and jumped up. "Here it is! Let's go see my new apartment!"

Dolores read the ad. "But I have to work."

"Call in sick, then. Please?"

"You have a Swiss bank account?" Dolores asked with concern. "You can blow two weeks' pay on rent every month? What if you have to pay a deposit today too?"

"I still have half my savings," Gillian said. "One forty four Waverly Place," she almost sang. "Four is my lucky number. That's how I know it's mine." She now kissed Dolores' hand.

"That's better than coffee," Dolores said. "I'll call in sick."

After breakfast, the two friends walked arm in arm "up" Waverly Place. Waverly Place is hard to describe precisely. First, it is not a "place." It is an odd, crooked

63

street that meets itself coming and going and around the bend, just past Sheridan Square, where people pick up the IRT subway.

Gillian scrutinized the address of every building she and Dolores passed. When they came to 144 Waverly Place, they saw a dingy brownstone building. It had archways above the front door and at the right side. At each window hung red shutters, their paint wrinkled and chipped. But the morning sun spread a warm yellow over the bricks. This made the building seem to absorb rather than reflect the rays.

To Gillian, 144 Waverly Place was the Taj Mahal. "My new home is alive!"

Dolores yawned and said, "I love the tacky cornices at the top. I'll bet they're not even made of real wood."

"I don't care," Gillian said, and she rang the bell.

An old man in a moth eaten, moss green sweater let them in. The landlord shuffled his right shoe as if a stone had lodged there. He led the young women up to the third story, where he opened a door into a small but very sunny room.

"It's probably gonna need paint," Dolores said. "Of course you'll ask me to help you with that."

It *was* a real find. A third floor apartment whose window overlooked the street. Just inside, to their right, was an efficiency kitchen with a small porcelain sink. The small bathroom did have a clawfoot tub with a shower sprayer attached to the faucet. The toilet tank was high up the wall, with a cord attached for flushing. "I love it!" Gillian exclaimed. "I think I'll hang beads here in the doorway."

Dolores pulled Gillian aside and whispered: "You can afford this on forty cents an hour?"

"Plus tips," Gillian said. "I get lotsa good tips."

"I believe you," Dolores said.

"But this'll wipe out my savings."

As if he had read Dolores' mind, the old man raised his bushy salt and pepper eyebrows and said to Gillian: "I ain't said you could have it yet." His mouth was pinched in like a hard little "o" because of his shrunken gums. When he spoke, his dentures clacked.

"I can vouch for her."

"Yeah?" he said. "Who are you?"

Dolores pressed him in full New Yorker mode: "Do you or don't you want a good tenant? She can afford it. If the bedroom's not okay, then it's no deal." She pointed at a closed door in the wall behind the kitchen and bathroom.

Afraid that Dolores would ruin her chances to nab this apartment, Gillian winced.

"That's a locked door," the old man said. "This used to be what they call 'a suite'." He walked over to a space to the right of the window and pulled down on a leather strap that was near the ceiling.

"A freakin' Murphy bed," Dolores said. She pulled Gillian aside and whispered: "Pretend you're not sure."

Gillian fiercely whispered, "Are you nuts?!"

"Trust me," Dolores whispered back. She said to the old man, "She'll have to think about it."

"What're you? Her agent?" the old man said. To Gillian: "Okay. Forty eight dollars first month's rent plus a forty eight dollar deposit. In advance. That's my offer."

"I'll take it!" Gillian said. She felt true happiness for the first time she could remember. She was sure this was the sign she had waited for, the sign that her whole future would be golden.

Worried, Dolores sighed.

The old man, Norbert Floding, seemed as thrilled as he was capable of being.

Gillian arranged to pay the landlord within the next twenty four hours. She was so excited that she almost fell down the steps to the sidewalk outside. While she pulled Dolores back down Waverly Place, Gillian smiled at everyone they passed. They came to the Northern Dispensary. A triangular, red brick structure, it is a simple Georgian building surrounded by a tall wrought iron fence whose bars stand from the sidewalk like spears. Thick zigzags of fire escapes obscure the rear of the building. It is a severe, settling fortress covered with cracks.

An intimate of Freud, Dolores said, "The N.D. is schizophrenic. It sits between Waverly Place and ... Waverly Place." She whispered, "I heard about a sinister dentist who's worked there since it was built. He lurks just inside the doorway. He's hungry for victims. He'll ask you, 'How're your teeth, my pretty', and then you'll faint. He'll carry you inside and I'll see you again nevermore."

"That's quite a story," Gillian said.

"Speaking of 'nevermore', Edgar Allan Poe lived near here on Waverly Place. That's where he wrote *Fall of the House of Usher*. A dreadful book. A wonderful book!"

"How'd you know that?" Gillian said.

"They made us read it at St. Michael's," Dolores said. "And Edna St. Vincent Millay lived in some Waverly Place garret while writing her exquisite poems."

Dolores piloted Gillian back toward Sheridan Square. Because Gillian was oblivious to traffic, Dolores had to keep her from stepping into the path of a Yellow Cab.

The two women sat down on a bench in the heart of Sheridan Square. Light penetrated the maple leaves, and their shadows, which made ragged shapes on the women's clothing. Gillian wanted to talk about Jānis, but she was afraid it would upset Dolores. She decided to let it go for now. She would just keep Jānis in her imagination until she would see him again the next Saturday night.

A small statue of General Philip Henry Sheridan stood in full sun. Something about him had been captured at its peak energy forever. To Gillian the sculpture was not merely stone, the General not merely a symbol of military pomp. General Sheridan had not looked this large, this vibrant before that moment. She found his sword fascinating. And the way his left palm bore down on its hilt. It made the scabbard push out slightly near Sheridan's hip. Gillian could almost hear the general's sword clang against a Confederate cavalry sword. The sound she imagined was like a bell, or a cymbal, or steel pipes. Or the high hum of electricity in wires. To Gillian the sound was cut into separate jolts and magnified a hundred times. In the distance, Dolores talked of salami.

"Eat something, Cinderella," Dolores said.

Gillian was glad Dolores was in a better mood. She stared at the General. "I'm not hungry," she said.

Dolores was talking. "Maybe next weekend," she said, "we can go to The Rivoli and see 'Portrait of Jenny'. Don't you just love Jennifer Jones?"

"If we go," Gillian responded, "it'll be because I love Joseph Cotten."

Chapter 13

MACDOUGAL STREET, GREENWICH VILLAGE

After dinner, Jānis steered Gillian into the dark, smoky Caffee Reggio, a popular jazz club. "Reggio 119" was stenciled on the café window.

Jānis asked Gillian if she'd like a cappuccino.

"A what?"

"And so, your first. Do you trust me?"

"I think so," Gillian said.

"Just like being in Rome," Jānis said.

Domenico Parisi himself stood by his gigantic brass espresso maker.

"Dom, here, brought the first espresso machine to New York," Jānis said. He introduced Gillian.

"Welcome to your lovely friend," Dom said. When Gillian extended her hand, Dom kissed it.

Jānis' smile showed he approved.

Dom gestured toward one of the classical Italian Renaissance paintings that graced the café's walls. "From the school of Caravaggio," he boasted. "Sixteenth century." He crossed his arms over his chest and surveyed his crowded café. "Look at my guests," he said. "Some are poets. Some are writers, painters. For only a few coins, where else can they get such inspiration? You know: *la dolce vita*!"

Gillian now looked like New Yorkers' idea of a Midwesterner—wide eyes, mouth agape—until she noticed Jānis' quirky smile.

"Two cappuccinos please," he said to Dom. "Medium sweet."

"Please sit here," Dom said. "A special table for two special people." Their table fronted a small stage, elevated only a foot high. At the back of the platform sat an upright piano on one side and drum traps on the other. "Just in time for the live music," Dom said.

One at a time, musicians straggled on to the stage: first a bassist, then a guitarist and drummer, and finally a pianist. Center stage there was one standing microphone. This ensemble lent an intimate, salon like feeling to the room. The musicians began to warm up.

"I like it here," Gillian said. "It's crowded, but it's cozy too."

"Did you enjoy your dinner?"

"I loved the lobster," Gillian said. "And I do believe Caesar salad is my new favorite. And I've never had sour cream and chives on a baked potato."

"For you, in the Village, there will be many 'firsts'."

A sultry, olive skinned vocalist took center stage just as Dom delivered cappuccinos to Jānis and Gillian.

"We are very lucky to have Miss Libby Holman at Reggio 119 today," Dom said. "It has been years ago since she sang here." Dom pointed toward the upright piano. "And she has brought the famous Josh White," he added. "This is *impromptu*. Can you believe it?"

Jānis lowered his voice and said to Gillian, "Miss Holman is a civil rights activist."

Gillian had only a vague idea what "civil rights activist" meant.

Jānis encouraged Gillian to try her cappuccino. Dom looked on.

Creamy richness passed from Gillian's lips and across her tongue. She closed her eyes. Dom and Jānis waited for her response.

"As they say in the hills after a great meal," Gillian said, "I ain't mad at nobody!"

Dom laughed and Jānis smiled. Then the room grew silent.

Now at the microphone, fortyish Libby Holman introduced herself to robust applause. She looked out, over the crowd and welcomed them. Then she winked at Jānis. "They say I sing songs of scandal and desire."

It was Gillian, not Jānis, whose face colored.

"And you sing them very well," Jānis said to Libby.

Libby then looked at Gillian and said, "You have a very handsome man friend."

Gillian almost said that Jānis was not her man friend. Instead, she adapted to the mood and purred, "You have good taste."

Audience members near the stage laughed, approving.

Jānis looked at Gillian with surprise, then pleasure.

But Gillian felt annoyed. *This is not me*, she thought. It was as if someone else had channeled words *through* her. *If Jānis wants me to be like this, then that's too bad. I'm not a flirt. I don't trap men.*

"Come back to us," Jānis said.

"I'm here," Gillian said quietly. She wondered if Jānis could read her mind.

Libby Holman's band was ready. "In case you missed it two years back," Libby said, "I want to offer a song from my movie. It's called 'The Girl with the Prefabricated Heart'."

Again, the crowd cheered. Men whistled.

Gillian whispered to Jānis: "Is she a Negress?"

Jānis looked puzzled. "No," he whispered. "She's a Jewess."

Perhaps it was all the "s'" that drew Libby's attention back to Gillian and Jānis, for Libby asked Jānis if he liked her movie.

"The film was disturbing," he said, "but that was intended."

Gillian wondered how Libby Holman knew Jānis had seen her movie. She felt vexed by how much attention this seductive songstress had already paid to Jānis.

The musicians began to play the intro to this steamy blues tune.

Facing Libby Holman, Jānis said to Gillian: "She enjoys being a woman."

Does that crack mean he thinks I don't? Gillian thought. But she held back the heat she felt and wondered if Jānis noticed. Even if he did, there was no point in hiding her pique from him.

As in a strip joint, a raucous wolf whistle could be heard over the bizarre *oom pah pah* rhythms of the song's opening phrases.

> *Oh Venus was born out of sea foam*
> *Oh Venus was born out of brine*
> *But a goddess today if she is grade A*
> *Is assembled upon the assembly line.*
> *Her chromium nerves and her platinum brain*
> *Were chastely encased in cellophane*
> *And to top off this daughter of science and art*

She was equipped with a prefabricated heart.

The crowd cheered and applauded, and the song continued. The refrain included the line: "untouched by human hands."

Gillian did appreciate Libby Holman's performance, especially the quality of her voice, but the song's lyrics bothered her. The words made her afraid *she* had no heart. Maybe she would turn into an old maid and wear horn-rimmed glasses and low heals. She would spend her old age sitting in some paint-chipped rocker. Friendless, alone. She would bide her time while wrinkles ravaged the skin all over her body and while seasons flew by like paper leaflets in the wind.

Jānis smiled at Gillian. "Perhaps we should go."

For Gillian, this was not a moment too soon. As she and Jānis reached the door, Libby Holman finished her song:

There's no man alive who could ever survive a girl with a prefabricated heart.

LATER THAT NIGHT ...

Gillian and Jānis stood by the third story railing of the bright orange Staten Island Ferry and looked out on New York harbor. In the distance they could clearly see the Statue of Liberty. Her torch lit up the small island home, with its jagged, irregular shoreline.

Gillian was still upset with what she had felt when hearing Libby Holman's song. What if her own heart was "prefabricated?" What if she might never be able to love or be loved?

Jānis put his hands on her shoulders and said, "The film is called 'Dreams That Money Can Buy'. Miss Holman's part was about mechanical lovemaking, a *ballet mechanique*, a satire. I saw the tune upset you. But you can trust me. You can trust yourself."

By this time, Gillian had turned her face away to hide her tears.

"Please tell me what is wrong," Jānis said.

Gillian excused her behavior by saying, "I cry when I'm mad. Not when I'm sad."

"You cry so you won't hit someone," Jānis said. "Or maybe when you are mad at yourself?" He put his arm around Gillian's waist, as if the two were slow dancing, and held her.

"Your kindness ..." she said. She leaned her face against Jānis' shoulder, absorbed his alluring scent. She was still thinking about what Jānis had just said. She admitted to herself that she cried when she was angry. And when she was confused or frustrated. *He can read me like a book*, she thought. *Maybe I can trust him.*

The Staten Island Ferry was nearing the Lady of the Harbor, and Jānis turned Gillian to face the statue. "See how majestic and powerful she is?"

Gillian sighed. She was relieved Jānis had so adeptly brought her out of her pique. "Was she the first thing you saw when your ship arrived?" she asked.

"Yes, but first we went to Ellis Island with our papers. They tried to make us change our names to be phonetic English. We refused."

"We?"

Clearly Jānis felt emotional. "My friend Kārlis and I. We left everything to come here." Then Jānis rallied. "But let us enjoy the rest of this night together." He cupped his hands, lit two cigarettes at the same time and placed one between Gillian's parted lips. Little smile lines curved like parentheses at the corners of his mouth.

Only Gillian's trace of a smile betrayed she "got" this reference to the film "Now Voyager," which she had seen at Loew's State theater when she was thirteen, alone. It was one of a half dozen movies about doomed lovers she favored. In this moment, Gillian was Bette Davis and Jānis was Paul Henreid. The cigarette was moist from Jānis' lips, and she took this in. Just as in the film, their cigarette smoke intermingled. It was like communion. Embarrassed by the thrills now shooting throughout her body, Gillian sounded like Bette Davis when she said: "You may call me 'Camille'." When she laughed, earth tones she had never heard spilled out in her voice. It was the first time she had felt how delicious it was to flirt with a man. "And do you have a sick wife at home?"

Jānis smiled, and the two of them let down their guard. "No," he said. "I am, as you say here, single."

Gillian wanted Jānis to know she was eager to hear about his past. "I want to know more about Latvia," she said.

"When it is the right time," Jānis said

Having rejected the "howdy folks" culture of St. Louis, Gillian could understand Jānis' restraint. His expression told her not to probe, and so she said, "I would love to know *you* better."

Jānis took Gillian's hands in his for the first time. "I will tell you one part of my story," he said. "I came here from Sweden by ship."

Gillian tried to keep Jānis' touch from opening her up. She was afraid he might reach all the way inside her. Then what would she do?

144 WAVERLY PLACE

At the end of the evening, Gillian and Jānis sat on the top of the steps of her apartment building.

Jānis lit a cigarette and offered one to Gillian. "Are you happy in your new home?"

"I love it," she said. "I finally have a place of my own."

They sat in silence for a few minutes and smoked.

Gillian wasn't ready to let Jānis see her flat, and she was afraid he would ask to come up with her.

But he didn't. Instead, he rose up and said, "And now it is time to say goodnight."

Gillian wanted to prolong the moment. "I think I owe you an apology," she said.

"For what? My best day in many years," Jānis said.

"For being a crybaby."

"There *is* a way you can make it up for me," he added.

Gillian looked at Jānis hopefully. "Yes?"

"Meet me, and my friends, next Saturday night. Let's make it Harry's Bar. Then we can start making our own history."

Gillian missed the import of Jānis' last line. And so she chirped, "Let's shake on it," Gillian said, and she laughed at Jānis' confusion. "Here. Shake hands with me. That means the deal is sealed."

Again, Jānis seemed bewildered, but he held on to Gillian's hand a little longer than she had expected.

"I say *yes*," Gillian said. "A handshake means I'll keep my promise."

Chapter 14

144 WAVERLY PLACE: A WEEK LATER

Intense sunlight penetrated the curtains in Gillian's flat. Smiling, she lay in her Murphy bed. She thought about how clever and lucky she had been to get this apartment with its big window and its clear view of Waverly Place. Her life felt rich and distilled and open. She figured Greenwich Village was the best place for a person like her to live. People here were intriguing. Markets and specialty shops and galleries were colorful, and often surprising. She measured her new freedom by these, and by her own rooms.

Gillian propped herself up so she could get more sun. She pulled the sheet back and basked in the light. She wanted to get up and dance in front of her window, where buzzard necked Mr. Angellini would gawk at her from across the street this morning as usual. His elbows would be propped on a pillow. No matter what time of day it was, his hair was tousled as if he had just gotten out of bed. Dare she dance naked while he sipped his iced tea from a tall glass and scratched his hairy chest with his free hand? He had those binoculars too. Would *he* get a surprise today!

And Gillian could hear Mrs. McBride's croaky voice at the core of a flock of neighborhood gossips. The widow would probably be wearing her small print floral house dress and kickoff, toeless black slippers. Mrs. McBride earned notoriety for poking her index finger into the chest of some young butcher shop boy who had rubbed her the wrong way. Gillian imagined dumping a glass of water out the window. In her fantasy the liquid cascaded down and spread onto the crown of Mrs. McBride's head. But Gillian knew she wouldn't really do this because she enjoyed these characters. She relished the sounds of kids' bicycles squeaking, and women's high heels clacking, and grocery boys whistling at the women in high heels.

Now Gillian got up, sprang back her Murphy bed, and put on her new silk *shantung* kimono. It was a gift to herself for having found a job and surviving a month on her own in the Village. The kimono's orange and yellow colors twisted like flames around the neck, sleeves, and borders of black silk. The colors contained symbolic information. She was sure they were code. Impressions of the Far East emanated from the kimono's intricate designs. They enchanted her skin. She imagined tiny women with unnaturally small feet and black bangs cut straight across. Little yellow men with Fu Manchu mustaches who drank green tea and wrote poems about dragonflies and mountains and cherry blossoms. She envisioned monks in meditation.

It was Saturday, and Gillian could do anything she liked. Today she would be alone. She touched the cheap Degas print that she had bought in a sidewalk sale. She had hung the artwork by her door, which was on the inside wall of her large main room. The print's colors were soft and pastel. The blurred ballerinas looked totally bored with tying their slippers. Very French! Their wrinkled dance instructor slouched in a rickety chair. Every day, Gillian could see the print's dance teacher, knees spread under her long drab skirt. The teacher read a newspaper. It was much better than having a mirror there, for Gillian could observe in the Degas print only what she wished to see.

Below the Degas was a straight backed wooden chair. Because Gillian thought chairs like that should be set against a wall, she rarely sat on it; rather, she used this back alley find, unearthed by Dolores, as a clothes hamper. So what if the two women had spent so much time, not to mention a lot of varnish, to make it look good?

Gillian could have parted with almost anything she owned now except the bamboo birdcage that hung at the inside corner of her main room and kitchen. The cage was light and small. She would put no bird in it, because she loved only to look at the cage and touch it and imagine whatever lovely bird was trapped inside had long ago flown free. She hoped the bird had found delight its own good food and perched, now and forever, on a branch of a sun dappled tree.

Gillian slipped through the curtain of orange beads that hung from her kitchen door frame. Because everyone who was Bohemian had beads like this, she had them. She loved the way the beads rattled and clicked when they brushed against her body. She set up her aluminum stovetop percolator and checked her Frigidaire for food. Only milk and ground coffee. Her kimono sash got caught in the refrigerator door. Gillian often closed the refrigerator door on her clothing just before something nice was about to happen. When she released the sash, she immediately found the sole donut she had left in a bag by her little black alarm clock on the kitchen counter. Though the donut was *molto al dente*, she chomped it downed it in a few bites.

The hallway pay phone rang with commanding volume.

"I'm going to spend my Saturday alone," Gillian shouted through her door. "I might have a man up here!"

Gillian succumbed on the seventh ring and ran into the hallway to pick up the payphone receiver. "Hell-o? Dolores... What made you think I wasn't in? ... You are calling from the deli downstairs... No, I don't have a hangover... I was going to spend the day alone... I am not being rude... All right. Bring up the *Times* when you come. I promise to pay you back... Look, we don't have to talk anymore if you're coming right up... Okay... Yes, the coffee's on, but it's going slow."

Gillian felt ashamed for begrudging Dolores a visit. She reminded herself how many ways her friend had saved her. Gillian felt guilty that she had somehow betrayed Dolores, who had made Gillian feel appreciated and worthy of love. By the last night Gillian had stayed overnight at her friend's flat, Gillian knew it was time to find her own place. She wanted not to keep going back to the Y and not to keep taking advantage of Dolores. Gillian would forever be grateful for Dolores' having been there for her when she found her flat, and she marveled, anew, how it all happened.

Gillian buzzed Dolores into the building, and soon Dolores pounded on the door. "Let me in, Gillian. I need a coffee!" Dolores burst in. She held a shopping bag in one hand and flung her other arm around her friend's neck. Today Dolores wore black ankle length tights, and an off the-shoulder tunic blouse and low wedge peep-toe espadrilles. "I would've brought you daffodils," she said, "but I was saving my cash for today."

"I like your outfit," Gillian said. "Where—."

"Goldin Dance Supply on West Eighth Avenue."

When Dolores leaned forward to hug Gillian, she received in return Gillian's stiff, upright hug. For Gillian, there was no leaning in, no opening to her friend's welcoming arms.

However, Gillian did let herself be conscious of the way her kimono swished when she walked and of wearing nothing beneath it. She brought out their coffee. She had to admit it was pleasurable to spend time with Dolores. Being with her friend was as comfortable and safe as being alone. Dolores knew what it was like to get painful menstrual cramps, who got more than a little crazy when the moon was full, and who smelled like talcum and rose water. Gillian sensed that she could indulge her weirdest self when she was with Dolores. She was sure the one here with her knew the same sensations, appreciated the smallest beautiful details, and felt the same crazed insolence when things didn't live up to her expectations. "I really did want to be alone today," she said. Even to Gillian, however, her own words sounded half-hearted.

"Not when you see what I've brought you," Dolores said. She took a quick look in the shopping bag. "What do you think it is?"

"Something from the Salvation army," Gillian stated.

"Something much better, though with that attitude I'm not sure you deserve it. Don't tease me. I'm sensitive you know."

"It could be tragic to give you coffee when you're like this. A little more, and you might devour the City"

Dolores took off her shoes. "You just parodied me?" She lay back on Gillian's loveseat, and pulled each leg of her tights up slightly at the knee. "I can take it," she said. "Do I look like an odalisque?"

"Of *course* I don't know what that is. But you look awful comfortable. I mean awfully comfortable and maybe even wicked."

"That's the secret of being an odalisque," Dolores said. "Only mildly wicked though. It also helps to look kinda sleazy. Aren't you going to ask me what I've got in this bag? I mean, besides the *Times*, a bottle of rather mediocre port, a long piece of greasy salami, and my tacky coin purse?"

Gillian treasured this playful banter with Dolores. Now she joined her friend on the floor. Her kimono pleasantly slid away from one thigh. "Maybe it's a bomb."

"I've never seen you in uniform before," Dolores continued. "You know? You match your kitchen beads."

"I also match my bedspread. And sunset."

"*Trés dramatique*," Dolores said.

Gillian liked the way Dolores looked her in the eyes when they talked, and the way her face opened and gave and received. "What is *your* obsession, Dolores? Besides coffee?" she added. She watched her friend stare into her glass cup.

"I'm obsessed with whatever I'm doing in the moment," Dolores said. "Like being here with you. Understand?"

"You look so serious!"

"It takes less energy to be serious than to be manic," Dolores said. Out of her grocery bag she took a small package wrapped in brown paper. "This, my dear, is a gift not to be taken lightly."

"Why?"

Dolores almost stood up. "That was a foolish question, my girl. What else would come wrapped in brown paper with this shape?"

"Pornography?"

"You used to be so innocent. Now open it and see."

It was a book: *Trilby*, by George du Maurier. "Look how old it is," Gillian said. On an inside page Gillian found an exquisite engraving of a young woman. "Ooh. I like this," she said, reading. "'She had a very fine brow, broad and low, with thick level eyebrows much darker than her hair, a broad, bony high bridge to her short nose, and her full, broad cheeks were beautifully modelled. She would have made a singularly handsome boy.' This sounds like *you*, Dolores."

"*Hélas*!" Dolores shouted. "Trilby O'Ferrall. Half Irish Bohemian!"

Gillian blushed because of the way she felt about Dolores, the way she knew Dolores felt about her. This wanting to be seen as beautiful by someone else who was beautiful felt illicit.

Gillian tried to open her heart, but doing this felt oddly like pain. Her own reflection in her friend's eyes frightened her, because to give too much might reveal the intensity of love Gillian needed. Sometimes it was like walking up the side of a cliff. Sometimes it was like diving off the top of that cliff. Deep feelings seemed dangerous to Gillian. When she looked at Dolores now, she was aware that her need for love was fierce and that she must conceal this. From far away she heard her own voice ask what the book was about.

Dolores, who had gotten up and poured them both more coffee, joined Gillian on the floor. "This rug itches," she observed. "Now. What if I told you the whole book is about a young artist who loved to sketch Trilby's beautiful feet?"

"Maybe I wouldn't read it?"

"*You* have beautiful feet, Gillian." Dolores quickly looked back up. "And what if I said it was about the *le Latin quartier* in Paris when the most exciting painters were there? Now you're getting interested. Here's the good part: Through hypnosis a diabolical musician named Svengali makes Trilby sing like an angel. Without him she sounds like a chicken. Ah, I see it in your eyes. Enough. Here. Read it."

"You are my dearest and only friend," Gillian said.

"Shall we plan our day?"

"I need to be back by late afternoon," Gillian said, "'Cause I have plans with Jānis tonight at Harry's. He's bringing his Latvian friends. You're invited too."

"That's awfully short notice."

"Please, Dolores? I want you to come."

"We'll see," Dolores answered.

Chapter 15

THAT NIGHT

The slow motion overhead fan in Harry's Bar wafted air around the ceiling but had little effect on the rest of the bar. This heat problem was chronic, because only two windows in the place would open. One was in the men's room and the other high up on the sand colored wall opposite the oak bar. Harry customarily kept the green door closed. This was his way of controlling who got in. Harry's was a dependable place for dependable drinkers. Regulars complained about the heat, but they kept returning, because Harry's beer was cheap and his drinks potent. After attending shows and dinners elsewhere, customers often arrived already half drunk. Despite patrons' inebriation, Harry always managed to keep the tone of his establishment mellow.

Below the open window above her "personal table," Mabel Levitsky started on her first bottle of Manischewitz. Harry kept it in stock just for Mabel and charged her about half the wholesale price. The light above Mabel's table was illuminated. The talkative proprietor of Levitsky's Treasure Trove by day, Mabel was an ardent devotee of wine by night. Rather than talking to other regulars in Harry's Bar, Mabel communicated only by the distance she kept from most others and by the rare eye messages she directed at the selective few she trusted. Patterns her cigarette smoke made in the air were like smoke signals floating up from the prairies of the Old West. However, just because Mabel seldom looked at other people there didn't mean she wasn't listening. She already had tuned in to the Latvians, who sat at a table at the other end of the wall they shared.

Pleasantly high, the Latvians were into their third bottle of red Bordeaux. One of them, whom they addressed as "Atis," was a bulky man with dark brown wavy hair and ruddy skin. Each of his hands was as puffy as a catcher's mitt, and he held his wine glass in a death grip. Kārlis, also dark and big, but more muscular, seemed to be the practical one on whom the others relied to arbitrate their volatile political discussions. He seemed unaware of how good looking, and how intelligent, he was. The third, Pēteris, sat at the corner, where he could lean against the wall. Pēteris' nondescript looks were diminished further by his frown and frequent coughing. The moment turned, and the Latvians looked as if they were about to pounce. They all stared at the green door just before Jānis entered.

Jānis wore a light tan jacket with an open collared shirt. His high waisted, ivory colored slacks with turnup cuffs were expensive and perfectly pressed.

"Here comes the old bear slayer now," Atis said. "Look! His hair is slick. Handsome clothes, Jānis. Come close so we can smell aftershave. Say to us if this American girl is still … 'fully flowered'."

Jānis stared at Atis but said nothing.

Kārlis frowned.. "You see, Atis? That is the difference between you and Jānis. *He* is a gentleman. I think you are too small, maybe too fat, to get a girl yourself. And your skin turns sour the aftershave."

Jānis panted slightly from the heat and took off his jacket. He joined his friends. "Let me catch up to you," he said. "Pour me some wine. Smell. See? No aftershave."

"But too much soap," Kārlis said, his accent much thicker than Jānis'. "And much Vitalis. Smells like machine oil and vodka!"

"You are smelling your own Vitalis," Jānis said.

"Say more to us about her," Atis almost drooled, "besides she is American and naïve and lovely and ripe for love."

Jānis checked the wine label. "'Castel Château Malbec, 1949'," he mocked. "Since it is now 1949, I think it cannot be a vintage year." He smirked, poured himself some Bordeaux, and brought out his beautiful cigarette case, which he put on the table. "Gillian has not been long in the Village."

The surly Pēteris opened his eyes. To hear better, he often closed his eyes during their conversations. "Maybe she knows not much," he offered. "Advantage for you I think," he said to Jānis, "but I think no American knows much, my friends."

"*Her* friend maybe does not like me," Jānis continued. "But girl friends of girls can be protective. Got her away from me fast the day I met them. Perhaps Gillian may give in to those who are stronger?"

"Perfect for you," Atis said, winking. "You did that with … what was her name? Esperanza? The gods! From *España*. Maybe because her name means 'hope'? Too bad that one had no brain."

Jānis relaxed, let the teasing go beyond him as he always did. He touched his shirt collar. He cupped his hand and looked at his own immaculate nails. "I am sure this one is different," he said. "Such rare eyes. And intelligence in them. She has good instinct. She is on the edge of—."

"And very young," Atis said. "You will develop her potential, no? She is pretty. That is all there is for you I think."

Jānis hesitated, as if being careful about choosing his words. "I respect beauty, yes. She has potential, yes. But there is also something else."

"These American women," Pēteris said, "who are bored and come here to 'make their fortune'. They follow any man who is nice to them. We are only escorts. A man's suit of clothes at their elbow."

Jānis visibly began to lose his normal cool.

"You, Pēteris," Kārlis said. "Why don't *you* take a Latvian woman then? You could just stay inside our little group of war hounded spirits. Keep our ethnic purity."

"You know there are not many Latvian women here," Pēteris answered. "Not under thirty years old."

Kārlis yawned and poured more wine for the others. "What about Lilja?" he asked Pēteris.

"She loves Juris Grislis," Pēteris complained.

"Because you have been so much among the *nospiesti*," Kārlis said.

"Not depressed, Kārlis. Displaced," Pēteris answered. She loves Juris because he is also Catholic."

"A minority," Kārlis said. "Not *kauls no musu kaula*?"

Pēteris was sad. "'Bone of our bone', but not of our faith," he said.

Jānis tried to cheer Pēteris up: "Do we not enjoy freedom here? And do we not have enough money for good wine and good food?"

Pēteris scowled. "You are paid to be political. I wait tables at The Lion's Head."

Atis grasped Pēteris' forearm to restrain him. "Why do you care if Jānis wants an American girl?"

"We should love only our kind," Pēteris insisted. "Maybe the" (here he grabbed his crotch) "*sēkliniek* of Jānis betray him. Remember the oath we together took?" What Pēteris then said in Latvian can be translated as: "Not even among the foreign will my voice be drowned out." Pēteris continued: "Americans make the joke on us. 'Romantics', they say. We are *brīvības cīnītāji*. We have no home until Latvija is again free and we return to her."

"I remember we are Latvian Nationals," Jānis said. "But we did not swear to miss our … opportunities here. We must do the sensible things for success. And, Pēteris: Do you believe I would marry a girl not Latvian? To marry is different."

"To love is different," Pēteris argued, "so what you want with the American girl?"

Jānis clasped Pēteris' arm. "Why do we argue? Do you worry that I will be in love?"

"I worry," Pēteris frowned, "you will not keep your promise. That you will join the other broken off branches of our people."

"Let us rejoice," Jānis said gently. "Let us drink to the goddess Laima, to good fortune, to destiny. Drink, Pēteris. It improves the mood! As they say in The Village, 'There are many hours before midnight'."

Atis smirked. "Pēteris has a headache. I made him come here."

Pēteris coughed into the back of his hand. "We had a meeting. That is where we should be right now."

"We can meet tomorrow," Jānis countered. "I follow what is inside me about this girl. You all know that is right. You would choose the same. Are you not my friends?" He gently put out his cigarette, clasped his hands behind his head and leaned back in his chair. "You will feel jealous when you see her. You will not care about the meeting. Let me have her. Let me see who she is. *'Ja jūs atbilstat mīlas priecāties'*, the old poet said."

"'If you meet love, rejoice," Atis translated.

Pēteris scowled again. "She does not know our ways."

Kārlis turned to Jānis. "Why did you not meet her alone here?"

"He is afraid?" Atis guessed.

"I see I cannot please my friends," Jānis said, only half joking.

"She entertains," Kārlis said, "and we do not yet meet her!"

"Remember it when she comes," Jānis said. "Have more wine."

Pēteris had more than enough political zeal for all the other Latvians. "The Latvian Relief fund is drowning," he said.

Now Atis scowled. "Bah! It is richer and richer. Ten thousand affidavits right now for our displaced brothers. Do you not hear what we hear, Pēteris?"

"More are needed! More still are in Latvia."

"And will be sent for," Jānis said calmly.

"When? How can we find them?" Pēteris burst into a fit of coughing, his face crimson and his eyeballs bulging. "The air in here is bad."

"You have this cough all your life," Atis said. "This is because you are never comfortable."

"And never comfort*ing*," Kārlis retorted. "Drink your cough away, Pēteris. Drink until the soul leaves the body out of disgust."

Then there was silence among the Latvians. Silence *heard* like the moments after a scythe cuts a swath through dry grass and the second after someone's death has been announced. Kārlis had drawn a bow, aimed and released an arrow. It had hit the target of his friend's soul with dead accuracy.

Pēteris smoldered and looked down, ashamed. Kārlis looked directly at Pēteris as if to say he understood and was sorry. Kārlis knew that what a man spoke might be either an access to or barrier against what he was. His words might reflect what he was or reject it. Kārlis believed that Pēteris must accept his new life and stop holding on to the pain of missing their homeland.

Chapter 16

Mabel Levitsky held her cigarette between the tips of her thumb and forefinger—her hand flat like a spy in some *film noir*—and blew cigarette smoke out in dense puffs and swirls from her nostrils and mouth. She eavesdropped on the Latvians. She pinched the stem of her wine glass as one would a pair of tweezers and said nothing when Harry brought her next bottle of Manischewitz wine. Silence in the rest of the bar drew Mabel's attention to the Latvians' table. All had stopped talking. In unison they turned toward the green door.

It opened, and Gillian entered. She wore a sleeveless rose pink, split necked tea dress that showed off her shapely arms. Along with her, the bouquet of *L'Air du Temps* wafted into the room. She glanced at Harry, then at Mabel, and finally at Jānis' friends, all without leaving the bar's threshold. Now her gaze tunneled through to Jānis with an intensity that magnified her wholesome beauty. The Latvians shot up from their chairs and stood at attention until Jānis introduced her.

Harry smiled deferentially. He brought more Bordeaux for the Latvians and Gillian on this, her night off. "Where's Dolores?"

"She might come later," Gillian said.

Harry gave Gillian the royal treatment: glass newly polished and sparkling, white towel wrapped bottle, decanted with a flourish. He asked her to taste it. When she pronounced it "excellent," he bowed, his bald head shining. Then he whisked the towel away and left them all to the business of getting acquainted.

Jānis' friends acted like gentlemen for a change. They showed their Old World manners, which made conversation easy and agreeable. Atis held his wine glass delicately, his pinky finger raised. He drank in tiny sips, which caused Kārlis' thick eyebrows to wander upward and a suppressed grin to twitch at the corners of his mouth. An apparent miracle had cured Pēteris' cough and had relaxed his scowl so completely that he looked almost pleasant. The Latvians had risen to an unspoken challenge and engaged each other in a contest of charm and other gallantries, and they enjoyed every minute of it.

Gillian responded to this *human* ambience. With the help of the Bordeaux, Gillian felt the red wine take her beyond inhibition and into the intoxication of their flattery. She reveled in being the center of attention. They all moved forward in time together. Gillian was sure this evening must be what she knew she deserved: to be thought lovely and interesting and worthy. To have a table full of men competing for her least response.

Gillian enjoyed the Latvians' banter while she watched Jānis' reactions. She felt them both right on the edge of touching each other, and she intended to keep this advantage the entire evening. The seductive energy of Gillian's being a grown woman had begun to emanate from her. Until now, she had never felt such force was positive. But Gillian's power wasn't the same as her mother's, which was set like a trap, baited and glinting. No. It wasn't the same at all. Gillian felt new, overwhelming life radiate from her body. She wondered if the others could feel it too. Intimacy, like a delicious nakedness, shared with four men at once. She inserted a Chesterfield into the ebony cigarette holder she had bought from Mabel Levitsky and waited for Jānis to light it.

When Kārlis asked Gillian to tell them about herself, she replied that there was nothing much to tell, which caused Jānis to exclaim "Impossible!"

"But I don't have any interesting stories to tell you about my life," she said.

Jānis' gaze glinted with silver. "This is nonsense," he said. "Think of what has made you who you are. Think of your parents and your education and your friends. Think of choices you have made."

Gillian had no desire to talk about her choices. Jānis surely didn't know what he was asking. Or did he? She feared that telling them the details of her life would ruin everything. She had come here to forget about her past, and she wanted to make no excuses for who she was. Above all, she didn't want to talk about her mother. Or her late father or her dead baby sister. Further, she was not about to admit how little she knew about herself, and she couldn't let Jānis know that she might need his help to find out who she was.

"Perhaps she's an elfin child," Atis offered, "left under a spreading fern. In that case, fairies raised her. That is her story."

Gillian smiled. "Thank you, Atis." She felt Jānis' gaze on her body. She then gave him a look that said: *I haven't given you permission to do that.* "And what about you?" she asked Jānis.

"That," Jānis said, "would open what you call the Pandora's Box. These stories. They are quite real but not pleasant. You see, we lost our country. Therefore, we came here."

"You have advantage," Kārlis told Gillian, "if you have no past. You cannot lose what you do not have, no matter where you go. But I remember. Sometimes when I walk in Manhattan I smell something like baking bread. It is like I am a boy again. But when the smell goes away, I feel pain, like when I left my country forever."

Kārlis' emotions penetrated almost to Gillian's core: "When was that?" she asked.

"In 1940," Kārlis said. "When Bolsheviks did a second 'land reform'. Our farm … one hundred acres. They left us two and a half acres. What you call, 'squatters' lived in our house. So much stealing of our republic. Remember? Mussolini said: 'If you pluck the chicken one feather at a time, people will not notice'. We did try to keep our constitution. But they took away our rights. First one, then the next, then the next. When we had no more hope, we came to America."

Atis spoke next. "My father had a watch shop, and I help him. The *krievi*—."

"That is Russians," Jānis translated.

Atis continued: "… charge him for being too patriotic to our republic. He did refuse to march with other farmers for support of Stalin. They execute him, along with thousands of others. A bullet in the back of his skull."

"My God," Gillian whispered.

"There are worse stories," Jānis said. "University students demonstrated in Rīga. The Russians killed a hundred and twenty five of them in one day. Both Kārlis and myself were in Liepāja and so lived."

"Did you all know each other there?" Gillian asked.

Jānis said, "No. Kārlis and I met Pēteris and Atis here."

"When they captured the Rīga telegraph building," Kārlis said, "Jānis and me were in Liepāja. Russians next took the radio station and post office. Newspaper in Rīga said 'stay away from Liepāja'. Friends gave us money and we came here. Days and days on a ship. Sick all the way over. But Lutherans in New York have helped us find work and each other."

Gillian asked whether they had seen their families since then.

"No," Jānis said. He put his hand over his heart. "But here we carry them with us. We are rich in history and talents and memories. Highest literacy in Western Europe, not just the Baltics. My friends, here, and I attended university. We had opera, art museums, ballet. Someday Latvia will be free again. We will never forget our mission. We will never lose our roots." He shifted in his chair, gave the others a look that said: *Enough of this now*. The other Latvians nodded.

"It is thirty years since our National Government was established," Kārlis said. "Fifteen since our great Kārlis Ulmanis, *Vadonis* of Latvia, routed all socialist factions from inside our government. He wore no soldier's uniform. He was only a farmer, but he began a new era in our history ... with not one shot fired. When he moved among our people, they covered his path with flowers. Peasants told him their troubles, and to them he responded with compassion and wise counsel."

Suddenly, Atis gulped down the rest of his wine and said: "As in the older days, let us saber fight!"

Jānis laughed. "No," he said.

"Let us show the beautiful young lady how you can hear sound before action is coming," Atis persisted. "Let us show her now."

"I would rather sit, talk," Jānis said.

"What did Atis mean?" Gillian said.

"She wants to see," Atis said to Jānis. "Show her."

Sullen lines reappeared on Pēteris' face. He emerged from his long silence: "Not to Americans," he said. "I don't believe—."

"Why not" Jānis said. Serious now, he said to Gillian: "You must promise not to judge before you see. You *will* believe it."

"After that introduction, how could I not want to see?"

Jānis rose and escorted Gillian to a bar stool. He stood with his back to his friends. "Here we will show how we can hear sound *before* something will happen," he said. He pointed back at the Latvians' table. "They cannot see my hand, but they know where it will be moving."

Gillian's half smile showed she was willing to suspend judgment only to a certain point. "But they can see your shoulders moving when your hand moves?"

"That is not it," Jānis said.

Mabel jumped up, which almost knocked her chair over. "Does it hurt to be so crazy?" she shouted. She had taken her wine bottle by the neck and now held it protectively against her sagging bosom. "*Nem Zich a vaneh!*" she shouted. Then she made an unsteady beeline for the green door. "Even if I was drunk I wouldn't put up with that *drek*!"

Amused, Jānis softly commanded: "Pull the jukebox plug."

Mabel clutched her wine bottle to her chest. "Pull it out yourself," she said. She tugged hard on the green door before she went out into the hot evening.

Jānis focused only on the door. "She will come back."

Gillian, too, watched the door. "I doubt it," she said. Then she noticed that the Latvians all peered at Jānis. They looked like a little battalion about to charge. At the same moment, they all turned back to look at the door.

"There!" Jānis shouted triumphantly.

"What?" Gillian asked. "I don't see anything."

Jānis made a creepy hissing sound.

The green door of Harry's Bar opened, and Mabel wove her way to the jukebox. She reached down and unplugged it. "*Meshugaas*," she mumbled, head down. She then retreated from the bar once more.

They continued to laugh in a release of tension and a feeling of joining fully, until Jānis shifted his gaze toward the back of the bar. "Ssss! Harry is coming."

"Why are you making that sound?" Gillian asked.

"To show you what we *hear* before someone comes in," Atis said.

"But why *that* sound?" Gillian asked.

Jānis' eyes glowed again. "The sound of the cobra," he said.

Gillian sighed. "I don't understand."

"Americans," Pēteris sneered.

"I will teach you," Jānis said to Gillian.

Except for Pēteris, the other Latvians had stood and flanked Jānis. All watched the door to Harry's office.

Harry opened his office door and stood there looking confused. "What the 'H' is going on out here? Where'd Mabel go? Jesus, have I got a headache. Gillian, let me know if you need anything." He slammed the door.

"What do you think of that?" Jānis asked Gillian.

"You mean Harry coming out when you said he would? It's either a co-incidence or we're all sharing the same dream," Gillian said.

Jānis moved to the center of the small, rectangular room, where Atis posed *en garde*.

"Ssss!" Jānis caught Atis' arm, which had suddenly shot out at him about waist high. "He would have hit my flank, but I could *hear* when, and where, he would try to cut me."

Gillian just couldn't fathom these odd foreigners. Nothing but air between them. "Cut you with what?" she asked..

Atis blocked Jānis' arm just before it hacked down at him. "Ssss!"

Gillian smiled quizzically. "Even *I* could duck a hiss."

His own smile indulgent, Jānis responded, "We hear this snake sound right *before* something is going to happen. We use this to saber fight. This time we will show you but not make the sound."

Kārlis and Pēteris stood about six feet away, back by their table. Jānis and Atis faced off, each with his legs about a foot and a half apart. It did look as if they were going to fence, but they held nothing in their hands. They stood with their knees flexed, right foot of each pointing at the other's. Atis had barely begun to flash his forearm dagger like, when Jānis countered as quickly with his wrist and forearm. However, before Jānis could finish his move, Atis came back under his arm with a thrust that Jānis again put aside with his own arm. They did not touch.

Gillian found this exhibition by the Latvians strangely hypnotic. "Good re-flexes," she muttered. "I *think*…"

"Warming up," Jānis said, his arm making angular movements and jabs in the air. "We will do this until one touches the other two times. In a match, it would be five."

Now exasperated, yet also excited, Gillian protested: "But how can you touch Atis when you're standing so far apart?"

Jānis held her gaze for a few heartbeats longer than he had to. "Watch," he said. "We will finish our saber play." He advanced toward Atis, who retreated in response.

Gillian felt stupid. "You mean I'm supposed to imagine you're holding real sabers?"

Jānis turned back to Atis. He looked fierce, and happy. "You tease me," he said to Atis.

"This is not some stage play, young woman," Atis said. His right knee was now bent in a forward lunge. Just as Atis' thumb began to point at Jānis' midriff, Jānis extended his right arm a few inches above Atis', his wrist bent slightly down.

Then Jānis made two quick, almost level hops backwards and said, "Atis drew my parry and was going to cut me on my left cheek."

On her bar stool, Gillian sat on the side like a referee in a tennis match. She had only a vague idea of what she was seeing. "How do you know he would cut you on the left cheek when his hand was three feet away from you?"

Delighted, Jānis laughed. "Experience," he said, "and the sound of the cut about to be made."

After admiring the muscles defined in Jānis' "saber" arm Gillian said, "I don't believe you." Her mouth tightened. "You do not have a sword."

Jānis corrected her: "Saber," he said.

Almost irritated now, Gillian asked, "What's the difference?"

"The saber fighting is more dangerous," Jānis said. "Germans, Hungarians. They duel for fun. No masks, no protection. Our instincts grew from the *spirit* of an opponent. His pattern of attack … it can be felt by emotions and seen by the eye *inside*."

"Fighting with real sabers is one thing," Gillian said. "Fighting with nothing is something else." But she sensed she was about to grasp something crucial about these people, maybe even about herself. She just didn't know what questions to ask.

Again Jānis spoke with patience: "Energy from you comes in thinking, feeling, imagining. It comes out from you and into the space around you. If someone is trained as we are, he can sense that energy. No training can teach this instinct for where the energy comes from or where it is going. But if you already have the instinct, it can be developed. *You* have that instinct for the energy of colors. I learned this when we first met."

"I do?" Gillian asked. However, she felt too curious about the saber play to soak in Jānis' compliment for more than a moment. "Why fight with real sabers, then, if the knowing is inside you?"

Jānis and Atis stood at ease. Jānis now looked at Gillian like the lover he hoped to become to her. "Because there is nothing like feeling the saber make a hit, a cut, on a worthy opponent. You feel it here," he said, placing his hand near his stomach, "and here," he added, touching his forehead. "No motion is

91

wasted. You feel every muscle like it is some instrument, playing the music of the moment."

Jānis' arm extended from right of his shoulder at chest height, his hand out flat, palm facing downward. "Flank feint, parry two!"

Atis jumped into action. "I'm about to snap at your ..."

"Head!" Jānis shouted.

Atis had moved and now pointed at Jānis' flank.

"Parry two," Jānis responded. He brought his arm away to the right of Atis' right arm. "Atis loves flank feints."

"I like cheek cuts better," Atis said.

"Be careful, Atis. Now to the head," Jānis said. "See him retreating?" Jānis made a return to Atis' head. He extended his arm fully and made a slicing motion. "See my thumb press down for the cut?"

"Ssss!" The Latvians did this in unison, stopping their action to look at the green door.

Chapter 17

THE NEXT MOMENT

"Is this a fight?" Dolores challenged from the now open door. She looked beautiful and ultrafeminine tonight in her white and navy dress. Belted at the waist and hemmed just below the knee, her blouse neck plunged, displaying her lovely cleavage.

Because Dolores normally wore slacks, Gillian had never seen her legs. Dolores' slim ankles and legs were shaped attractively by her white, peep-toe pumps. Surprised at how steady Dolores was in these stacked heel shoes, and delighted with Dolores' appearance, Gillian came to her. Under her breath, Gillian said, "I love your outfit. Come up to the bar with me."

Dolores ignored her friend's request and sat at Mabel Levitsky's now vacant table. Jānis turned to Atis. "You parried four," he said. "An error."

"No more, fellas. Okay?" Gillian said, laughing. Dolores kept looking away from her.

"Can I get drunk without having to do some kind of routine?" Dolores asked the Latvians. "After what I just saw, I *need* a drink."

"All right," Gillian said. She felt as if the top of her head was about to come off. Jānis joined Gillian at the bar and Atis approached Dolores' chair.

"You got any Mogen David?" Dolores asked Gillian from across the room. Dolores took out a cigarette holder about a foot long, fumbled with her pack of Viceroys, and inserted one.

Pēteris coughed and came over to Dolores' table. "We could buy you better wine," he said.

Dolores propped her legs up on the empty chair opposite hers. "Wrong," she said. "It was a joke. But talk some more, honey, so I can hear your accent again."

Jānis went to the Wurlitzer and plugged it back in. Its arrays of colored light flickered on and Jānis selected a tune. Though, for ambience, Harry liked the volume at a tasteful level, the words of Ivory Joe Hunter's rendition of "Jealous Heart," filled the bar. Jānis returned to the Latvian table, while this rhythm and blues version of the old country tune played in the background.

> *Jealous heart, oh jealous heart stop beating.*
> *Can't you see the damage you have done?*

Gillian left the bar top and walked slowly past Jānis. Her hips swayed in gentle, suggestive motions. She grasped a bottle and glass in one hand and an unlit cigarette in the other. She knew Jānis watched her move through the other Latvians, who had gathered around Dolores' table. Gillian walked in slow motion. She felt as if Jānis was aiming a powerful beam at her to draw her back to him.

> *You have driven her away forever jealous heart,*

Ivory Joe Hunter sang.

Dolores observed Gillian. Her eyelashes fluttered. "Want a light?"

Pēteris coughed. "A woman lets a *man* light her cigarette."

"Honey, I've been waiting five minutes for four men to light mine," Dolores said. Looking intently at Gillian, she lit her own cigarette. "If you're smart, you won't depend on a man for anything," she said to Gillian.

Atis tried to take Dolores' hand. "But you would like this 'trouble'?"

"Not from just anyone," Dolores said, her insincere smile transparent to Atis but not to Gillian. Clearly, Dolores succeeded in making a big impression tonight.

> *And I know she loved me at the start,*

the jukebox played.

Gillian set a bottle of tawny port on Dolores' table and inhaled her cigarette. "Look at the gorgeous label, Dolores," she said. The label was black, with mauve letters, framed within a filigreed gold.

"'Douro Amandios Old Tawny Port 1945'," Dolores said. "'By Amandio Silva & Filhos of Portugal'. Harry obviously has better taste than I have," she added.

Gillian still felt the pressure of Jānis' gaze on her neck.

The other three Latvians openly gaped at Dolores, their arms draped across each other's shoulders.

Dolores pointed at the bottle. "See? She knows me well."

Kārlis wrinkled his nose. "It smells strong," he decided.

Through the years her memory will haunt me,

the voice of Ivory Joe sang out from the jukebox across the room.

Dolores pinched Kārlis' cheek. "Down, Igor," she said. "Gillian. Want to sit down?"

"*I* will," Kārlis said.

Pēteris sat down at Kārlis' right. "Which of us do you want?" he asked Dolores.

Dolores moved her chair back a few inches. She smiled sweetly and said, "I had no idea there was a shortage of women in the Village."

Atis bent over and removed Dolores' feet from the chair. He let his fingers remain an extra second on her ankles. Then he sat down. "Of course she will choose me."

Dolores poured herself some port.

"Jealous Heart" ended:

It's so hard to know she'll never want me
'Cause she's heard your beating jealous heart.

"I was more interested in you all before I came in," Dolores said. She glanced at Jānis and frowned slightly to let him know she got the intention of his juke-box selection. She then suggestively placed her long cigarette holder between the rows of her beautiful teeth and took a slow drag. She let the smoke go up one nostril like a tiny, slow cyclone.

"But you did not know us before," Pēteris said.

Dolores closed her eyes, cat like. "Exactly," she said.

Then everyone laughed.

But Gillian was surprised at Dolores' behavior. She felt Dolores' *allure*, and pondered why her friend was putting on such a show. Dolores obviously had no interest in the Latvians.

When Gillian could catch Dolores' attention, her thoughts shot out: *What the hell are you doing?*

Dolores looked away.

"You're only sober," Kārlis said. He put his arm around Dolores. "You like this?"

Dolores shrugged Kārlis' arm off. "Too soon to tell," she said.

Jānis remained at the bar. He smoked intently. When Gillian came back to Jānis, he leaned his body sideways, like a diagonal line, toward her. Gillian handed Jānis the full color brochure of the Indianapolis Union Station, and he whistled with appreciation.

"This is much greater than I imagined," Jānis said. "I want to go there someday, see this for myself … with you." He carefully folded the brochure and slipped it into his rear pants pocket. For a moment, Jānis let his guard down. His sincerity showed in his face, and Gillian quickly responded: "Only if we could come back to New York afterwards … not go on to Missouri."

Gillian's anxiety turned to relief when Dolores and the Latvians seemed to reach a temporary truce. She relaxed enough to settle on a bar stool, closed her eyes and let everything disappear. The voices of Dolores and the other Latvians sounded far away. They talked quietly. Dolores asked questions, her voice colored with ironic tones. Pēteris coughed intermittently. Kārlis laughed nervously. Atis was silent. Gillian thought she might go to sleep if she could keep her eyes closed a few moments longer. In her mind dusky smoke curled upward, swirled in big spirals that turned pale lavender at the top. She tried to look above the smoke, but it changed to a dark orchid color. She thought she was seeing the inside of her own eyelids. Red blood vessels and blue eye shadow blending into other fuzzy shadows. Far away, she heard Jānis' voice.

"What do you see?"

Gillian felt as if she were swimming backwards very slowly, pulling herself up and out of blue water with each stroke until she reached a foreign shore. Heaviness pressed her body down.

Jānis repeated: "What do you see?"

"I see purple smoke," she said. When the room came back into focus, the light hurt.

"Yes," Jānis said. "Just now, you look even more beautiful."

Gillian looked down at the familiar scratches in the bar top.

"The smoke is the essence of you," Jānis continued. "Purple is a most high color."

Fully under Jānis' spell now, Gillian responded, "Is it? Then I see you surrounded with purple." Tears tried to form, and though she didn't move, she could feel her touch go out of her body and into his.

Dolores shouted from across the room: "So these are Latvians!"

Jānis went to Dolores' table. With his back to his friends, in a low voice, he said only to Dolores: "You want a friend for a lover?" It was impossible to tell by his expression whether he had asked this out of spite or to reveal how perceptive he was.

Dolores' pupils briefly contracted, but she soon recovered. "As I said before, you're wrong about that."

Jānis smiled as if he had all the knowledge in the world and went back across the room to the bar.

Dolores undid the arms of the Latvians from around her, rose from the table, and walked up to Gillian at the bar. She put two dollars on the bar top, turned to Jānis and said, "You don't know anything about me. Or about my friendship with Gillian."

"I yield to your passionate belief," Jānis answered.

"What *are* you two talking about?" Gillian asked.

Dolores looked at the words *Olive E. Nichols*. "Everything," she said.

Gillian tried *not* to admire Dolores' breasts.

Jānis noticed. "You *should* admire beauty," he said to them both. "Wherever you find it."

Dolores looked down.

In this moment, a sense of Dolores' fragility hit Gillian powerfully. Dolores' fingers, bending a matchbook cover back and forth, signaled peril, perhaps transmitted that their friendship was sinking while four men observed from the shore.

Dolores' eyes conveyed she was "going down" for the last time.

Why did she come if this is the way she would act? Gillian didn't want to be the only reason that Dolores had come tonight. She had to admit that the "air" here had altered, had been charged with a new kind of excitement, and had changed from mere warmth to a pleasurable, but scalding, heat. She sensed that the magic had turned to a sort of danger, cloaked by an aura of preservation. *Dolores can take care of herself,* Gillian thought.

Dolores put her hand on Gillian's. "Don't you worry. You're *both* safe," she said. "See you around."

Gillian sensed she had lost control of the situation. Jānis had captured her and Dolores was fading. She didn't know which of the two had made her feel more uncomfortable, but she already knew with whom she'd be leaving Harry's Bar tonight. She felt she couldn't afford to gamble when it came to this Latvian, and so she was willing to let Dolores slide on the strength of their friendship. *About loyalty* ... Gillian stopped herself from thinking about paying the piper and opted for the high dive. "Would you call me in the morning, after ten?" Gillian said to Dolores, who went to the green door.

Just before Dolores stepped out into the stale night air, she turned back and smiled wanly at Gillian.

Gillian had not noticed Jānis' triumphant little smile. She barely realized that before she met the handsome Latvian, she had almost let Dolores into her inner world. Through her senses, through her inner vision to her core essence. The richness with which Dolores imbued everything she shared had already filled Gillian with delight and pleasure. This closeness had begun the first time Gillian stayed overnight at Dolores' flat. However, Gillian still had not fully let Dolores in. After meeting Jānis, Gillian knew she needed thrills, that pleasure without *touch* was not enough. Thus began a tug of war between loyalty to Dolores and excitement about the Latvian.

Jānis said, quietly: "Let us have one more drink, and then I will walk you home."

Chapter 18

PRE-DAWN: THE NEXT MORNING

Gillian and Jānis walked down Seventh Avenue, past Sheridan Square, to Christopher Street. It was 2:00 a.m. when they reached the Northern Dispensary, which lay in shadow. The odd building looked like a smoky amethyst that matched the circles of glass framed in a section of sidewalk in front. A triangular halo of light came from Waverly Place and 4th Street beyond. The Dispensary's ironwork spears were softened by the near absence of light. Its roof melted into trees and sky.

For the first time, Gillian felt afraid of the place. It reminded her of something: black water. Something that had happened a long time before. Something about death. Maybe her sister's, maybe her father's. Death was black and soggy, and it trudged, and it stopped in corners to whisper, and it waited at the bottom of murky pools of water. Her own death must be in the slow motion of drowning: that experience of losing air and colors, and consciousness. Missing time, having her entire life snake by like 8mm film slithering across a cutting room floor. And yet the present moments were also imposing upon her imagination, slow and crystalline. The darkness around her, and suspended time and dizzying motion … did she also feel this way about love?

The couple stopped walking. "Shall we have a cigarette?" Jānis asked, and Gillian nodded. As he had on the night of their Staten Island Ferry ride, Jānis placed two cigarettes between his lips, lit them both, and handed one to Gillian.

Jānis and Gillian came to the front steps of 144 Waverly Place and sat down together on the top step. Jānis waited for Gillian to speak. As if she already had revealed her thoughts to him, she said, "Sometimes I can't remember how old I am. Sometimes it's as if I'm still five or six. It's like the layers of an onion, each age still alive, and I'm operating on all levels at once. And yet sometimes my feelings get stuck at one level. I try to go forward, but I can't."

"Because of things you have not faced from the past," Jānis said, "at the moment they happened. To face them would give you too much pain."

"I'm not afraid of pain," Gillian protested. "At least, I don't think I am. But some things are out of our control, aren't they? I mean, isn't there a difference between what you already are and what happens to you by chance?" She let Jānis take her hand. His was warm.

"What you are," he said, "makes you choose what happens to you next, and after that. In this way, you create your future."

Gillian felt heat spread throughout her body. It was as if Jānis had just sent a bolt of sensation from his hand through hers. She struggled to continue. "I don't understand how that can be. What if there's something missing inside you? What if something important has been missing your entire life and keeps you from being whole?"

Jānis released Gillian's hand. "And what might that be?" He took out his gold cigarette case. "What 'something'?"

Gillian was afraid to say the word "love" aloud. She believed that finding "true love" would transform her, make her unfold, propel her forward. But she wanted someone to give love to her *unearned*. She stood back now and waited. She had a right to this love "the world" had largely withheld her entire life. Besides, she had proof she could not make it happen by herself. Someone else had to recognize her value, move toward her, accept her … and take her.

Jānis smoked, cupped his hands as they sat on the stairs of 144 Waverly Place. A breeze tousled his black hair. Even in this heat and humidity, his shirt collar stood up as if freshly starched. His limbs formed angles. He looked away. He seemed to be waiting for something from her. Some signal?

She blurted "What are you thinking?" She wished she didn't feel so stupid. She had said she didn't understand. Maybe this is what made him go silent.

"About how quiet it is," Jānis said, "and about if you like me. And," he added, "about when you might sleep with me."

Her eyes wide open, Gillian said nothing.

"And you have never slept with a man before," Jānis answered. "You do not feel … desire?"

"I've never wanted to," she lied, for she did want to sleep with this man. She felt awkward, and wilted by the long evening. No. The real reason was that she needed to give herself some time. She said, "I'm not ready." She thought about "Freddy," a boy from her high school in St. Louis. Freddy told everyone he was Gillian's boyfriend, but he was clumsy, and he didn't clean inside his ears. Gillian remembered thinking that Freddy's good looks seemed shaky, as if in a few years he might even become homely. Worse, he had no imagination.

Jānis smiled but didn't move toward Gillian. "In my country," he said, "we do not know when, or if, we will see each other again. Time could be short. Sharing feelings is more important. You have let me hold your hand. You have given me all the 'signs'. You feel … ready."

Gillian found something touching about what Jānis had just said. She decided that he must be telling the truth because he looked so uncomfortable in that moment. Yet, her head took its usual control of her heart. "I've only known you a few weeks," she said. She realized how flimsy her excuse must sound to this intense man.

Jānis looked boldly at her now. He measured her face and her body, and then her face again.

She knew he had put her on the spot again, so she said, "How many women have you slept with?" She waited out the moments of silence that followed.

"Parry two," Jānis said and waited for his meaning of Gillian's deflection to sink in. "You really asked me how many women I have loved," Jānis said. "None, I think. I know what loving Latvia is. What loving my parents is. But the most love I have felt for anyone was for my twin brother, Matīss."

Gillian was surprised. "You have a twin? Is he here too?"

"Dead." Jānis neither spoke nor moved for a long time after that. Finally, he seemed to measure his hands and said, "Matīss' death, the loss that was to me, has not changed who I am. I have been me my whole life. What you see outside is who I am inside. It is wrong to *not* act on what I feel, what I sense, what I think. Who cares if others approve?"

Gillian wanted to reach out to him physically. She held herself back. "But if it doesn't matter, why do you care if I like you?"

"This is logic. I will not argue with this," Jānis said. His eyes misted. "It does seem you have caught me in your trap. But I feel you hold yourself back. Someone told you to talk much when you are afraid? For you it dulls the physical appetite? This is not true. There is our Latvian custom. And I think you need something from me."

"Wait a minute," Gillian stalled. "You haven't explained the contradictions I just pointed out."

"You are right. But I think *you* contradict."

"Why?"

Jānis smiled. "Head return, parry five," he said. "You want me to touch you."

"What makes you say that?" In an odd way, what Jānis had just expressed made Gillian trust him. Her not responding had nothing to do with the fact they had just met or that she had not gone past the kissing stage with any man because of sheer, blatant inertia. This inertia formed the foundation of everything else she was. "You've caught me," she said. "Now please explain yourself."

"But I have! I would not force you. I can wait as long as you. But this will not make me stop thinking about it. Now please answer my question: You need love?"

Gillian tried to think of something that could get her out of this spot. Obviously she couldn't lie to Jānis, for he would know. Nor could she remain silent. That would also reveal her feelings. She landed on "I'm afraid of that word." After a moment she added: "You still didn't tell me how many women you've slept with." *There*, she thought.

Jānis laughed. It sounded earthy, full-throated. "Round and round," he said. "Maybe you are right to make it hard for me. I tell you it only makes *wanting* more intense."

"Good!" Gillian said, her eyes shining. Now she relaxed, and this helped her make her decision. "Not tonight, Jānis, but maybe soon." Hope flickered in his eyes. "I'm afraid you're a hypnotist and have me in your power."

"Your own power," he answered. "I will not excuse you. This night was wonderful. But it is late. You have not disappeared. That is good," he said. He pulled Gillian to her feet.

"You have just touched me," she said.

"It does not count as a real touch," he said.

Gillian kissed Jānis briefly at the side of his mouth and hugged him for several moments. She smelled the aroma of his neck. She could feel *his* tension.

She could not feel her own. Right then she almost changed her mind. She would take him up to her apartment.

But Jānis bowed slightly and kissed the back of Gillian's hand. "Good night," he said. He glided down to the sidewalk before walking back down Waverly Place.

Gillian watched him go, hoped he would turn around. Instead, he seemed to get smaller and smaller until he finally disappeared into the darkness.

Chapter 19

Gillian let herself into her apartment building and checked to see if she had mail. To her, a letter box was a phenomenon. She loved owning whatever was in it, even owning its usual emptiness. Gillian's mailbox proved she lived at 144 Waverly Place, even if she got only bills and a rare letter from her mother. When she came home every day, her mailbox seemed to be waiting like an immense potential. It extended her inner life, held her desires, waited to be enriched, waited for that one signal that could change everything. Gillian needed to feel herself expanding from the tight circle of her emotions. She needed to know someone wanted her, and so she never gave up on her mailbox. Every day, she opened it slowly.

Today Gillian found a pink envelope curiously postmarked Poplar Bluff, Missouri, where her Granny lived. Gillian knew what Granny looked like only because of an old photograph. The picture had been shot outside Granny's log cabin in the summertime. Wiry and small, Granny wore sturdy black shoes and a long, plain cotton dress buttoned all the way up to her throat. Her hair, like white cotton candy, was wound in a tight knot at the back of her head. Behind wire rimmed spectacles, her eyes showed no emotion. Her mouth, a straight line, barely showed. In the photo Granny gripped the handle of the wringer mechanism at the top of a white enamel washer. Her hands were rough, and her knuckles deformed by arthritis. Wet clothing hung from, and was wrung halfway through, two rollers at the top of the hand cranked machine. In the picture, a few feet behind Granny was an ax whose head was embedded in a stump used for chopping wood. In the distance was a ramshackle outhouse, a half-moon carved out of the door's top. Gillian could remember having met Granny only two times: once when she was eight years old and at her father's funeral. To Gillian, Granny felt as distant as the Ozarks, where Granny, and two previous generations of ancestors, had lived.

The envelope bore Hannah's thick, flamboyant script. Each word ended in a sort of whiplash. Each line spaced itself far from the next, as if to give Hannah extra cushioning. The envelope was cold. It smelled of jasmine, which Gillian found sickening, the way stinging red ants smell on the hottest summer days.

By the time Gillian had climbed the first flight of stairs, all her energy drained away. When she reached the second flight she felt dizzy. Her mother's history swept over her like a fuming dust storm, and Gillian decided she didn't want to open this letter. Her apartment looked small and uncomfortable inside. She wanted to smash into bits everything she loved in these rooms. It was as if she had been shot with some drug of frenzy. She was convinced that everything she wanted, everything she did, was useless. She felt a familiar emptiness. In desperation, she kept trying to discover who she was. Maybe some special kind of love could help her? She had accepted substitutes for this love, embellished what she felt, and still wanted more, something that could live up to her vision of what it feels like to be loved that way. Even Dolores' friendship left her empty.

The overhead light in Gillian's room looked harsh. She switched on her table lamp and tapped the pink envelope on the palm of her hand. She was exhausted. Still, she decided she had better get it over with, start tomorrow out fresh. When she opened her mother's letter, the jasmine smell sickened her. However, she thought this was probably because her apartment was so muggy. She turned her big window fan around to vent the hot air out.

Hannah's letter was written on cheap pink stationery. Against the background of Gillian's rusty orange rug, her mother's handwriting looked as if it were bouncing across the page. It read:

10 June 1949

Daughter:
Had some landlord "problems" back in St. Louie. Decided to move back to the hills, as your Granny is not well. Says I leave her

layin here like an ol yeller dog. Love the woods but hate using the washboard and chopping wood for the stove! The old timers think you are nuts being in that city. They wonder if you are wearing green eye shadow and too much rouge. Do you wear lots of rouge? Anyway, if you get enough of that place you will have to come here. Not that there is enough room. We got a cabin. That's all. The well's good and there's a pretty fair market in town. Not like St. Louie of course.

I almost forgot. Can you send me say $10 to tide me over for a while? My savings ain't gonna last forever. Garden's not so hot on account of not enough rain. Have been doing some sewing and mending work. Sold some baby clothes in a store downtown. Its called Sew Fine Fabrics. Isn't that a scream? Well got to go. Pot's boiling over and your Granny's yelling for me. Your Granny's neighbor man Eban Gunter's coming for supper. He hunts down here and swaps me meat for home cooked meals.

Well take care, Your Mother

Gillian thought about the ten dollars, and she did have an idea about what her mother meant by "landlord problems." Gillian hated the way Hannah displayed her voluptuous body and the way Hannah turned *neon* when a man came within view. Hannah often looked mesmerized by her reflection in every mirror, meeting her own eyes as if she were appraising a rival. Hannah's vanity somehow robbed Gillian of her own self-esteem and left her uncertain about her own female instincts.

The enervating events of the entire day, and evening, had made Gillian fall into bed without brushing her teeth. Yet she lay awake a long time, thinking about other children she knew when she was growing up.

As a child, Gillian had a girl friend named Beverly. Beverly told Gillian about a boy named Stevie down the street and how they had mutually discovered the difference between boys and girls. When Hannah found Gillian and Beverly one afternoon with their dresses up and their panties down, she spanked them both, told them they were "dirty," and sent Beverly back home with a note safety pinned to the neck of her dress. The note read: "I am a dirty little girl."

Gillian had thought about sex for a while now as "dirty." However, what she felt while fantasizing about it was totally different. Her ideal man was clean

107

and sensitive, intelligent, handsome. Gillian found it easy to substitute Jānis' face for that amorphous man of her fantasy life. Gillian lay in bed. She imagined the Latvian as the man making love to her. She closed her eyes in the darkness. She pictured herself and Jānis gazing into each other's eyes and conversing while the tension built. She experienced their hands feeling without touching. And when they caressed each other at last, hands melting into each other's skin, it was like delicious crackles of lightning. White light felt. She needed this love.

And yet, she wondered whether even Jānis might be enough. After years of imagining *the one*'s face, his voice, his touch, his bearing, she was afraid of the reality of the man she had just met. He might be dangerous, might make her leap, then fall. He might make her die again and again in delirious possibilities ending in brutal disappointment.

All her life so far, Gillian had been falling, then lifting herself up again. This might be nothing compared with the risk she intended to take now. She still felt Jānis on her skin. He pulled her as with strings pulsing yellow and orange and red—a reality as essential as it was disturbing. A man's attraction. She knew he shared some part of her which she habitually denied, for the feeling of him seemed to resonate in her very identity. She perceived that the source of his brightness might well be an impenetrable darkness. She felt these things at gut level, for no words could convey such sensations.

What Gillian understood was so far below consciousness that when she lay on her bed Jānis stood there, immersed in white light. She felt no danger because gold rays surrounded him. Through her window milky white moonlight spread across the room. Her pillows met her like warm puffy clouds. Dressed in a long white gown and Grecian sandals, Gillian walked toward Jānis with her hands open, supine like Jesus', at her sides. He stared *through* her. "I will be with you again soon," he said. "I will drink only to you. Then you will love me." Now at the edge of sleep, Gillian caressed his cheek and kissed him just to one side of his mouth, which she found to be sexy. Then she slept.

When Gillian sank to a deeper level of sleep, ecstasy left her. Something pulled her lower, into her innermost self. It was dark there. Unpleasant black waters absorbed whatever *lived*. A huge, ancient tree grew out of that water, and its mirror image extended far below. Gillian was compelled to dive among the tree's underwater branches. If she wanted to surface, to breathe air again, she had to choose the right limb. But then, though nothing outside her made her do this, she had to dive again. This compulsion to dive, to move from one branch to another, continued for what seemed forever.

She pulled herself even lower each time, looking for something she hoped was air. Finding the right limb also meant she could swim back up to the light. Since nothing but herself caused her to lose breath and light in these obsessive dives, she relentlessly continued. The mysterious force within her propelled her through pain and near suffocation to find some part of herself that could answer her innermost questions: *Why was I born? Who am I? Why am I here?* These riddles drove Gillian onward, even if she acknowledged her quest only in dreams.

Chapter 20

THE EAST VILLAGE: JULY 1949

One Sunday morning, with a package in her hand, Gillian followed Dolores up to the roof of Dolores' building. Dolores' huge Mexican sombrero bumped against the stairway walls. Dolores cursed and zigzagged while trying to get a heavy cardboard box up to the tarred roof above her apartment.

There Dolores had already set up a card table and two folding chairs, a red Coca-Cola cooler and a small potted palm. She spread out an oil cloth, worn through in patches, and began stacking old mismatched china plates, cups, bowls, and glasses. She finished off her bottle of Black Label beer and hummed "Ah, the Apple Blossoms" while she let several Viceroy cigarettes burn out on a concrete ledge beside the table.

Like a mirage, shimmers of hot sunlight rose upward from the tarred roof. "I sweat like a pig!" Dolores said to herself.

Gillian just looked bewildered.

"I *am* a pig," Dolores added. She pulled another beer out of the cooler and sat down on one of the folding chairs. "And I am a very depressed pig," she added. She propped her feet up on a corner of the table and lit up yet another Viceroy. "Have a seat," she said to Gillian, who dutifully sat down in the other chair.

"How can you already be soused?" Gillian asked.

A few feet away, a pigeon landed on the ledge.

Dolores ignored Gillian's question and addressed the bird: "Pidgey pidgey. There's no food up here. Go poop on someone else's veranda."

The pigeon toed his way closer and eyed the cooler. The hot sun revealed the beautiful iridescent lavenders, greens, and mauves of the bird's tiny head feathers. It also made Dolores' Saint Anthony medallion glow like a UFO, which interested the pesky bird.

"I'm tired," Gillian said, "and it's hot up here."

"Get out!" Dolores shouted at the pigeon. She picked up a chipped brown mug and threw it against the concrete wall ten feet from the table. It made a cracking sound before it fell, intact, to the rooftop, rolled over several times and landed upright. The pigeon swooped over to it, perched on its lip, and looked inside.

"You got guts," Dolores said to the pigeon. "Wanna beer?"

"You know I hate beer."

"I was talking to my pigeon friend here," Dolores said. "Have a Coke then. Or a 7UP." To the pigeon she said, "You been around. I bet you've seen some weird stuff in your short birdie life." She leaned over to accentuate her cleavage. "Lots of people would pay just to look," she said to the pigeon.

"You are so drunk," Gillian said. She helped herself to a 7UP.

"7UP," Dolores said. "Like you. So clean, so … lemony."

The pigeon jumped back on the ledge and turned its tail to Dolores.

"That was your big chance, ingrate," Dolores said. "If you had a pedigree, you'd be *capon* on my dinner plate tonight."

The pigeon disappeared below the ledge.

"I've brought you a present," Gillian said. She held in front of Dolores a medium sized package wrapped in lemon yellow tissue paper and tied with white satin ribbon.

Dolores turned away. "I'll open it later, okay?"

"It's really you."

"I'm sure I'll love it," Dolores said. "Don't you notice anything?"

"Please, Dolores. Open it now."

"Later."

Gillian whomped the package on the table. "All right then!" She murmured: "You're so bitchy today."

"I need to be bitchy today."

"And hostile," Gillian said.

"That's a good word: hostile. You didn't learn that in Missouri."

"Snob," Gillian said. "I read that there's more illiteracy in New York City than in all of *Miz-zu-rah*."

"That's because there are millions more *people* in New York City than in all of *Missouri*." By emphasizing "Missouri," Dolores had pounced on the way Gillian said the name of her home state.

"All right. Missouri. But I'm tired of you teasing me about where I come from."

"Drink your soda," Dolores said. "Oh, by the way. Did you know that, until last year, there was lithium in 7UP?"

"The things you know ...," Gillian responded. "Why should I care?'

"Maybe you started drinking it back in Missouri because lithium is a sedative," Dolores added.

"And I'm still drinking it because I like the taste," Gillian said. "Are you depressed, Dolores? Or just mad that I'm late?"

"Another late date with Latvia man?" Dolores almost spat.

Dolores' jealousy repelled Gillian, who looked defiant but said nothing.

"Come on," Dolores said. "It shows all over you. Aren't you mad at me? Wouldn't you like to pop me one in the jaw right now?"

Gillian dribbled 7UP down her chin and sighed. "Why?"

"Because I deserve it," Dolores said. "If there's a wild woman trapped inside you, I'm here to make you let her out."

Gillian wiped the 7UP off her chin with the back of her hand. "You can try," she said in a monotone.

Dolores fingered the wrapping on her present. "That's a start," she said, "because you gotta have guts to survive in this City."

"You read that somewhere?"

"No," Dolores said. "My shrink told me that."

"I'd rather be a jaded, worldly woman," Gillian said.

Dolores laughed. "Okay."

"Some things about people in the Village I still don't understand. Like, I came up here thinking we're gonna have lunch and you have no food, but you have enough dishes for twenty people." Gillian said this as if she and Dolores had been talking about it all along,

"I have an exciting plan for these dishes."

"It's almost one o'clock. I'll take you to lunch." Gillian looked for somewhere to put her soda bottle. My treat," she said.

"Throw that bottle against the wall," Dolores said. "I'll clean it up."

Gillian held the bottle firmly by its middle. "It's half full. It'll splatter."

"Go on, Gillian. Throw it!"

"My hand won't let me!"

Dolores took the bottle from Gillian's hand and hurled it against the concrete wall. "God, I loved that," she said. "That *sound*!" She stood up, picked a salad plate from the top of the stack, and sent it flying at the wall.

Gillian looked mortified. "What if someone hears us?"

Dolores broke another plate against the wall. "They can't have my dishes!" she shouted.

"What'll you eat off ... after?"

Dolores hurled a coffee cup, overhand, like a fastball. "I bought these cheap at a junk store yesterday," she said, "so I could do this with you." This time she heaved two plates at once. They joined the other shards at the base of the wall. She stuck a huge dinner plate in Gillian's hand. "Here's a really good one. Don't let me down!"

Gillian faced the wall. "My arm's not as good as yours."

"Move closer then."

"What if the pieces ricochet off and hurt us?"

"Christ, Gillian! Trust me."

"Dolores, I can't."

"Would you throw the fucking plate?"

Gillian hated it when Dolores used that ugly word. This made her hurl the platter violently against the wall.

"Damn! That was great! Do it again," Dolores said. She gave her friend a stack of saucers.

Gillian threw saucer after saucer against the wall. "Listen to that! Here Dolores. You better throw a few while there's still some left."

"I see I have created a monster," Dolores said. With one hand, she heaved an entire stack of six dessert plates at the wall. "Maybe that was a bit excessive," she said.

All at once Mrs. Noticias from downstairs appeared on the roof with a policeman.

"Ladies," the cop said, "you are disturbing the peace. You are also littering."

Mrs. Noticias pulled the cop aside. "Meester Officer," she said. "You think we should call the hospital?"

"Yes sir," Dolores said. "I'm planning to impale myself on shards of broken dishes, and I'm taking all of you *with* me!"

Gillian looked terrified, but she spoke calmly: "We're both very depressed, Sir," she said. "We both have … 'female problems' right now, and you know how women get."

Mrs. Noticias clung to the officer's arm. "*I* never get thees way," she said.

"My friend speaks truth," Dolores slurred. "And I feel even worse than she does because my boyfriend dumped me for a flashy redhead," she lied. "I am at this moment venting on my dishes. Why, anyone else would be taking pot shots at the pedestrians down there."

Mrs. Noticias looked shrewdly at Dolores. "Maybe you could use some new dishes." She muttered, *La sabelotodo.*"

"That means 'know-it-all'," Dolores said to Gillian.

Gillian barely hid a smile. "Officer, we'll clean this up right away."

The policeman looked at the heaps of broken dishes and then at the two women. "Tell me you weren't throwing them at each other. Do me a favor and don't cut yourselves. Next time you get 'depressed', take a couple of aspirins."

"The one in the sombrero," Mrs. Noticias said to the policeman. She indicated Dolores.

The officer piloted Mrs. Noticias off the rooftop and the door closed behind them.

Dolores gazed with admiration at the mess they had made. "The cop won't be back if we're quiet," she said. She sounded oddly sober. "Let's clean this up and then you can take me to lunch."

Gillian pushed the wrapped present toward Dolores again. "Here. I want to watch you open it."

Dolores read the gift card out loud: "'To my beloved friend. Love, Gillian'. Dolores thanked Gillian. Then she unwrapped her gift carefully, slowly, and opened the plain white box. "Oh! It's absolutely mad! Where'd you get it?"

"I made it for you."

It was a peasant style blouse, in fashion thanks to Carmen Miranda movies. Unlike the one Dolores often wore, this one was special. The loose fitting cotton blouse with short, puffed sleeves had a square neckline with eyelets. Through the neckline, and the edge of each sleeve, Gillian had woven bits of lavender ribbon.

Dolores pressed it to her cheek. "I love it! And I have just the skirt to go with it."

"They still let me use the machines at the Y," Gillian said. "In exchange, I teach other women how to use them." For the first time, she gave her friend a full on hug.

The two friends laughed for a few delicious, tension relieving minutes. Then they began to clean up the broken dishes.

Chapter 21

GREENWICH VILLAGE ... AN HOUR LATER

Below street level on Christopher Street, the Lion's Head was paneled, ceiling to floor, in dark walnut. Cathedral lamps with thick onion skin shades hung midway down from the ceiling. These, and the paneling, and the square oak tables in their brown leather upholstered booths, gave the tavern warmth and privacy. A gaunt teenage boy played classical guitar in a dark back corner of the room.

Gillian took off her floppy straw hat. It was adorned with blue and yellow cornflowers. Today she had not put on enough face powder to obscure her freckles.

"Oh, no," Dolores said. "I think Pēteris is our waiter." She stuck an unlit cigarette in the corner of her mouth. The humidity made her curly hair stick to her face. She wore her new blouse with a gathered cotton dirndl skirt that accentuated her narrow waist. It was striped with navy blue, "sat" at her waistline and flowed to a wide hem. Dolores grabbed an ashtray and a bottle of ketchup off the table behind them. She had a stranglehold on the neck of the bottle. She peeled a corner off the label. "Del Monte," she announced. "Ever notice how these things only come off partway? I stuck a shredded one on my fridge a few months ago to commemorate the sacrifice of so many tomatoes." Dolores' tone changed abruptly. "I suppose you called your boyfriend to tell him we'd be here?"

"Jānis told me about this place early this last night, after he asked me a dozen times what I'd be doing today. He said, 'Take your friend out for lunch at the Lion's Head,' and then he gave me two dollars." Gillian unwrapped

Dolores' fingers from the ketchup bottle. "You haven't even seen the menu," she said.

"You never know when you'll need a transfusion," Dolores said.

Pēteris entered from the upper level bar and stood at their table. He set down two glasses of ice water. "I should not bring water unless you ask for it," he said to Gillian. "However, I try to be kind. Your friend believes I do not give you good service? That is why she takes this cat-sup bottle from the other table."

Gillian intended a friendly smile. Instead, she just looked awkward. "Hi, Pēteris."

"Ladies," he said.

They both waited for him to speak, but he just stood there.

"Any famous writers here today?" Dolores asked.

"I would not know," Pēteris replied.

Dolores blew out a big puff of cigarette smoke in Pēteris' direction. "I remember you," she said. "You're the perpetual optimist," she added with a *soupçon* of sarcasm .

Gillian shot Dolores a warning look and said, under her breath, "It takes one to know one." She asked Pēteris for a straw.

Pēteris brought one soda straw back from a little supply counter.

Gillian told Pēteris she was glad he was their waiter.

"Thank you," he said. "However, I did have no choice in this."

"See, Gillian?" Dolores said. She asked Pēteris if he could *"spare"* another straw.

Gillian ordered a hamburger platter and Dolores ordered turkey breast on whole wheat with lettuce and mayo.

Pēteris bowed with feigned submission and left their table.

"You *will* need ketchup with your French fries, Gillian."

"Okay, Dolores," Gillian said. She grazed her fingers along the smooth wall paneling. "Pēteris was okay just now, don't you think?"

Pēteris returned with two small salads and left the women again so fast that it made them giggle.

Gillian held her fork in her left hand and brought some lettuce and tomato to her mouth on the back of the fork.

Dolores' eyes widened. "What're you? British now?"

"Jānis taught me to eat 'Continental'," Gillian said.

Just then, two men burst through the door. They had tied bright red scarves over their noses and lower faces. They wore long brown tunics, sashed over their dark baggy pantaloons. Like low flying daggers, they moved toward Gillian's table and pulled her out of her chair. Pēteris saw them, put down the lunch tray, and headed toward them.

"What is this?!" Dolores shouted. But the two men were hustling Gillian out the door. "Call the cops," Dolores said to … anyone. She grabbed Pēteris by his belt and jerked him halfway across the room.

"But I will lose my job," he balked and covered a tiny smile.

"Screw your job! We've got to get her back."

Once outside, Pēteris and Dolores saw the kidnappers running down Christopher Street as they dragged Gillian along behind them.

"There they are!" Dolores said.

Pēteris was calm. "They will go to Spring Street," he said.

Dolores pulled Pēteris at a good clip across Seventh Avenue, which eventually tore his sleeve. "Are you in on this too?" she asked. "What the hell is going on?"

"You can see for yourself," Pēteris said. "They will take the IND."

Dolores didn't wait for Pēteris. She put tokens in the turnstile and clomped down the steps and into the urine smelling, dimly lit subway. "Gillian! Gillian!" But the subway train's door closed.

Pēteris sauntered along with Dolores and took her arm on the platform. "We just board the one next," he said.

Dolores leaned over to look at the back of the train that was taking Gillian away. "This is awful," she said. "Where are the cops when you need them?" She gave Pēteris a "drop dead" look. "You either have no feelings or you're just plain crazy!"

"This was the plan," Pēteris said.

Dolores was furious. "What the hell do you mean?"

"Jānis said to me this morning: 'Do not tell the friend about this part. Geelion must be afraid. This will enhance the joy'."

"Oh. She's not in danger, then?" Dolores sighed, then relaxed. "I'm still mad at you," she said to Pēteris. "You could have trusted me," she added as they boarded the next train.

"The plan. It did work fine," Pēteris said. "The Latvian Wedding Game." He gestured toward an empty seat. "You see? Even in this hour of rush we have luck."

Dolores stood and held on to a bar high at her right side. "Wedding?! Oh, great," she said. "So Jānis didn't let Gillian in on this?"

Pēteris just looked at Dolores.

"Well? What are we supposed to do now?"

"We follow them all the way to the flat of Marija and be shouting much," Pēteris said. "We will act afraid and with anger."

Dolores rubbed her stomach. "Will there be food?"

Gillian got off the subway with her two "abductors," Kārlis and Atis, who had to unmask at Spring Street when transit officers boarded their car. Now they were in Lower Manhattan, a terrain unfamiliar to Gillian. In contrast to the crazy quilt structures she was used to in the Village, apartment buildings and shops here were more uniform in size and shape. Here, the streets felt unprotected. She clung to Kārlis' arm when a leathery faced derelict, who conversed with people only he could see, thrust his grimy hand toward them.

"He has been too long on the 'tea'," Kārlis said laughing. "This is a lesson to anyone who smokes marijuana. You want to enhance? Okay. You want to harm? Not okay."

Gillian looked withered from the heat and from her fake kidnapping adventure. "It's weird that you're both being so chatty," she said. "Twenty minutes ago, you kidnapped me in the middle of lunch. I'm still hungry. Please tell me why we're running around like this."

The two Latvians now flanked Gillian on the train platform, and they climbed the stairs together. Gillian walked unevenly, somehow managing also to keep up with the Latvians when they crossed intersections and turned corners. She tried to catcher breath. "By the way," she said, "I knew it was you."

Kārlis winked at Atis. "How?"

"I know the Latvian scent now."

"Very good," Kārlis said.

Kārlis and Atis tied on their bandana masks again. "Now you must pretend you do not want to be here."

"But I don't even know where I am!"

Since Kārlis' body obscured the buzzer panel, Gillian couldn't see whose apartment he rang.

They were admitted by a buzz. Kārlis and Atis took Gillian while they ascended three flights of stairs so quickly that Gillian felt woozy. Then they stopped in front of someone's flat.

"Everything happens to me on Sunday," she panted.

"You are a sweet girl," Atis said. "Straighten up skirt please. Tuck in the blouse also." Out of modesty, he looked away.

Now Gillian faced the closed door. She sensed that whoever was within that apartment literally tugged at her. Jānis' presence braced her, for she could sense his support.

"Who comes?" Jānis shouted.

Kārlis told Gillian to say her name, which she did. "And please take off your shoes when you go inside," he added.

Gillian could hear someone playing a stringed instrument at turbo speed. A woman sang this bright tune in another language.

Jauns un traks tu, puika, esi bijis, lauzdams manu zelta gredzentiņ'
Jauns un traks tu, puika, esi bijis, lauzdams manu zelta gredzentiņ'
Vai domā'i manim jaunu pirkti, vai saukt man' par savu līgaviņ'
Vai domā'i manim jaunu pirkti, vai saukt man' par savu līgaviņ'
Vai saukt man' par savu līgaviņ' . . . .

The door opened to a small parlor, lit with dozens of tall white candles. Gillian was next aware of the herbal aroma that was distinctly Jānis', and she felt his hand curve around her waist from behind the door. He led her into the main room of the apartment. Kārlis and Atis followed them in. Several small electric fans generated a cross breeze that made the space cooler than Gillian expected. She took off her leather sandals. Immediately, someone handed her a pair of shiny rust colored slippers. Each had an elastic band over the center, and Gillian enjoyed how soft and comfortable they felt.

Gillian expected to hear a knock at the door. She looked back over her shoulder. Bright candlelight illuminated what Gillian knew must be some Latvian emblem, displayed on the back of the door. It was comprised of three buttercup yellow stars above the top half of a shining yellow sun on a royal blue field. More than a dozen short rays formed a half circle above this sun. Just below and standing upright, a red lion faced a silver griffin. A larger red lion on the left and a gray griffin on the right framed the central design. Two intertwined, leafy oak branches formed the base of the escutcheon and were tied by a ribbon of burgundy red-white-red.

"This was my country's true coat of arms," Jānis said, "when we were free. When the Bolsheviks annexed our country in 1940, Stalin made it against the law to display it." He had tears in his eyes. "It is part of one of the oldest national flags in the world. There you see the sun of freedom."

"It's beautiful," Gillian said. She felt how proud Jānis was, how homesick. She *took in* the flag's glorious symbols. "Where are we, Jānis?" she finally asked. "Is this your apartment?

For the moment, Jānis released all his unhappiness. "It is Marija's," he said. (He pronounced her name as *Mar-ya*.)

Marija had a mane of wavy, golden hair and the large almond shaped eyes typical of Baltic women. She wore a stiff, embroidered matron's cap that stood up vertically about eight inches around her head. Embroidered around the rim were red-brown amber beads. Around her waist were strands of dark leather, entwined with cherry amber beads. Though Marija was young, she had one lower tooth missing.

"Marija will be your best bridal maid," Jānis added, "for she plays the *kokle* and she has learned more than one hundred wedding songs from centuries ago. She has written one for us."

Gillian froze. She had so many questions in this moment, but she could not speak. Maybe the preacher was late? Or would it be a priest? She had no idea what Jānis' religion was. And further, Jānis had not proposed to her. Was this real? Or some kind of cruel joke?

Over Gillian's head Marija slipped a long white linen gown, embroidered with red, blue, yellow, and mulberry color flowers. Then she tied a golden fabric cord around Gillian's waist.

Gillian admired the stitching and the bright colors. She asked Jānis what was happening. Jānis held her more tightly. "You will see in a few moments." In the warm candlelight, Jānis' face and clothing glowed. He wore a tunic much fancier than those of Kārlis and Atis. The yoke of his white linen shirt, which he wore over white batiste pants, was embroidered with rich red and gold thread.

Overwhelmed with expectation, Gillian wasn't thinking clearly enough to ask Jānis about the garland of flowers that adorned his head. Furthermore, never having met the "bridesmaid," Gillian hesitated to ask her to confirm what she hoped was about to happen.

Marija placed a wreath of flowers on Gillian's head and stood beside her. She smiled at Gillian to encourage her and began to sing again with an oddly zany gusto.

Jauns un traks tu, puika, esi bijis, lauzdams manu zelta gredzentiņ'
Jauns un traks tu, puika, esi bijis, lauzdams manu zelta gredzentiņ'. . .

Jānis acted as if this was an everyday event. Apparently mellowed by wine, he led Gillian to a table on which two huge wooden bowls overflowed with a variety of fruit Gillian had never seen assembled in one place: white and red grapes, pears, oranges, apples, bananas, and mangoes. There were little brown, kiln fired clay bowls, one with dates and figs. Another clay bowl was filled with cracked cashews, pecans, and almonds. There was an odd, shallow bowl that contained what looked like cranberries atop a bed of cottage cheese. Petite pastries adorned little silver trays. On terra cotta platters were pirogues filled with minced ham or sausage or sweet cheeses. There were six bottles of wine imported from Latvia.

When Gillian realized that this was a wedding feast, she asked for a chair. She hoped she wouldn't cry. *Maybe he does love me*, she thought.

When the buzzer sounded, Marija stopped singing.

Again, Jānis asked: "Who comes?"

Pēteris stood outside the door with Dolores. "Say your name."

"You know damned well who it is!" Dolores shouted to the door.

"You may not come in," Kārlis shouted from inside Marija's flat. "We do not know you."

In vain, Dolores tried to turn the knob. "Let me in!" she demanded. "I want to make sure Gillian's okay."

Pēteris laughed. "That is good," he said. "Now tell Jānis you are very angry that they have taken your friend away."

"You better let me in," Dolores said, "or I'll call the cops."

Pēteris winked at her. "*Very* good."

Kārlis pressed all his bulk against the inside of the door and said, "Dolores Valencia, you must promise not to tell anyone what you will see here today. Then you can come in. Do you promise this?"

Dolores felt no duty whatever to obey the Latvians. She did, however, promise.

Jānis peeled Kārlis off the door and unlocked a dead bolt. "Come in," he said. "You will not get back your friend, at least not as she was."

When Dolores burst in and rushed to her friend's side, she found Gillian dabbing her eyes with the sleeve of her gown. Marija handed her a linen handkerchief.

"I love your top," Marija said to Dolores.

Dolores, who had put a protective arm around Gillian, quickly figured out that this was not just a wedding game and that there was no use fighting the inevitable outcome. And so much food! She exclaimed, "Thank God! I'm starved!"

Marija sat in a chair with her kokle across her lap. The instrument was like a long zither, crafted of varnished beech wood. Marija began to play and sing their wedding song again. The Latvians laughed and talked with Jānis, who tried to spot Gillian. Unable to see her clearly because of the leafy garland that encircled his head, Jānis adjusted this crown.

Finally, Gillian came to him, and her smile was radiant. "You can't know how much this means to me," she said.

"Don't worry," Dolores said. "I'll protect you from these, these pagans." She stuffed an entire sausage pirogue in her mouth and then moved back a few paces when Jānis approached them.

"Your new blouse is perfect for today," Gillian said to Dolores. Gillian told Jānis that he looked wonderful. "I especially like the flowers in your hair. But I wish you'd told me to dress up."

"If you were a Latvian woman," Jānis said, "you would wear what Marija wears, only something finer." He kissed her in front of everyone. "I knew you would want your friend to be here. We will perform a ritual in the tradition of my country. Even Pēteris approves."

Gillian felt too queasy to eat anything.

Jānis continued: "A kind of … marrying."

Dolores paled. "This is real?"

"As real as it *can* be," Jānis said. "Let us proceed. Dolores Valencia, you must pretend to be very protective of your friend. Pretend she is here against your will."

"That will be easy," Dolores said. "Then what?"

"Gillian must pretend she hates me."

Gillian brushed against Jānis' hand. "That won't be easy," she said.

"It is our tradition," Jānis said. "Dolores, please take Gillian over there by Marija."

Dolores relented, but she also retorted: "The girl's singing the top tune on the Latvian hit parade?"

Jānis started back across the room. He pretended not to hear Dolores' quip. "You need not know the song," he said to Gillian. He then stood with the other Latvian men by a high, narrow wooden table on which lay an old brown book, with Lettish words gilded on its spine and cover. On the wall above the table hung the Latvian flag with its dark red and white stripes. Dolores hooked one arm into Gillian's and brought her friend over to stand beside Marija, who now sang in heavily accented English:

> *Ray-dee-ant Spidola, come to ree-ver Daugava,*
> *Where Lacplesis, your true below-wed, waits.*
> *No finer pe-ir weel wed tu-gay-der,*
> *Join-ed tu-gay-der by reever,*
> *Tu-gay-der, and-lass-lee.*

During the second verse, under her breath, Dolores whispered to Gillian: "I'm so glad she's seen-ging in Een-gleesh."

Gillian gently elbowed her friend.

Pēteris turned to Dolores. "Tell us what your friend will be giving in this union."

"What?"

"It is the tradition," Kārlis said, "that the family of the bride brag of what she adds to the wealth of the bridegroom."

Dolores told them Gillian had little money. Gillian's face turned ashen, and so Dolores added: "But she has other riches: beauty, courage, kindness. Both a sweet nature and a high intellectual curiosity."

Jānis then beamed.

"I like that," Dolores said. "I might give the bride away after all."

"Then bring her to me now," Jānis said. "Kārlis, open the sacred book. We are ready." Jānis reached for Gillian, held her hand in his two hands, and pulled her to his side. "Dolores, come," he said. "Stand at her right. Marija will now sing the song she wrote for us."

Chapter 22

144 WAVERLY PLACE: AUGUST 1949

"I want to make love with you again," Jānis had said tonight as they stood on Sixth Avenue, smoking, waiting to cross. Intense humidity made it hard to breathe. Now it was after 2:00 a.m., Sunday morning. Jānis was out. He wanted to find a shop still open where he could buy more cigarettes.

In her small kitchen, Gillian paced the linoleum floor, which looked dull tonight. She could hear her alarm clock ticking on the countertop. She washed her hands with Lux liquid and ignored a banana peel draped across dirty dishes in the sink.

She undressed now. She kicked off her shoes, let her clothing drop to the floor and stepped out of the little pile it made. She snatched her kimono off a hook on the inside of her bathroom door and slid the kimono over each shoulder. She searched her Frigidaire in vain for something to eat. There were only a couple of raw eggs and a shriveled grapefruit half. Yellowed celery hearts. An almost empty bottle of milk.

She slammed the refrigerator door on the dangling black sash of her kimono and cursed. She felt embarrassed that she had no clean sheets. Same ones on since Jānis last stayed over, two weeks ago. He had knocked on her door in the middle of the night and had gone right to sleep on the bed beside her. She had lain on her side and admired Jānis until dawn. Then she fell asleep and dreamed she was walking alone on Christopher Street at night. Garbage cans overflowed onto the pavement. In her dream, when she reached the end of the street, a very ugly man came out of nowhere. She awoke and saw Jānis watching her, his face almost touching hers. They had made love in the morning, and afterwards had a breakfast of *crêpes Suzette* and espresso before he disappeared, as he often did.

Now Gillian turned out the light. A white yellow glow, from the streetlight below, infused her long room. She closed her eyes, caressed the strings of orange beads that hung in her kitchen doorway, let their cool nubs slide over her face and body. The ends of the chains brushed along her ankles. They swished along her thighs when she stroked them, let them go. They felt to her like streams of water, down spouting over her head and along the hollows of her neck and between and around her breasts, and around and down her belly. Soon Jānis would be here with her. Soon, they would …

The sound of Jānis' key in the lock jolted Gillian out of her reverie.

"I bought cigarettes," Jānis said. After he closed the door, a veil of light from the window outlined his body. When he slipped his hand through Gillian's kitchen beads to touch her face, his fingers were cool at her cheekbones and ear. He kissed her neck. "Why are you standing here?" he asked. He wrapped more of the bead chains around her waist. He pressed the beads against her thighs. He slid his fingers over them and over her.

Gillian wanted to prolong this moment, to savor these feelings. "I need to tell you something again," she said. She leaned away from him. The beads felt odd, but nice too. "I was five. I almost drowned. I was lying at the bottom of a pool, at the deep end. A girl pulled me up by my hair."

Jānis' smooth cheek stroked across Gillian's. He took both her hands in his. "You told me this already," he said, "because it is important. You have not let it go." With his hand he cradled her cheek. "Maybe you think surrendering to our lovemaking is like drowning."

Gillian blocked Jānis' astute observation. Instead, she spoke of what had been nagging her. "There was something else. Funny. This darkness brought it back." When Jānis kissed the bridge of her nose, Gillian could feel his eyelashes brush her forehead. "The funny thing is," she said, "I don't know if I really did what I'm about to tell you about or dreamed I did it. I went back to the pool a few months later, in September. I didn't intend to. I was just walking home from school. It was late afternoon, and the water was black with leaves. It

128

looked like a storm was about to break. I walked down those three steps and stood in the shallow end for a long time with the water up to my chin. I don't know why I did it. The water was horrible, and it smelled bad."

Jānis lit a match. Its flame made the beads and his face flicker and seem to catch fire. He handed Gillian the cigarette. "You did it because you had to prove you were not afraid anymore."

She touched his neck. "But I wasn't afraid *while* I was drowning. It was pleasant, really." She gave Jānis the lit cigarette and watched the end of it glow orange, bathe his face. She liked the way he held his fingertips perfectly flat against his mouth when he smoked.

"But all your life you have been afraid of it. The dark. As children, we feel *everything*. Fear … sometimes it tastes like copper on your tongue. Other times it slices your stomach like a blade. But we cover the wounds. Yet we feel them our lifetime while we grow. You are strong enough now to let that story go."

Gillian thought: *What can my almost drowning mean to this man who has seen death really happen to so many?* She shook off her self-pity.

Jānis kissed Gillian's hand. "Maybe you are afraid of *me*?"

"Put out that cigarette, will you?"

Jānis let go of her. "Shall I put it out in my hand?"

"Like you did our first time?" Gillian asked.

Jānis spread the beads back from Gillian and drew her body against his. "Admit you were impressed. I asked you, 'Do you dance?'"

"Did you put out the cigarette?!"

"In this ashtray. Here—on the counter behind you. Do you not know where your things are?" Now Jānis' herbal scent encircled Gillian like a wreath. "You were afraid our first time," he said.

At his touch, Gillian felt a wire of energy tighten inside. Then she kissed him. She muttered, "You tricked me, Jānis." She felt her back grow moist and her abdomen ache. "You held my hands above my head," Gillian said.

"And we 'danced'."

"Laying down," Gillian said. "You told me Latvian girls like it."

"*You* liked it!"

"I like it better now," Gillian said.

"Because you are no virgin now."

Gillian moved through the beads. "I'm frowning."

"I can feel you."

She leaned toward Jānis. Then she kissed him, feeling his lips open.

Jānis moved away. "Want your own cigarette?"

"No! I want you to make love to me!" He came back to Gillian, and she felt his lips on her earlobe.

"No more talk about drowning," he whispered. His hands firmly grasped her bare waist, under her kimono.

Gillian took his hands away. "Can't promise that. Now where did you really put out that cigarette?"

Jānis took her gently out into the main room. "In my hand."

"Liar," Gillian said. Her stepping on Jānis' toe was an accident. She said, "Ha! Serves you right."

Jānis looked as if he were waiting to hear something important.

Then she asked: "Do you love me?"

He pretended not to hear. "You would not do that on purpose, step on my foot on purpose. No. You would not do that."

"You're sure?"

"If, as you say, I'm a liar, what would words of love mean?"

Jānis had gone over by the window. He felt around for the Murphy bed strap. Up near the ceiling he grabbed air.

Gillian caught the implausible scent of cinnamon and orange blossoms now. She lit a candle. "It would mean *everything*," she said.

"Don't do that," Jānis said, his voice almost a whisper.

"I want to see you," she said. She went to him and unbuttoned his shirt. She admired his almost hairless chest, which he once told her meant he was "highly evolved." This made touching him all the more pleasurable. Then, with her hands inside his shirt and on his stomach, she loosened his shirttail from his pants.

"You look like a ghost," Jānis said. He blew out the candle. He reached around her and gently put his hands on her breasts. "I want to feel you," he said. "I can see you with my fingers. I can smell your perfume." He smoothed the kimono off her shoulders. "Like reading braille," he said. "Take off your kimono now."

"The blind leading the blind," Gillian said. "Take off your pants now." She felt his lips on her throat. "Are you smiling, Jānis?"

"No."

"Of course not. You can't get your pants off."

"Shame on you," he whispered. He grabbed Gillian hard around her waist. His weight pushed her down to the floor. "I could tickle you to death!" He took her kimono in his hand and said, "I will throw this out the window! It will float down to the sidewalk. And in the morning, all of Waverly Place will know I had you. In the wind your kimono will ripple like a flag!"

Gillian pulled away from Jānis and sat up.

"I *will* throw it. Give in to me."

"I think you're smiling, Jānis," Gillian whispered. She knew tonight she would indulge him completely. Jānis lay down with her on the orange rug and kissed her shoulder. She imagined Jānis smiled, and it was enough. She could smell his woodsy scent. It was his own aroma, strong as cologne but much better. He kissed her lips now, and when she opened her eyes she saw blue rays emanating from Jānis' eyes.

"Remember me," he said. He had his hands in her hair, fingers curved at the sides of her head. He kissed her, moved, moved inside her like waves. The sound of his breathing and the pressure of his mouth and body rocked her out of her loneliness. Waves pushed and lapped toes and thighs and hips and bellies and shoulders and lips. Waves like drowning and pulling and re-membering and … surviving. Jānis' touch startled her skin now like a cool breeze on summer's back. And he was still inside her, raising the nerves in her skin to quickness. Alive, alive, static charged and tightrope walking the edge between passion and abandon. The sound of their bodies lapping. Sound *felt* like rain on the skin, resonating threads that stretch from womb egg through a man's and woman's ecstasy. Not moans, now, but swaying, weighted pleasure pressing, waves pressing, sound pulling. Waves, sound, bodies, and hands and skin. Electrically, electrically, pushing on that tight wire, that current vibrating in Gillian, inside her body.

Gillian felt that her back on the thick pile rug was far away from the front of her. Her back was gone. It was as if a window barrier between her self's room and life outside had opened. And there, on top of her, was Jānis' smooth chest and belly, his thighs. And she was back in her life somewhere, at five and twelve and twenty. So far, so far behind her, she lay in the black waters, her legs and arms floating. Almost still now. A soggy leaf curled at Gillian's lips and a pale moonlike light entered through a door ajar that was her childhood bedroom. These visions reflected, filmy, inside her eyelids. Waters now, came slowly, calm now, adjusting to her weight, blending, and circulating. She sighed now at the moon.

Chapter 23

SEPTEMBER 1949

A few autumn leaves had fallen in Washington Square, and the sky had taken on that piercing blue that only fall imparts. A golden light spread down the buildings and across people's faces. Though colors are lovely in September, when discerning people walk in the afternoon, they feel vague regret. Because the air is crisp at night with something so wistful it has no name, perceptive ones often feel insecure. They note a peculiar angst that means days of warmth are waning, and it is time to live it up before trees turn bare and birds leave for the winter.

This time of year, who would argue that a world without change could be a good world? Would anyone deny that there are peaks of experience whose endings are tragic? After all, when summer's promises have gone unfulfilled, one begins to perceive autumn as a cheat. We cry, "I want my money back," but summer turns away. We then find ourselves at the weaker end of some muddy tug of war. Like squirrels in the fall, we begin to take stock of our food. Unlike squirrels, we also begin to assess our cache of love.

By 11:00 a.m. in Grand Central Terminal, the humidity had settled like a dank velvet curtain. Passengers sweated. They fingered their now slick train schedules and their wrinkled tickets while they hurried through the long underpass. Near the oyster bar, two men stood facing opposite corners where a pair of vaulted, tiled archways intersected. The archway was known as "The Whispering Gallery" for the same kind of acoustic properties as those of the St. Louis Union Station's oyster bar.

One of the men was Jānis. He faced into a corner of the archway and spoke in English. His lips moved fast. He occasionally looked over his shoulder to make sure no one was near. Listening at the opposite corner, about thirty three feet away, another man appeared to be reading his train schedule. This man also glanced over his shoulder.

Jānis crumpled up an empty matchbook and threw it into a food smeared waste can. Then he walked slowly over to the refreshment stand, where he took a long time looking through magazines before buying a paper cup of coffee. This Jānis drank casually until the man to whom he had been whispering slipped out of the terminal. Finally, Jānis checked the Arrivals board just before he exited for the subway.

Later that day, through a back door marked "Deliveries Only," Jānis entered the Biltmore Hotel in Grand Central Terminal. He took the cool back stairway at an easy pace and emerged from a door accessing the hotel's third level. Only Elsie Canad stood in the hall. Elsie was a mixed race hotel maid in her mid-fifties. Over the years, Elsie had taken special care of the Biltmore's Room 300, a meditation chapel.

"Folks start stragglin' up here around five, even on Fridays," Elsie said to Jānis. Then she laughed. This made her fulsome breasts, belly, and hips to jiggle. "I been here some twenty years now, Mister Y, and you know, I seen enough folks sittin' in here, readin' their trashy paperbacks. (Elsie thought Jānis' name began with a "Y." He had not corrected her.) "And men lookin' at half naked girlie pictures in *Glamor Parade*. 'I'm prayin', they say." Elsie pushed her damp, frizzy hair away from her face. "And I seen some pretty young things too with their little hearts all broke up, cryin' like doomsday done come. Ain't no real church in here I tell you. 'Cept to me."

Elsie and Jānis came to the closed chapel door.

"Are the others here?"

"Yes, Sir," Elsie said.

Jānis looked back over his shoulder before he opened the chapel door. Soft lighting from above bathed this Gothic room, enhancing the light oak pews and sanctuary, backlit stained glass, and dark red drapes. Fresh white carnations adorned the altar. Jānis' friends stood along the left wall, just inside the door. "We can keep the door closed?" Jānis asked Elsie.

"As always, Mister Y," Elsie replied.

"Remember: Get yo' business done before five o'clock," Elsie said to Jānis. "Don't you tell no one I let you do this again," she added.

Jānis smiled. "People will be in the bars by five," he said.

"Well *I* won't be," Elsie said. She walked down the hallway outside the chapel. Her hips tossed back and forth. She took a few random swipes at the wallpaper with her feather duster and then headed for the elevators.

Jānis closed the chapel door behind him and turned to his friends. Kārlis stood farthest from the door. He looked intelligent and brave. Atis wore a hopeful, thirsty look. Pēteris was half asleep in the heat. Also present were Helmars Rudzitis, a silver haired Latvian who carried himself like a diplomat, and a Yugoslav, Colonel Milanov, to whom Jānis had whispered in Grand Central Terminal.

Jānis spoke to the latter: "Colonel Milanov, please tell us what they are saying in Belgrade. I am amazed you got out."

Milanov leaned against the wall beside the back pews. He rubbed his shoulder, where in humid weather his old war wound throbbed. "They questioned me again and again," he said. "They called me finally 'a mere nuisance'. You see, that Old War is no longer alive to the Bolsheviks. They now boast about the next great war, which they say will be fought on the North America continent."

"But you have news," Jānis said to Milanov, "about Communist infiltrators in City Government?"

"Only rumors," Milanov said. "In Europe there are many rumors about many things."

"What about names?" Kārlis asked.

Rudzitis, who had left the group to pluck a carnation head from the altar bouquet, said, "Code names only. Informants warn that we are being watched in the Village—however, not heavily. At least for now." Rudzitis lifted the carnation to his nose and exclaimed "Beautiful!" He then buttonholed the carnation of his wide lapel.

Pēteris sat near Rudzitis in a pew, his knees drawn up under his chin. "I have seen an informer in Harry's Bar," he said. "That is on Greenwich Avenue. A so-called musician."

"But this means you are in danger," Milanov said. "They have found where you like to go."

"We know who they are. We must be careful," Jānis said. "But there is something else. I do not want my girlfriend to be involved."

Rudzitis sat down heavily beside Jānis. "Why not? I presume she knows nothing?"

Milanov asked Jānis if "the girlfriend" was his lover.

Nodding, Jānis added: "She does not know what I do for Latvia. This work underground."

Pēteris coughed. "Jānis, I did warn you about this."

Milanov said: "You must think if there is anything she could have passed on to them, not knowing. Any little thing. A slip of the tongue?"

Rudzitis clapped Jānis on the shoulder. "The heart goes, and one must follow, right my friend? Any informer would quickly discover that she is an innocent."

Jānis' mouth tensed. "They would not believe it. At most they might try to scare her. She is hungry for knowledge," Jānis continued, "but she takes this thing and then that thing. Then she puts them together like so." He formed a cross with his two index fingers. "Sometimes she is right. Sometimes, however, *this* is really *that*." Jānis then moved his hands apart and spread his fingers, palms forward. "I tell the girl something. She hears other words. What worries me? I talk in my sleep."

"What of importance could she hear?" Rudzitis asked.

"Talk she has heard when we go to Harry's Bar," Kārlis said. "She looks only at you, Jānis."

"We have a code word for the new work we are doing," Jānis whispered. "Absinthe."

Milanov cocked his head. "Provocative."

Pēteris asked Jānis what he had told Gillian about absinthe.

"Not much."

Rudzitis shifted his weight from one foot to another. "Which has made her even more curious?"

Jānis thought for a moment. "Yes," he said, "but then she knows I have many secrets. I did promise I would tell her more about it one day. You know. About the liqueur. I must find a way to make her think this word is only a word. She will then not be harmed."

"You must not let this danger stop your work," Milanov said.

Kārlis looked at the floor. "But how can Jānis protect her?"

"Only by not seeing her," Milanov said.

"Innocent ones pay for activism," Pēteris said, glowering. "I did warn you about this, Jānis."

"Those the innocent *love* control their destinies," Atis added.

Seated now on the lowest step of the chapel's elevated sanctuary, Kārlis loosened his shirt collar. "It is one thing," he said, "to get the American Lutherans to give money to the Latvian Relief Fund. It is another thing to expose Communists in New York City Government."

The others looked at Kārlis as if he had been shouting. Jānis opened the door to make sure no one was listening in the hallway.

Kārlis continued: "If we go on, we can expect to be 'punished'."

Atis remained silent, his fleshy knuckles white from his repeatedly clenching and rubbing them.

"What if we printed in *Laiks* what we have found" Rudzitis said.

Milanov looked eager. "Not a bad idea," he said. "However, even if it will be anonymous, they will look for those who found this out."

"This danger to us is necessary," Kārlis said. "And, Rudzitis, if you publish in your newspaper what we know, you will be in danger too."

With a pale blue handkerchief Jānis wiped his face. "You have all seen stirrings in the *Times*. You have heard the talk in bars and coffee shops. The U.S. Government and its citizens are getting ready to roast these Bolsheviks alive."

"*If* they can find them," Rudzitis said.

Milanov looked earnest. "You believe America will support you?"

Pēteris yawned. "We are way ahead of Americans and the FBI."

"Do not be sure," Jānis said. "The FBI will take the credit. And city officials will keep the public from knowing Communists infiltrated."

Atis finally spoke. "So? They will be eager to get them rid of."

"Not by us," Kārlis said.

Rudzitis looked at Milanov. "I see now," he said. "To save face, they will not want this known. They will want to take care of this themselves, quietly."

"Which means," Milanov added, "that the danger comes not only from the Communists."

The men grew silent. Through the chapel's backlit stained glass window light filtered and cast colors on the floor. Only Jānis remained standing. He directed his eyes upward, toward the source of the light. To Milanov he said, "I remember when our people drove the Bolsheviks and the German *putch* out of Rīga. In their prison yards the bodies of Latvian soldiers were still warm when our National Army came in to deliver them. And the blood of civilians will forever stain the fringes of the Rīga Meza Parks. They were thrown together in one burial pit." Jānis turned red. "I do not believe in 'Father, forgive them'. No numbers of years will whiten those monstrous acts," he said. "We look to the future when we will again sail the four miles across lovely *Kizezers*. We will again bathe and fish in the sea at *Lilasts*. In the Valley of the *Gauja* we will again hear the sweet music of the Rose of Turaida. We will walk along the banks of lower *Daugae*. Through us, the Naves Sala will no longer be an isle of death. From the carnage that happened there we will rebuild our Republic. We will go home at last."

Chapter 24

144 WAVERLY PLACE: OCTOBER 1949

Intense cold from the window woke Gillian. After the movement and heat of lovemaking, hours of half waking had tired her further. She felt suspended, lay cocoon-like in layers of blankets. Jānis had gone, but his pillow still bore the imprint of his head and the scent of his hair. She gathered his pillow to her cheek and ran her fingertips along the hollow. She remembered how he had said her name as if it stuck in his throat.

Gray light hovered just outside Gillian's window, which she closed so she could shut out the feeling of this month. She dreaded this time of year, even though its vivid colors pulsed in her senses. She knew the sky's painfully lovely blue meant an end. The sky's vitality would perish into grayish white, like an old spinster coming to the end of her life. In this last expenditure of energy, the brilliant leaves would fall, turn brown and decay in icy slush.

However, as heat hissed out of the steam radiator at the end of Gillian's main room, she turned down her blankets, spiting October. She was still voracious and alive, for she was truly human, and to be human meant going on despite the cycles of nature and weather and even emotions. She could fly through them, emerging within love like some rare, invincible butterfly.

Because Gillian had buzzed no one into her building, she was surprised to hear two tentative knocks on her door. It was Dolores. She left her fashionable boots in the hallway outside of Gillian's door. When Gillian met her eyes, Dolores flushed and moved awkwardly toward her, extended her hand but dropped it again at her side. "Your landlord, 'Mr. Whatsit', was downstairs," she said. "He let me in."

Gillian snickered: "The widowed Mr. Norbert Floding," she intoned. Laughter cascaded from her and ceased, then began anew.

Already reduced to helpless hooting, Dolores pressed her arms against her stomach. "Stop it!" she howled.

"No. Seriously," Gillian chortled. A snort that punctuated her hee-hawing got the two friends laughing even harder.

"That was gauche," Dolores said.

Gillian grinned broadly and, with wicked sass, retorted, "So what?"

"You look like the Cheshire Cat," Dolores said. "Do you know that *creature* was demented? Like schizoid."

"Always disappearing and reappearing," Gillian noted.

"Exactly!"

The two friends shared more delicious laughter and, during just this space, Gillian let herself feel the intimate bond between herself and Dolores. However, the moment she caught Dolores perceiving this, she looked down, for her mind held secrets that she was afraid her eyes might reveal. What she could share with Dolores would depend on how well she really knew herself.

There were times when Gillian believed if she could stop feeling the distance between herself and Dolores, and act on pure impulse, the void inside her would fill up. Her pain would stop. Before Jānis, she had imagined Dolores holding her, comforting her. But Gillian believed she must put up barriers and had not told her friend. She locked this more generic love longing away in a corner of her emotions, snapped a lid on it, and forgot about it.

Dolores now sat on Gillian's loveseat like a patient in a doctor's waiting room. She eyed objects around her is if they were unfamiliar and vaguely threatening. "When I told you I'd stop by this morning," she said, "I had everything rehearsed."

"On the phone, you said you wanted to talk out some things," Gillian said, not feeling up to it after all. "You said I'm inaccessible and obsessed with Jānis."

Dolores glanced around Gillian's room. "I was just being honest," she said. Her focus shifted to the copy of *Trilby*, which lay closed on the coffee table. "You haven't finished it."

"I read the first third before—."

"Before things got so hot and heavy with Jānis? Please don't be mad at me, Gillian. This is what I wanted to talk to you about," Dolores said, looking both determined and apprehensive. "I shouldn't have supposed the book would ever mean to you what it does to me."

Gillian wanted to be kind. She wanted not to feel like a bad person, so she sat beside Dolores. She said, "*Trilby* upsets me."

"Why? Because *Trilby* makes you feel pathos?"

Gillian stared at her rusty orange rug until it blurred. It seemed to emanate heat now. This disturbed her. "The book made me feel sad. I was tired of feeling sad," she said. "I was sick of everything being wrong and losing control of my life. Right now I'm happy. Please don't judge me for that."

"I'm not judging you," Dolores said.

"I'm sick of thinking of myself as some kind of victim. I don't ever want to be a victim again. I feel lucky in my apartment."

"Sometimes bad luck is just an accident," Dolores mused. "Say a flowerpot drops off a fifteenth floor window ledge and crowns some poor sap, taking him out. I think good luck depends on *who* a person is inside. If you're living right, you're smiled upon as if by God."

"I'll have to think about that," Gillian said. She spread her hands out, chest high, and looked at them. "What I'm afraid of is that we can't help who we are. We must live with that. But we're also victims because things can just happen to us, like falling in love. We feel some things, but we don't feel other things. I know I love Jānis and I know I love you. But I love each of you differently."

"Well, thank goodness you don't have to suffer for your love of Jānis," Dolores said, with wistful sarcasm. "What makes you think there won't be any pain? Right now you're secure. You haven't fallen yet. You're high on your impossible illusion about some guy who can save you. Are you even having a real relationship with Jānis?"

How petty, Gillian thought. If Dolores cared about her, she should be glad for her. Instead she was sitting close to Gillian, trying to make her feel guilty.

"Are you trying to incinerate me with your eyes?" Dolores said.

Gillian turned away. "What do you know about me and Jānis anyway? What right do *you* have to give me advice?"

"Actually I'm glad to see you angry," Dolores said. "It shows you have some fight in you." She moved away from Gillian. "All right. Here's something for openers: What does Jānis do for a living?"

"I don't know."

"Kind of routine info," Dolores said. "Okay. Where and how does he spend his time when he's not with you?"

"He doesn't say."

"And you don't ask him? You don't want him to share all that other big part of his life with you? How dopey is that?"

"Thanks," Gillian said. "I know you're disappointed with me."

"More like *afraid for* you."

"And maybe you feel abandoned," Gillian said.

"Like a child. Let's do Jung, not Freud. Jung's more, more *humane*."

Gillian got that it would be best to change the subject. "Then let's talk about something else."

Dolores sighed.

"I don't even know what *you* do," Gillian said, "when you're not working and when you're not with me. What about your 'boyfriend' that you won't talk about? You know everything about me." Gillian looked at Dolores' sad eyes and then at her own hands and then at Dolores' hands. "You're a terrific person, Dolores. You're quality." She had successfully changed the subject again.

"I'm afraid for you! I'm afraid he's going to hurt you terribly."

"If that happens, it'll be my problem," Gillian said, "and there's nothing you can do about it."

"I don't want you to go through that. Please believe me!"

Gillian touched Dolores' hand. "I do want to believe you," she said. "And I still want you to be my friend."

"Then promise me something," Dolores said.

"Yes," Gillian said.

"Promise we can still do things together, that you'll spend time with me, so we can have a present and future. Not just a past."

"Yes, and I promise I'll stop hiding things from you," Gillian said. She put her arms around Dolores and felt her friend's tears on her own face. "I promise I'll spend more time with you, starting today, but you must accept that I'm in love with Jānis," Gillian said.

Dolores looked miserable. "Let's, please, change the subject."

"Okay."

"You know I read a lot, Gillian, which is a how I spend most of my alone time. Sometimes I read three books at once. It wouldn't hurt *you* to read more."

"I really don't have the time," Gillian said.

"Every Sunday you have time. I wouldn't be able to think straight if I didn't read. You know, in a book everything is organized. Everything is orchestrated. It makes you feel life might have patterns. God knows, my apartment has no organization. And when I look at the clutter I feel that is me inside."

Gillian smiled at her friend. "You could put your books down for a Saturday morning and tidy up. Then you'd feel right with yourself."

"A waste of time. Do you know I'd rather dig ditches all day than do one rack of dishes?"

"That's pathetic," Gillian said. "Want some coffee?"

"Thought you'd never ask," Dolores said. "Wanna come over *chez moi* and do my dishes for me? Do you, huh?"

"You could sweep and dust for me and I'll do your dishes and we can go to Lorna's. Remember? I haven't met her."

Dolores ignored the reference to her mother. "And we could drink Tawny port to keep us going."

"Too sweet for me."

"How about beer?"

"Remember? I only drink beer when I'm desperate," Gillian said. "I love to pour a good beer but I can't stand the smell of it."

Dolores assumed her odalisque position and squinted. She pointed her finger at Gillian and affected an accent that sounded like a cross between Transylvanian and Spanish: "You mean, my dear, you are averse to beers and ales of all kinds? Can you possibly be making a *jugement absolu*? That is, *being* absolute?"

Having no talent for mimicry, Gillian could answer only as herself, defensively. "You think I'm wishy-washy!"

"I believe," Dolores said, "you don't know your beer from your doorknob. Let us review your situation. You have been looking for, what shall we say? Ah! Some spiritual type orgasm, and—."

"Dolores!"

Dolores continued. "As I was saying, you have been looking for the ephemeral? The unsayable? The esoteric? The practically ineffable, the … ."

"If you mean the unknowable, tell me how you see that."

"You," Dolores said, "are, as the philosophers say, a *tabula rasa*. A blank tablet, or, rather, putty for space and time to … *impress*."

Because Gillian couldn't think of anything to say, she faced straight out into her long room.

After she set her coffee mug on the floor, Dolores continued, now doing a takeoff on Sigmund Freud: "You vant to take zee ultimate journey. My dear, you vant zee escape. Yes, I haf encountered zees before in young vomen. Why, I myself vas vonce 'een love'." Now Dolores resumed speaking normally: "I believe, however, no living person could meet your impossible standards. Why? My dear girl, it is simply because that person doesn't exist in real life. Oh, the beauty of the imagination!" Here she made a wide stage gesture. "Oh, the wonders of escaping reality!"

Gillian showed her irritation. "You lost your accent." But she knew there was something true about what her friend had said. She had tried to ignore this, for it created too many questions, and questions change the way a person experiences things. Gillian rationalized against the truth of her friend's words. "You're jealous," she said to Dolores.

Flecks of lime green flickered in Dolores' dark brown eyes, and the flesh on either side of her mouth tightened until her face was hard as a mask. "You have a lot to learn," she said, her voice not merely icy but also like the hard earth of winter.

"I'm sorry," Gillian said.

"What you're really sorry for is wanting to hurt me just then. Well, I'm glad, because it means I hurt *you*. I finally got through to you. And, incidentally, the reason you don't mind not knowing about *all* of Jānis' life is that you don't want the responsibility of that. If he's a mystery, both of you can keep his image intact. That's really creative, Gillian. It may be almost as creative as giving birth."

Gillian stiffened. "My God! You're not wishing that on me, are you? You'd enjoy that?"

Dolores looked abject, repentant. She also looked confused about what she had just said. But there was an obvious heat in her cheeks. "I don't know why I said that."

Gillian perched now at the edge of the loveseat. "Enough, okay? I don't want us to ever be vicious to each other again. Dolores, I need you to accept that what I do and how I feel are my choices."

"Yes, okay. But admit," Dolores said, "that you tend to wait for things to happen to you. Then you're stuck with them. Admit you don't act on all your feelings, especially if you're scared."

"Actually, for once in my life I *have* acted, and I want to follow it through. Don't you see? Even if I'm fooling myself, I have to keep going with this or I might as well be dead. I'm not always brave, but something made me have the guts to let Jānis into my life. Do you know how important that is to me?"

"Yes," Dolores said.

"Maybe I just don't deserve your friendship," Gillian said.

Dolores tried to smile. "Maybe I just enjoy a good fight."

"True! Thinking about what's drastic makes you high," Gillian said, her voice warm with now compassion.

"Yes," Dolores said. "At least you do see that."

"But it doesn't help me," Gillian said.

"You'll have plenty of time to figure it all out. You *are* eventually going to try to?"

"I'll have to, won't I?" Gillian said.

"Even if you're eighty?"

"Then I'll have false teeth and be in a wheelchair in some old folks' home. Who would there be to take care of me?"

"Your kids? You'll name the girl Dolores of course."

"I don't think so," Gillian said. "Oh, there's nothing wrong with your name. I mean I don't think I want kids. That would be vain. I also know I'd be a rotten mother. I'm too nervous."

Dolores stretched out her legs. "How could you be married and not end up with kids?"

"I'm afraid to ask Jānis if he and I are really married. For now, I'm fine with having my own place. It might be weird, actually living together. I'd probably make an awful wife."

Dolores moved to the edge of the loveseat. She stared at Gillian's hands for what seemed a long time, then spoke: "What about Jānis?"

"I don't understand half the things he says to me," Gillian said.

Dolores' eyebrows, normally penciled in a gentle arc, formed chevrons.

"Jānis is different. He says he doesn't belong here and he says that Americans are shallow. He talks a lot about Latvia. He says he 'lives for the day' when they can all go back."

"Do they really believe," Dolores asked, "that they *can* go back?"

"It's all they talk about. And you wouldn't believe some of the other stuff they say. Like, they say they're telepathic. I don't mean telling the future or anything like that but being able to read certain people's minds."

"Why not everyone's?"

Gillian laughed a new throaty laugh. "Jānis says most people's minds aren't worth reading. He talks about a lot of things I've never heard of. And he talks in his sleep."

Dolores' cheeks reddened.

Gillian did not see her friend's response. "One night he said 'absinthe' and woke himself up. When I asked what he was dreaming about, he told me to go back to sleep. I know it's a drink, but I can't get him to tell me any more about it. Since that night, he did tell me it changes colors and that there are only a few places where they still make it. Then he changed the subject. He does that when I ask him about other things too. And then some things he keeps repeating to me over and over, and he gets mad at me if I don't remember."

"He can't think you're slow," Dolores said.

"Jānis knows I'm not. He says I'm stubborn and I already know everything, inside. He says I'm repressed, that I am attracted to violence. I don't act on my thoughts. He believes I can do anything I will myself to do and that I see more about a lot of things than I'm willing to admit."

"Well," Dolores said, "do you think it's true?"

"You know I hate violence. I have no idea what he means when he says I know more than I admit. Why does he make such a big deal about these things? Everything's life or death to him. He says I've got to understand why I do what I do or I'll end up in some looney bin."

Dolores looked as if she were about to say something.

Gillian was not finished, however. "Lately he's been even more distant. We haven't spent much time together, and when I do see him, he's so … twitchy. The others don't show up much at Harry's anymore. When they do, they stop talking as soon as someone comes in. Half the time I don't know when he is in Harry's. I turn around and there he is, talking to the others as if I'm not there."

"Charming," Dolores said, an edgy *timbre* creeping into her voice.

Gillian continued: "I've been working longer hours at Harry's because I want to save some money, and when I get home I just flop on the couch."

"No wonder I have seen so little of you," Dolores said.

Gillian looked confused and sad. "It's like I'm a robot. Eat, sleep, and work. I only have time to think at night sometimes, rarely, and then I lie awake for hours and feel even more tired the next day. Harry says Jānis has made me his slave, but Harry doesn't know Jānis. When Jānis and I are alone, he *is* good to me. As long as I am with him and he wants to make love," she continued, "I know things are all right. But I am surprised at how little else I'm doing these days, besides keeping bar. When I have enough in savings, I'll cut back on my work hours. Harry says *if* that time comes, he'll get more part-time help."

Dolores looked at *Trilby* again. "When you have time," Dolores said, "reading might relax you."

"Maybe I'll shock you and do that. Anyway, there's no reason why you and I couldn't take in a movie now and then. I have been lonely sometimes, but not unhappy. It's hard to think of anything except Jānis."

"Try it," Dolores said. "Risk leading part of your life as Gillian, not just as Gillian-slash-Jānis. Be my friend sometimes too?"

"Of course. Things are just weird right now. It's not making me unhappy though."

"Couldn't you use some basic companionship?"

"Yeah," Gillian said. "I guess so."

"That's what yours truly is here for," Dolores said. "Be my friend, Gillian."

"Thanks."

Dolores relaxed and settled back on Gillian's loveseat. "For what?"

"For saying my name," Gillian said.

Chapter 25

NOVEMBER 11TH (ARMISTICE DAY), 1949

Though it was warmer than usual for early winter in New York, the green door to Harry's Bar was closed. Today, the air inside was stale, yet it wasn't so much an odor as a feeling. A leftover something hung here like a presence, like the past, unresolved. It also felt like the future, unknown. Blue cigarette smoke filled the room but obscured nothing. Rather, the smoke colored expressions on people's faces and seemed to muffle their conversations. A sense of anticipation and a feeling of laziness permeated the bar. Patrons appeared likely to go along with whatever was about to happen. It was as if they had come in empty and would wait for some event to fill them.

As Harry passed Gillian to draw a beer for Joe Capetti, he acknowledged the heat without sympathy. "Unseasonably warm, don't you think," Harry said to Joe. It was a statement.

Joe, who owned the laundromat across the back alley from Harry's, sat at the end of the bar. An *émigré* from Italy when he was seven, Joe merely nodded. Beer came first, especially in hot weather. "Ah," he said. He wiped the foam off his luxurious salt and pepper mustache.

"God, Harry. I wish you'd prop that door open," Gillian said.

"You *know* I gotta control who gets in here," Harry said. He looked sideways at the green door. His neck wrinkles, formed by decades of gravity's pull, piled up like a stack of flapjacks. Now he leaned an elbow on Gillian's bartop design.

"But it's seventy degrees out there! And about a hundred in here," Gillian said.

"It won't make no difference if I open that damned door," Harry said with unusual petulance.

"Okay, Harry. But look at that steam on the stained glass."

Joe Capetti looked up and grinned. "*I'll* say!"

Harry pointed a pudgy index finger in Joe's direction. "That's from *your* dryers."

"Naturally, I came in here to get away from that heat," Joe said.

"You came in here," Harry said, "to get away from Louisa. Want me to run a tab for you?"

"I can't have steam blowing out the front of my laundrymat, can I? It wouldn't look good. And Mabel over there bitched to me about not letting fumes in her parlor, and I'm real scared of her, right Mabel?"

Mabel looked up from her table, where she hoarded the window that was open high on the wall above her. She blew streams of smoke out her nostrils. "Damn straight, Joe," she said.

"I look at it this way," Joe said. "You got this church window, and I got the steam to christen it. Ha ha."

"That window is the one classy touch," Harry said. "When I got it free from a church they were tearing down, I knew it would bless me."

"Well it don't belong in a bar," Joe said with finality. He wiped his mustache again.

Gillian rang up a check for a pale little man who'd been drinking Brandy Alexanders since three o'clock. (To "richen them up," Harry made Brandy Alexanders with vanilla ice cream instead of milk.) On his upper lip the little man had meticulously drawn with a black eyebrow pencil a very thin, Errol Flynn type mustache. Gillian recognized him as the man in the fedora she had seen in Levitsky's Treasure Trove. He slid an extra dollar into her hand and said, timidly, with a thick accent: "Because you're so pretty."

Pleased and embarrassed, Gillian looked away. By the time she turned back to thank the odd little man, he had disappeared into the temperate November air. In his place stood a tall, cancer-thin man who had yellowish complexion. Gillian was sure she had seen him before.

"Gimme a beer, sister," he said. His skin, hair and teeth were all the same tone of yellow. He had a small, flat nose with outsized, ovoid nostrils. His eyelashes and eyebrows were light, semitransparent. His hair was thin, unhealthy looking and cropped close, so that it did not reach the front of his flat forehead. Squinting at Gillian, he watched the beer foam as it rose in the glass.

Gillian figured he was waiting for his beer to spill over the mug's lip like most other beer drinkers did. But Gillian had perfect instincts. Just when the foam looked as if it would flow down the sides of the mug, she released the tap lever, and the white suds balanced neatly on top.

The ugly man's pale, bony hand covered two thirds of the mug. He grunted and swilled half his beer in a few gulps. Then he wiped the foam off his lips with his bare forearm. He then began to gape at every bar customer. Mabel Levitsky met his gawking with a look that said *Fuck off!* The ugly man smiled appreciatively and swiveled back around on his bar stool.

"I'm Georgie," he announced to Gillian without looking at her. "Where you from, sister?"

Gillian recognized him now ... from Village Cigars. "Missouri," she answered. She wished she could vanish.

Georgie swigged another beer Gillian already had poured for him. He looked over his shoulder. "You like it here?"

"It's interesting," Gillian said. She tried to get Harry's attention, but he was carrying on an animated discussion with Joe Capetti.

"You're not very friendly," Georgie said to Gillian. This time he looked directly at her.

"I guess I just don't feel like talking today," Gillian said.

Georgie laughed, fully baring his ochre teeth. "You like music?"

Gillian said nothing because Harry acknowledged her S.O.S.

"I'm a bassist," the man said. "Play jazz at the Village Vanguard sometimes. It don't pay enough. You should come hear my band."

Harry replaced Gillian in front of Georgie. "Need another beer?" Harry asked. Then he added, lamely, "Ever bet the trotters?"

Georgie looked surprised to spot Gillian at the other end of the bar.

"A bartender has instincts about people," Harry said. "I got a tip that it'll be 'Fools Gold' in the seventh tomorrow."

Georgie's laugh was like a cough. "Who's your bookie, pal?"

"Guy name o' Roscoe," Harry said.

"Yeah. I know 'im. But I heard 'Rain Dance'," Georgie said. "I don't bet the trotters anymore, partly because of not working steady. But also 'cause it's a racket. You know how they limp them out there for warmups and then finish them like fucking locomotives. Excuse my French. Or they look like goddamn thoroughbreds just before bets close, and then they break stride at the first-quarter turn. I'd do almost anything for cash, but the harnesses just ain't worth it."

"Maybe you need a better bookie," Harry said.

"Really, you don't know *what* to bet on," Georgie said. He trailed his calloused fingertips along the edge of the bar. "I got a gig in Miami next week anyway. Gonna get on a Connie and fly." No one within hearing distance of the man knew that a Connie was a four engine Eastern Airlines Lockheed "Constellation."

The green door swung open, and Kārlis, Pēteris, and Atis came in. They all looked surly.

"Happy Armistice Day," Gillian greeted the Latvians sincerely, but almost immediately she realized it was a mistake.

Pēteris came up to the bar. "For your information," he said, "this is also the anniversary of the Bolshevik Revolution. We came to America to get away from this 'celebration'. Give us a decent bottle of wine and spare us your version of what this day means to the rest of the world."

Gillian looked as if Pēteris had just slugged her.

Harry jumped to Gillian's defense: "Let's keep it friendly," he whispered between his clenched teeth. "If you don't like the talk here, you just go somewhere else." He got the Latvians' bottle of wine and uncorked it, but he held it tightly when Pēteris reached for it. "Why should we care about your personal gripes?"

Pēteris wrenched the bottle from Harry while the other two Latvians sat down. Slyness dented the corners of his mouth. "When you think about peace," he said, "think also about your 'A-bomb'."

"What's that got to do with the Armistice" Harry asked.

"The *kriev* have their guns out for America too. You are a fool if you don't see that," Pēteris sneered.

"I do read the papers," Harry said. "What they're doing with the atom is clearing roads and irrigating fields."

Pēteris glared. "Your press smells," he said. "Sovietsky prosecutor Vishinsky is a liar. Who do you think Bolshevized Latvia?"

Harry leaned casually over the bar, closer to Pēteris' face, his voice low. "It's 1949, pal. The war's over. Forget about it. It's ain't our fault what the Russians did to your country, so go drink your wine, relax."

Kārlis and Atis had been watching from their table. "Bring the wine, Pēteris," Kārlis said softly. "We won't wait for Jānis."

Gillian checked on Georgie, who quietly sipped his third beer and flipped through a small lined notebook. He occasionally squinted at the green door.

"I guess it's just a bad day for them," Gillian said to Harry.

Harry rubbed the back of his neck. "Every day's a bad day for them," he said. "I don't see why they have to come in here to air their gripes."

Gillian laughed. "Who else would put up with them?" She tossed a withered lime section into the sink. She wished things would calm down.

Only Georgie noticed Jānis enter Harry's and head straight for the men's room.

Behind the bar, Gillian filled wooden bowls with pretzels and shelled peanuts. Steam from Joe's laundromat muted the colors of the stained glass window behind her. The backlit shelves of glasses just below the window created a halo around Gillian's body.

Now Jānis stood by the Latvian table as if materializing out of nowhere. He glanced over at Georgie, then turned his back to Gillian. Jānis looked tense, his muscles defined like a dancer's on his taut frame.

Gillian came around the bar to see the Latvians better. She thought it odd that Jānis had not come in with his friends. She wanted to embrace him. She looked instead at the familiar shape of his head, his hair cut blunt and straight across the base of his neck. He had gotten in the bar again without her having seen him. It bothered her that he didn't speak to her when he came in. She wanted him to acknowledge her.

At that moment Jānis looked at Gillian, his gray eyes lit with silver. His mouth slanted upwards with ironic comprehension.

Gillian said to Jānis from across the room, "You came in through the men's room window, Jānis?" Her attempted joke failed miserably.

Jānis gave her what she called his *look of blades*. The one that meant he could do perfectly well without her. He then began talking again, with urgency, to the other Latvians.

Georgie had stood up and, for a moment, scrutinized Jānis. Then he slapped some coins on the bar top. When Georgie opened the green door, the Latvians stopped talking and watched him go outside.

Gillian hoped Georgie would never come back to Harry's. She began to wipe the bar down and listened to "So in Love," now playing on the jukebox. A couple she didn't know began to slow dance in the confined space.

So in love with you am I,

Patti Page sang.

Harry slinked up to Gillian, clicking his fingers to the Cole Porter song's gentle Latin rhythm. "Wanna dance?"

The song had been released in February, so Gillian thought she should be used to it by now. Instead it disturbed her.

> *So taunt me and hurt me,*
> *Deceive me, desert me,*
> *I'm yours 'til I die ...*

Gillian only slow-danced because she felt awkward when she tried to do Latin dances. Her mother had discouraged her from dancing at all. Even if Gillian rejected all her mother said, Gillian would still have felt awkward. Grownup rationalizations didn't matter. Willing herself to find the truth about herself didn't matter because, at her core, five year old Gillian, awkward and small, saw little angels dancing in the bushes outside her parents' house in St. Louis. And her mother laughing about it.

How foolish Harry looked now, this trotting, bald bulk, maneuvering up to Gillian. She had to stop him. She backed away, trying at the same time to look kind. "What about your customers?" she bleakly asked.

Still ebullient, Harry took Gillian's hand. "They can get their own partner," he joked, putting his arm around her waist, not gently.

Gillian's face was hot with embarrassment. She did a diplomatic maneuver out of Harry's reach. She prayed Jānis hadn't been watching. Something about the song ...

> *So in love,*
> *So in love,*
> *So in love with you, my love, am I.*

"It's my duty to keep your customers happy," she said to Harry.

Harry looked disappointed. "It's my bar, ain't it?"

"I think I should samba back to work," she said cheerfully. She felt defeated. Her body ached with tension. All she could think of was Jānis, who stood just a few feet away, his back to her.

"Well," Harry said, "the song's over anyway. Joe's probably dry."

The atmosphere in the bar had become so intense that Gillian's hands and arms felt as if they had been plugged into a light socket. As the final bars of the song faded, she wondered if Jānis would come to her.

Mabel made it to the green door almost undetected, until she muttered, "Sitting on *shpilkes*. All of you."

Joe Capetti finished off his umpteenth beer. "Cash me out, will ya, Harry? I could stay for more, but—."

Harry picked up Joe's empty glass. "So what's stopping you?"

"My wife Louisa again. She don't know what I feel like. Christ! I never say nothin' to her, you know? Even when my back's hurting."

"You work too hard," Harry said.

"Yeah. Well, I'll be seeing you," Joe said.

The jukebox began playing "The Hot Canary" and Gillian looked down at the scratches on the wood in the middle of the bar, which today looked like spikes and shields. The song's high-pitched, pizzicato violin made it sound like a canary was being tortured, and Gillian wished she could rip this outdated record out of the jukebox.

Gillian began to wipe each freshly washed glass like a marksman hitting a row of targets. Each time she clasped a wine glass stem, she longed to launch it, watch it somersault and smash against the opposite wall into a thousand little glitters. Every time her fingers pinched a shot glass, part of her brain urged her to hurl it down to the floor, to stomp down on it in one clean, hard motion. This made her hold each glass even tighter. She dried the glasses one by one. The bar towel she twisted into them squeaked at each pivot of her wrist. She placed the glasses on the bar top and began to store some of the wine glasses on the middle shelf of the glass cabinet.

"Gillian," Harry called to her.

Gillian stood up too fast. Her elbow hit one of the glasses still on the bar top and sent it flying to the floor in front of the bar. During one split second she enjoyed how lovely the glass sounded as it broke and how quiet the room had become.

Harry had already come around in front of the bar with a broom and long-handled dustpan. He swept up the mess and asked Gillian if she needed a drink. "It's okay," he added.

"Another accident," Gillian said.

Harry repeated, "You need a drink?"

"I break another glass and you offer me a drink."

Harry took the towel from Gillian's hand. "You been working here half a year yet?"

"Not yet," she said.

Harry emptied the glass chunks and slivers noisily into the metal trash can behind the bar. "No charge tonight for people named Gillian."

"I owe you a few, Harry," she said gently, turning her head slightly in Jānis' direction.

Harry smoothed back one of his few strands of hair. "I know this is about the Latvians," he said. He glanced at the corner table, where Jānis listened to his friends. Jānis' feet were spread apart, his legs stiff and his arms crossed. "They talk about a lot of nothing," Harry said.

Gillian willed herself not to look at Jānis, who had stopped talking but had faced her when the glass shattered. As if it explained everything, she said, "They call that table their American home." She felt heat spreading from her face through her shoulders and down her back. Without looking at Jānis Gillian could feel his eyes on her now. She poured herself a small brandy and began warming the snifter in her hands. She felt as if Jānis had put his hands on her waist. She could feel his breath on her face, and when she touched the snifter to her lips she knew for sure that he was watching her. Would he come to her?

"We should have champagne sometime soon," Harry said. He took off his long white apron. "*You* ought to be drinking champagne."

Jānis was at the bar now, beside Gillian. He looked irritated. "Not champagne yet," he said, his eyes on the snifter Gillian held. He looked at Harry indifferently.

Gillian knew Jānis felt no malice, but she also realized others thought he was too direct, often rude. Something made him unhappy right now. She just didn't know what. She wanted to break the tension in the bar. "Jānis thinks I'm unsophisticated," she said, but her hand tightened on the glass.

"He's right," Harry said gently, "but *I* believe 'unsophisticated' is a compliment."

Gillian's face hardened. "Thank you, Harry," she said. She believed she could never do enough or be enough to please this Latvian. She extended the snifter toward Jānis and toasted: "To us." Then she drained the glass.

Jānis cheeks tightened. "*He* teaches you nothing," Jānis said to Gillian. "Flattery does not show you the truth about you. Harry does not know you would love to break that glass on purpose. You should do this. It would give you pleasure. You could feel it on your skin."

"I am not in the mood for this today," Harry said. "You guys think you got a premium on everything. And, as for the war, I fought over there too, you know."

Jānis' voice was quiet now: "No one took your country," he said.

Harry looked at Gillian's mouth before he looked down at the bar. "The wars are over," he said. "Some people should forget the past."

Gillian felt her arms vibrating again. She was fascinated with Harry's clenched hands, his knuckles white and prominent. She focused on Harry's undershirt, just visible under his limp, green shirt collar. "This is not your business, Harry," she said. "You know I care about you, but this is not any of your business."

Harry glared at Jānis. Then he took his hands off the bar and walked into the back room. He slammed the door with intention.

"Why do you do that, Jānis?"

"What?"

Gillian gripped the brandy snifter but said nothing.

Jānis opened her fingers and took the glass. "Good, Miss. You both acted like fools. His 'samba' and your accident with the glass."

Gillian yearned to snatch the glass from Jānis. "You are dead wrong about what I want," she said.

Jānis lowered his voice to a whisper. "Fool," he answered.

At first Gillian felt shame. Then pride came flooding through her, and she wanted to transport out of there, out to Washington Square, where a bird's singing could wash away this awful tension, where sound could soothe her, not make every nerve be a bringer of pain. She told herself she did not have to be all nerves like this. She loved Jānis, but she did not share his bitterness. "A fool for love," she whispered. "I love you for how you used to treat me."

"What?"

"Nothing," Gillian said, "except you called me a fool. You didn't say my name."

He held the glass out to her. "Take it," he said.

But Gillian did not take it. She merely watched Jānis raise the glass high in the air and let it fall straight down. When the glass hit the floor, it sharply pinged and then shattered when his ankle high, calfskin boot stomped down on it in one clean, hard motion.

Chapter 26

Harry's bar had been closed for half an hour. In semidarkness, Gillian and Jānis drank Anisette, neat, at the Latvians' accustomed table. This drink had been her idea.

Jānis' jaws tightened. "Your Government thinks only the Germans are barbarians," he said, "and knows nothing about the NKVD and their stinking tribunals."

Gillian believed she felt everything Jānis felt, and this made her afraid. Something else goaded her: a sense that they were both out of control, both trying to keep up with an elusive phantom that held answers about their future together. "How can they understand?" she asked.

When Gillian's attention began to wander, Jānis closed his fingers around her wrist. "There is a prison in Rīga," he continued. "Before the Russians retreated, they shot all prisoners in the courtyard. They could have let them live!"

Gillian pulled her arm away. "I *can* feel what you feel," she said, holding his hand.

Jānis touched her throat. "Even you can be only this close to me. Only if Matīss was still alive could anyone know what I feel. My brother. But you have never had a twin. He was like a sword!"

Gillian kissed his hand. "You look like the Devil when you talk about him." She slid her finger down the vein that now bulged at the side of his neck. "Jānis. Tell me again about absinthe."

Jānis made a sound that should have been a laugh. "Absinthe is not only a drink but also is something dangerous. When I tell you that absinthe is greenish, potent, and deadly, you will think I am teasing you. You would not understand that death can sometimes be a luxury."

The word *death* shocked Gillian. She could think of nothing else to say, except, "I want to hear what happens when you drink absinthe."

"It does what it does," Jānis said. "That is why they made it illegal." Then he finally laughed. "You could not drink absinthe anyway. Even a little wine overcomes you."

"Not true. It took a lot of vodka for you to ruin me," Gillian said.

"Which you already had in your apartment."

"With the help of eleven white roses you gave me then?"

"With the help of your weakness for danger."

"And your dreamboat face," Gillian said. "But men usually give a girl a *dozen* roses, red roses."

"In my country, even numbers of flowers are bad luck. Twelve red roses are only for funerals."

"I see," Gillian said. "I did love the white roses, though." She reached her glass up to touch Jānis' lips. "Now will you drink this?"

"Bah! Anisette is not the same as absinthe!"

"Not as strong?"

"No," Jānis said. "And missing the most critical ingredient."

"What ingredient?"

"Wormwood."

Gillian knew that wormwood meant gall. "I don't believe you," she said. "You're making that up."

"Bitterness ..." Jānis continued. "There is no learning without it. There is life and so there is bitterness. There is not enough beauty to balance this."

"And the absinthe?"

Jānis looked very stern now. "Wormwood," he repeated. "A French exile created absinthe when Napoléon was only a Captain. The wormwood makes it bitter. There is no absinthe without it." He clasped his fingers together on the table, studied his thumbs.

"Then you *have* drunk it."

"Yes. The last time I saw Matīss. We were in Liepāja with friends from university. News spread that the Russians had searched my family's house, arrested Papa and shipped him to Siberia in a cattle car."

Gillian played with the edge of the green checkered tablecloth. "Why did they arrest him?"

"The Russians charged everyone with 'anti-Soviet' activities. We hated them. Only traitors cooperated. The rest of us hated their Cossack hides! Before they took Papa away, Matīss and I talked of how we would spit on any Russian soldier who stopped us on the street."

Gillian leaned over the table and kissed Jānis, who fully accepted her kiss now. "We can stop talking about this. It upsets you."

"I need to tell you about it because I am selfish. However, to say too much would not be safe." He patted her arm and then steepled his hands together on the table. His forearms made a straight line in front of him. His shoulders trembled.

"Darling," Gillian said. "Are you sick?" But when her own shoulders began to shake she realized that somehow it was she who should be afraid. "Go on."

"When we heard they had taken Papa," Jānis continued, "friends warned us we should get out of Liepāja, go to America. They told us they knew others who had escaped to Sweden by fishing boat and took steamer ships across the Atlantic. We had money, but it was not safe to ask in Liepāja about other ways to get out. So Matīss and I made our plan to depart separately." Jānis stared at the center of the table. "We drank absinthe together that night. It took a year to smuggle the absinthe out of Thessaly. The girl friend of Matīss ... We stayed with her our last night in Liepāja. She had ways of getting people to do what is impossible." He laughed. "She had friends and they had friends. You know. So, we got the absinthe."

That moment, Gillian believed the sound of Jānis' laughter would fill her for the rest of her life. It was like the sun rising on the flag in Marija's flat. LATVIJA. She remembered the rays, the light of life and heat that radiated from that sun. Gillian was also laughing, but tears dropped heavily across her closed mouth. The black rays emanating from Jānis' eyes could mean only one thing: death. The beautiful Latvian sun eclipsed. "What is the matter, Jānis?"

"What do you see?"

"Are you going to die too? You're *not* going to die!"

"Enough!" Jānis shouted. "I hate your sentimentality! I will continue about absinthe."

Gillian was afraid she would cry. "Now I don't want you to."

Jānis continued as if he had not heard her. "How delicate absinthe is. How perfect the method of preparing it. Do not forget what I will say now." He asked Gillian if she was listening to him.

She had been listening to the traffic sounds outside. "Yes," she said. "I won't forget."

"Good. I will begin. *Artemesia absinthium*. That is Latin for wormwood. Its leaves are aphrodisiac. To us drinking it is a kind of communion. Pagan. When you decant it into the tumbler it is yellow green because of the wormwood. The aroma: licorice, hyssop, fennel, angelica root, and aniseed."

"How in the world did you know that?"

"All sacred rituals are of truths. Absinthe is not just something 'cool'." He responded now to Gillian's puzzled look: "You think these two are opposite?"

"I am trying to understand," she said.

"Which is why I am trying to explain."

"What is anisette then?" Gillian asked.

"Imitation: anise, with star anise flavoring. You pour it from bottle to glass and it remains clear. Absinthe is clear, but then you drip water over a lump of sugar in a silver strainer and into the tumbler of absinthe. When water touches absinthe ... a miracle! It weakens the alcohol, the herb's oils separate, and then the liqueur turns chalky, like thin milk." Jānis sat back in his chair.

Gillian was sleepy, but she wanted to hold on to every second she had with this remarkable man. So, she supported herself at the table by leaning heavily on her elbows. "Someday, will you please tell me what it does when you drink it?"

Jānis sweated heavily now, his face glistening, his shirt darkened under the armpits and around his neck. "Not yet," he said. "I feel strange. I feel like all my energy is pounding in my head, like I have no legs. Do you ever feel like that?"

Gillian swished her fingertips across the oilcloth on the table. "When I'm nervous. Or afraid," she said.

He stopped her hand, held it. "You feel it in your body."

"On the tops of my arms. You know: a sense of danger, only it's nothing you can pinpoint. Like something is lurking. Sort of a bogey man."

"Bogey man?"

"He's the one you are scared is hiding in the closet when you're a kid. You're in bed with the lights out and suddenly it feels like your room is alive with crawly things. And they're creeping out from under your bed and from behind your curtains. Mostly they're small. But the worst is the bogey man because he's big and dark. And you know if he comes out of your closet in the dark, you won't see him until it's too late. It's all your imagination, right?" When she tried to shift her chair forward, it felt extremely heavy.

Jānis sat completely still. He was sweating even more heavily now. "That 'bogey man'," he said. "He is real. You hear about him in the papers all the time."

"Stop it," Gillian said. "You're scaring me."

"No," Jānis said. "You must face him some time in your life. You must grow up."

"I stopped believing in that monster a long time ago," Gillian said.

"You know what I mean. I am talking about real life. You must face him now. He can be the toast you burn in the morning or a drunk driver running over you in the street at night. Or even some politician. He can be an idea at its worst: a belief that takes away a man's freedom, his life."

"You said sometimes death can be a luxury," Gillian said.

"When we are too weary to keep trying, we forget about freedom. Everything is in the struggle. Everything. If we can stay alive, we have the freedom to fight. But it is a privilege we have to take with both hands because some other guy is also trying to steal it from us."

The overhead fan's lazy blades circled round. "I don't understand why you're so upset right now," Gillian said. "I don't know what you want from me." She stood up. "It's getting late. Come home with me, Jānis. It's been such a long time."

Jānis frowned. "No. Because we won't talk there."

"You won't just stay with me for a few hours?"

He shook his head. "I cannot. With your eyes, you are asking me 'Why not?'"

"There is no reason," Gillian said, "and because I'm tired and cranky, we'd better go. Will you help me lock up?" She turned off the lights in Harry's Bar except the one hanging above their table. Jānis gazed into the light, his chair tilted against the wall. Gillian thought he must be the proudest man on Earth. Now she stood by the door, yards away from him. She knew he wasn't *there*. In his own mind, he had gone back in his memory alone, back to Liepāja to be with his brother. And they were drinking absinthe together. Jānis and Mātiss were filtering water over a sugar cube and through a sieve, down into the yellow green liquid. The two of them watched the color change, waiting eagerly to drink the precious liqueur whose heart is wormwood.

Gillian tried to imagine what it would be like to see two Jānises, to meet a person who was like a sword. She thought if Mātiss was like a sword Jānis must be too. Still, she was having a hard time figuring out what being like a sword meant.

Jānis rocked his chair forward. There he sat, his chin held high, his eyes slicing through the green lampshade. He didn't even blink.

Gillian knew if she went to Jānis she might see those black rays again. "Coming with me?" she asked. Tension poured out of him. Sweat saturated his skin and shirt. When Gillian came to him now and put her arms around his neck, he smelled different: musty, acidic.

He didn't move. "You are a child," he said. "You need kindness."

She pressed her cheek against his hair. "Is that so bad?"

"Not good, your need for me to be kind," Jānis said. "A burden."

Gillian jerked her arms away from him, but he caught one of her hands and put it against his cheek.

"It is because you need me," he said. "It is because I promised myself I would not break. Not for anyone or anything. Not for poverty, or pain, or a woman. It is because Mātiss was killed in the Baltic Sea for being on one boat while I escaped to Visby for being in another. It is because I am no more safe now than I was then. And this is why you must not love me!"

Gillian stood behind Jānis now. She rubbed her cheek against his hair. "I can't help it," she said. Half asleep, she sat beside him for a long time, her head resting on his shoulder. The lamplight eased over the two, sheathing them. Outside its yellow circle, a deep plum color seemed to permeate the dark shadows. Gillian held her face next to Jānis', and thought: *Maybe later, my darling, you'll tell me what absinthe does when you drink it.*

Chapter 27

LATER ...

Seen through a light mist, colors on familiar marquees, in store windows, and on people's clothing looked soft, vulnerable. Accustomed noises had lost their crispness. A small fleet of taxis swished by. People's footfalls landed as if in talcum powder, their conversations sounding like phrases whispered in a large but low ceilinged room. And smells from the bagel man's wagon, and the heat from his little grill, could be perceived only like memories, or imagined events, whose vividness fades even as one tries to keep them.

"You look beat," Gillian said to Jānis as they waited to cross the avenue, but he said nothing.

On the other side of the avenue Jānis stumbled on a rise in the sidewalk but kept himself from falling. Gillian smiled at Jānis' catlike reflexes. He had looked, she thought, like a figure skater taking off by his toe pick. She now took his arm and they continued, neither speaking. This November mist seemed rancid, making it hard to breathe. Only a few bedraggled leaves clung to the tips of tree branches.

When they came near a playground Jānis spoke: "Let us sit on the swings. Here. You take the low one." He sat in the higher swing, his feet firmly on the scuffed up turf.

Gillian lifted her legs off the ground so she could make a big arc backwards. Going forward again made her feel pressure against her face and stomach and the soles of her feet. She kept wanting the effortless forward part of the arc.

She slowed to a lazy swinging motion, dragging the balls of her feet on the patchy grass. She had kicked away all the leaves within her reach. "When I almost drowned," she said, as if they had been talking about this all along, "it seemed like I was on the bottom of that pool for forever. Funny: I wasn't scared I was dying."

Now the pair's swings were seesawing. When they crossed in the middle, Jānis said, "A child does not think: 'I need air or I will die'."

"I meant I wasn't seeing something good."

"Bad and good can sometimes be two side of the same coin," Jānis said. "What we are saying matters little, really. Look how you have pushed the leaves away from you to keep your own space."

"I know," Gillian admitted, swinging back and forth. She had crooked her arms to hug the chains.

"You should see your eyes!" Jānis said. "Do not worry. I am not that tired. I can still move."

"You surprise me. That's all. What are my eyes doing anyway?"

"They are like two big moons," he said.

"I'm a little night-blind," Gillian said, "and I'm trying to see." She stopped swinging. "It must be three o'clock," she said.

"That is the time of ghosts," Jānis said. He crooked his fingers and wiggled them toward her face. "Whoooooo!"

"I love it when you're this way," Gillian said. It makes me feel like we still have a chance," she said.

Jānis pulled Gillian toward him by the chain of her swing. "*Pūst pīlītes*," he said. "You blow little ducks, talk nonsense."

Gillian held on tight. "It's not nonsense, Jānis. I'm talking about when you're cold. You know: cruel. Nothing can reach you. Especially not me."

"I need you to know who I am," he said. "Who *you* are."

"That's not giving me much credit," Gillian said.

"All the credit in the world, but you are still in your cocoon. Caterpillars do not look like much in the cocoon. But you know they will slowly creep out one day and dry their wings in the sun, and then fly."

"Butterflies don't live very long," Gillian said.

"The secret of their beauty."

"But it's not fair!"

Jānis brushed Gillian's bangs aside. "How do you know they do not feel those weeks as we do a lifetime? Have you seen pairs of them late in summer? They flutter up. Zig. Zag. They land and cling together with their wings fluttering. To watch them is to feel music, feel movement inside you. When they mate, it is their life. They're not just flying around to lift *us* up."

"It's not all bitterness then?"

"Not all," Jānis said. "We suffer too much to feel those moments for long. Yet, those short moments of beauty can feel endless too. While you live them. While you are free from keeping time. You are then free of your body, your mind."

Gillian started swinging again with a vengeance. Then she let the swing go in smaller and smaller arcs. She looked out over the playground and thought of her Pop.

"We should go," Jānis said. He had watched Gillian all this time. "I like the look on your face right now. You forgot where we are?"

Gillian nodded. Then she walked forward, off her swing. She shuffled through the sparse leaves like a child, kicking them up and off her toes. "Bugs," she said with odd satisfaction.

"Bugs?"

"There's usually a lot of bugs in dry leaves."

"Not in New York," Jānis said.

"Why not?"

"Jobs are too scarce. Besides, you have killed them," Jānis joked.

"I'm too much of a goody to be a bug killer," Gillian said.

Jānis took her hand. "I will walk you home," he said. "You will go right to bed. By yourself."

"But I'm not sleepy now!"

They came to Christopher Street and crossed to Sheridan Square.

Jānis rushed Gillian along. "You are going to sleep now," he said.

"I could stay out here with you all night."

"No. And, finally, no. Let me be alone this night. I will make it up to you some other time. I promise," he said. They came to the Northern Dispensary, where it was pitch black.

Gillian stopped walking. "Make it up to me now," she said. The darkness tingled. She held Jānis' face tightly in her hands. "I'll put on some coffee."

"You spoiled little girl! You know I would stay if I could. You know I mean what I say. You *will* go home. You *will* get some sleep, and so will I, only if we are apart. This is what I want."

When they slipped out of the darkness Jānis looked back over his shoulder at the Dispensary. Then he pulled Gillian quickly along the sidewalk, almost to the door of her apartment building.

Gillian tugged at his sleeve. "Say you love me."

Jānis looked exhausted and pale, his eyes lifeless in the shadowy streetlight. He supported himself on the hand railing. From the bottom step he said, "I must go."

"Jānis!" Gillian begged. "Come back and stay with me." She went down to him and pulled at his arm.

"I cannot."

"Then at least can you say you love me?"

"The only word I will say is *freedom*," Jānis said softly. "But I know what you want." When he put the palm of his hand to Gillian's cheek, his whole body shook. "Gillian," he whispered. He kissed her briefly and walked quickly back down Waverly Place toward Seventh Avenue.

Jānis had said her name. This validated both her existence and her importance to him. Though Gillian knew he wouldn't turn around, she peered at the back of his head. She could see his hands clenched at his sides. From that distance he looked small.

Just before he entered the black shadows of the Northern Dispensary, Jānis stopped and smiled at Gillian. It was a brief, painful smile. Then he disappeared.

Gillian lit a Chesterfield and, for what seemed a long time, she looked down Waverly Place into the darkness. She thought Jānis might still be waiting there. She should run into those shadows after him, tell him she would go anywhere with him, tell him she could not spend this night alone. *Do it*, she thought. *Follow your instincts.*

With her shoe, Gillian crushed out her cigarette. She walked briskly, then ran, down Waverly Place. She felt exhilarated panic spread throughout her body. It burned inside her legs. Surely she could catch up with him. Then she would embrace him, and they could be together tonight. However, when she reached the Northern Dispensary the blackness hit her like a slap. She stopped. Disoriented, she heard swishing, shuffling sounds, footsteps, men's low voices.

They rushed out at Gillian from nowhere, their fists pounding into her chest, her stomach, her face. "Jesus," she moaned, panic and pain making her stomach lurch. Fears of being raped overwhelmed her just as her knees hit the pavement. Then she fell backward, her insides on fire. She tried to keep her head up. She could hear her own voice from far away. Sounds like low growls. Then an awful groan coming up from somewhere beneath her body and sounding like a long, mindless hum.

She became detached. Out of her body now, Gillian was a spectator, watching each blow come at her in slow motion. She was unable to do anything but wait this out, and so she perceived odd things: the scuffed toes of a man's brown shoes and some red and blue striped tie swishing across her face. A garbage can that had fallen over, its contents spilled out and stinking on the sidewalk beside her. Her own arms flailed helplessly upward and came back across her chest to protect her, and the men's hands pulled them away. It was taking forever.

Gillian tried to see how many of them there were. Maybe three. Her now painful eyes were open. She thought they were closed because yellows and reds swirling and then faded, and then intensified again.

"We ain't supposed to kill *her*, one of the men said.

That was it. The beating stopped, bringing Gillian a sudden awareness of the pain throughout her body. Yet she also felt numb. She was conscious primarily of something wet, which she knew must be her own blood, dripping from her mouth through her wet hair to her ears and down her neck. She would lie there and play dead until her attackers finally went away. Then she would be able to get up. She would get up and call the hospital.

"She's *out*," one of the men said.

But Gillian was trying to focus on the man who just spoke, and though blood was all over her face she could make out the blurry image of a tall, very ugly man who had yellowish skin. He turned and walked away. She heard the footsteps of all three men grow softer and softer, and she knew they were clearing off now. She would get up in just a minute. When her head cleared. She would not need to call the hospital. No. She wouldn't have to do that. She would get up and call Jānis. Call Jānis ...

Chapter 28

Dolores was reading Katherine Anne Porter when Harry phoned.

"Gillian's at St. Vincent's," he said. "Some sonsofbitches beat her to a pulp last night. I'm going up there now. Meet me there?"

When Dolores hung up the phone, she left open the book she had been reading, just at the section that begins:

> *To Maria Concepcion everything in the smothering enclosing room shared an evil restlessness. The watchful faces of those called as witnesses, the faces of old friends, were made alien by the look of speculation in their eyes ... .*

At St. Vincent's Hospital, Dolores and Harry waited along the hallway in the Joan of Arc wing. Dolores chain smoked. A zombie-like Harry stared at the dark fleur-de-lis within the floor's square tiles. Every so often, Harry whispered a vehement "sonofabitch."

This morning the hall was a regular thoroughfare. Post-surgery cases, the extremely ill and the muddled limped, or were piloted in wheelchairs and on gurneys, past Dolores and Harry like a bandaged fife and drum corps. A few were attached, fetus-like, by intravenous tubes to what resembled halves of coat racks set on wheels. These the patients dragged at amazingly high speeds over to the sand filled ash cans that lined the Joan of Arc wing.

Electricity was apparently a miser at St. Vincent's. Where Dolores and Harry sat it was too dim even to read a paper. It was too dingy to cheer either the patients or their visitors. Only the subdued flicker of reddish Christmas decorations gave off color. Staff had put them up early. The Mid-Atlantic states' turkey population had not yet taken its annual nosedive.

Dolores waited for the Maid of Orléans to manifest. The assembled host desperately needed *Jeanne d'Arc* to perform tailor-made miracles to save them. Instead, there appeared a nurse in a white uniform and wimple, smelling of Pine-Sol. Her blue eyes were small but kind.

"Miss Rysert," Nurse said, "required surgery to stop internal bleeding. They also had to do some work to repair her mandible. She is deeply sedated. She may not know who you are. But with care she will recover from her injuries soon enough."

Harry stood up. "Who in God's name would do this to her?"

"All I can tell you," Nurse said, "is that the authorities are still investigating. A young man was killed early this morning too … about the same time and near the place where Miss Rysert was attacked."

Remaining seated, Dolores asked, "Do the police know who that man is … was?"

Nurse said that "two plain clothes somebodies are, at this moment, trying to talk with the patient. I don't have the authority to give you any more details, but you can see your friend as soon as the police have finished." She added that Dolores and Harry should stay only about fifteen minutes.

"Harry, I'm scared," Dolores said. "What should we do? I can take care of Gillian when she gets out." When tears came to the corners of Harry's eyes, she added, "It feels like sulfuric acid in my throat."

Harry was nearly hysterical. "I should've been there. I could've have stopped them."

"I'm afraid," Dolores said, "Gillian will never be the same. I have terrible new feelings when I think of her, like none of us can control what happens to us. Do you feel it too, Harry? Anxiety. Guilt and pity. Something like needles pushing into my eyeballs from behind."

The two plainclothes investigators marched out of Gillian's room. After looking directly at Dolores and Harry, one said something to the other, and they went right on through the nearest exit.

"Come on," Harry said. "Let's go in." He pulled Dolores by the hand.

Gillian lay in bed on the near side of a two bedroom. A white muslin curtain, which hung on metal rings from a frame to her left, partitioned the room.

At first Dolores stood just inside the door. She peered at the form lying deathly still in the hospital bed. Then Dolores moved closer to look at the almost unrecognizable face of Gillian Rysert.

Both of Gillian's eyes were swollen shut. Raised, reddish blue contusions covered her bloated face, hands, and arms. Bandages that covered the sides of her face had also been wound around the top of her head. Heavily sedated, Gillian whimpered intermittently, especially when she tried to turn her head.

"Jesus, Mary and Joseph," Dolores whispered.

Omnipresent Nurse returned to the other side of Gillian's bed by the intravenous unit. "I'm afraid she's going to be out for a while," Nurse said. "Perhaps you should wait a few days until she's feeling better. Pretty thing I imagine," she added. "Such a shame."

Harry was supporting his full weight on Gillian's bed rail. He stroked one of her arms just above where the IV tube was taped to her wrist.

Dolores touched Harry's shoulder and told him not to worry.

An NYC cop waited behind Dolores. "When you two are done in here I want to ask you some questions," he said.

Dolores told the cop she needed to ask him questions, "Like who was *killed* near the Northern Dispensary this morning."

The policeman whispered, "Her boyfriend. A friend of his identified him in the morgue about an hour ago."

Gillian half dreamt/half remembered the Friday afternoon her father failed to pick her up for the day's outing. She crouched on the window seat until her knees hurt, until the streetlights glared down on the front sidewalk and curb. She waited for Hannah to return from her job at Kline's. When Hannah finally came home late that night, she held a small paper bag with its top tightly rolled down. Hannah thrust the bag forward to Gillian. "Here," she said. "I brought you this egg salad sandwich."

"I'm not hungry," Gillian said. She peered into her mother's face. "Pop didn't show up."

Hannah paused for only a split second before she said, "He couldn't come because ... Well, I know this will upset you, but ..."

"What?" Gillian cried. She was sure she had screamed right in Hannah's face.

"He died at City Hospital," Hannah blurted. "They tried to save him, but his liver was too far gone. You know how much he drank."

After Chester's funeral, Gillian's mother had come into her room on a Saturday when Gillian was still in bed at Noon. "You: mourning such a man," she said. Hannah had intended this statement to sum up all the shortcomings she perceived in her late ex-husband—and in her daughter.

"He was my Pop," Gillian whimpered.

"Yeah. Chester. A worse drunk than my Papa. You know darned well my sweet Lettie died because of him."

"Why do you always say that?" Gillian had asked, weary of being contrasted with the sister she had lost.

"The sins of the fathers," was all Hannah responded.

Every time Hannah repeated this mantra, Gillian got closer to finalizing her getaway plan. She knew, however, her mother could legally access her savings account, and so she had closed the account and sewn the proceeds in the lining of her handbag. By the last time Hannah slapped her, Gillian was ready to go. She was armed with the one skill Hannah had taught her that could help her survive: sewing high fashion clothes. From a Vogue Patterns catalog, Gillian had created all her own outfits for school and uniforms to wear to work at Woolworth's after she graduated from high school.

At St. Vincent's there was no Thanksgiving for Gillian. For the next two weeks, Nurse kept her heavily drugged. Still, Gillian frequently awoke, screaming, because of her nightmares. Around 3:00 a.m. one morning, Gillian had awakened to the sound of Jānis' voice. He called her name. In the background, a vitals monitor rhythmically beeped.

"Gillian," Jānis said, "It is all right now." He was opalescent, transparent. Pastel colors defined his features. "I am going home again at last."

During one of Dolores' frequent visits, Nurse came to Gillian and checked the intravenous line that was bringing saline solution and morphine into Gillian's battered body. Nurse told Dolores that the trauma Gillian had undergone might affect her "for some time" and that if Gillian knew Jānis was dead, "she doesn't let on."

However, during one of Dolores' visits, when Dolores stood close to Gillian's bed, looking at her face, Gillian reached for Dolores' hand and squeezed it hard. But when Dolores called her name, Gillian did not respond. The pain that showed on Gillian's face was not just physical. What hurt Gillian most lay very deep inside her, so deep that sedatives and sleeping pills did not hide her suffering. They merely kept her from *expressing* it.

The police offered no more details about Jānis' death or of Gillian's beating. Nothing appeared in the *Times*. Not even a blurb. Neither Kārlis, Atis nor Pēteris had come to Harry's Bar since Jānis was killed. Dolores had wanted to send flowers for Jānis' funeral, but nobody knew what happened to Jānis' body after the medical examiner had completed his official autopsy.

Chapter 29

Three days later, just after dark, Kārlis stood in the alley at the back door of Levitsky's Treasure Trove. He knocked lightly on the door two times. Mabel Levitsky opened the door and hurried him into a living room small enough to be a parlor. She showed Kārlis to a settee. "I had to make sure you weren't followed," she said.

Viktor Levitsky presided over this assembly from his wheelchair. He had not bothered to affix his prosthetic legs to the stubs of his legs, which ended just above where his knees used to be. Kārlis tried to hide his shock at seeing this man, who literally had given parts of himself overseas in the first war as an Intelligence officer.

Also in the room was the odd little man with the penciled on mustache and the gray fedora, whom Mabel now introduced. "Mistrz Leopold Borisevich is a diamond cutter," Mabel said. She seemed to search the room for concealed eavesdroppers. "You will need his *connections* overseas," Mabel said.

"You want to ship your friend's body back to Latvia," Viktor Levitsky said. "Secretly."

"By sea?" Borisevich inquired, his accent pronounced. "Through *Szwecja*, Sweden, I presume?"

"Yes," Kārlis said. "We think it should be a cargo ship. This way, Jānis' coffin can be hidden among other cargo, in case there is an inspection."

Borisevich shook his head. "But you cannot just put a coffin on a ship without the official papers. As you well know, Latvians are still trying to get *out*. I think none are wanting to go *back* right now?"

177

"What do you propose?" Kārlis asked.

"There is the MS Stockholm," Borisevich said. "It is an ocean liner of the *Svenska Amerika Linden.*"

"Ah, yes," Viktor said. "Sleek, I hear, but not as luxurious as the ones that came before it."

"Yes," Borisevich said. "All the better."

"Put a coffin in some cabin?" Kārlis asked.

"No," Borisevich said. "In the hold, where there is the occasional automobile, trunks of belongings and so forth."

Kārlis frowned. "Isn't that the first place Customs will look when our dead friend arrives in Sweden?"

Viktor almost whistled. Instead he paused for a few moments and then said: "This is where Leopold, here, comes in," he said. "He will smooth the way with select crewmen. At night, while the ship is being prepared for its departure the next morning, these crewmen will unload the casket to a special waiting area in the Göteborg terminal. The crew will wait for Jānis' family to secure his coffin from this private area. Each of your friend's family will need a pier pass, which Leo will arrange via his contacts in *Göteborg.*

"How will you pay?" Borisevich asked.

"With this," Kārlis said, handing Jānis' gold cigarette case to Borisevich. "It's twenty four carat," Atis added. "Solid gold. Inside, you will also find one hundred American dollars."

Borisevich stepped forward to inspect the case. "I will take the cash," he said, "but we will need *Pani,* I mean *Mrs.,* Levitsky to sell the gold case first. She knows a Jewish goldsmith who "fences" such objects, melts them down, and makes them … untraceable. Many times she has done this for me, so that I can buy passage for Polish Jews who cannot come to America otherwise." Borisevich then handed Jānis' beautiful cigarette case to Mabel.

Viktor Levitsky clipped off the end of a fat Havana cigar and lit it. His cigar smoke formed puffs in front of his body. Then the pungent smoke spread like a veil over everyone in the room, as if to obscure these compassionate conspirators. "Who will claim the body when the ship arrives in Göteborg?"

"His aunt and two male cousins," Kārlis said.

"We will make the arrangements," Viktor said.

"For *this* part of your friend's voyage home," Borisevich added.

THREE DAYS LATER …

It was 4:00 a.m. under a new moon. On the street outside Marija's apartment, Kārlis, Atis, and Pēteris stood behind the long white unmarked ambulance that held Jānis' coffin. Kārlis had put a red rose in his buttonhole. Pianissimo, Marija sang *"Te ganiņi ganījuši."* Jānis' three compatriots quietly hummed a drone tone in accompaniment. The melody was fifty six seconds of heartbreaking sweetness for Jānis' voyage home.

Kārlis placed his palm on the back of his late friend's Maplewood coffin. He said, "Now you will again bathe and fish along the sea at *Lilasts*." Atis did likewise. "In the Valley of *Gauja,"* Atis said, *" you* will again hear the sweet music of the Rose of Turaida." And now Pēteris remained stoic. "May you again walk along the banks of lower *Daugae, mans dārgais draugs*."

With Kārlis at the wheel of the white ambulance, the Latvians had pulled all the way up to the Pier 97 entrance of the Swedish American Line. It was a red brick building with two one story tall, garage door style openings. Huge white letters, "Swedish American Line," lit up the building's West 57th Street side. At the foot of West 57th Street, Kārlis, Atis, and Pēteris left the vehicle.

The Latvians were met at the entrance of Pier 97 by two MS Stockholm crewmen. "Here are your pier passes," one of them said. "You'll need these to come with us when we take the body outside to the pier." Each tangerine orange pier pass was numbered. Each was issued "for official business" to a Swedish alias chosen by *Mistrz Borisevich*. On the lower left corner floated the three little coronets, two on top centered over the third on the bottom, of the MS Stockholm's logo.

The crewmen slid Jānis' double sealed coffin onto a gurney and rolled it into the cavernous terminal building. The only identification on Jānis' coffin was a sticker with navy blue lettering on a yellow background: "Swedish American Line" and an oversized "D" in the center, denoting Jānis' surname.

In the deeper shadows of the building stood Colonel Milanov, the Yugoslav, and the Latvian elder, Helmars Rudzitis. "Do not light your cigarette, Milanov said to Rudzitis. "Better to stay here while they say goodbye to their friend."

"We show to Jānis the respect in prayers," Milanov said, "and in action."

The Latvians followed the MS Stockholm crewmen into the terminal. The iron scaffolding supporting the top length and sides of the building looked skeletal. At the far end, a huge American flag was suspended from a catwalk above the passenger area, where a high blue painted picket fence formed an "L" for passengers queuing up to board the ship.

The crewmen told the Latvians that they should remain on the pier, at the dock, and not board the MS Stockholm. Each of the Latvians, in turn, placed his hand on Jānis' coffin and said: "*miermīlīgs aijāt.* "Peaceful sleep, my friend." Kārlis' weeping was bitter, almost silent when the crewmen escorted Jānis' coffin down to the far end of the gangplank that led to the ship's hold.

With its superbly raked bow and cruiser stern, the 525 foot Stockholm was powered by two *Götawerken* diesel engines and had a hull like that of a warship, slender and streamlined. Looking more like a large, private yacht than a transatlantic ocean liner, the Stockholm was one of the prettiest passenger ships on the North Atlantic. The hull of this Corvette of ships was painted a gleaming white. On its yellow funnel the line's famed three golden crowns were emblazoned on a round blue shield.

The Latvians longed to remain on the dock until the Stockholm embarked. However, they knew they must avoid being detected, for Jānis' sake. With the five IRT Powerhouse smokestacks standing like sentinels behind Pier 97, Kārlis, Atis and Pēteris murmured together a final prayer for their friend's journey home. Having arrived at this same pier nine years ago, Kārlis knew that, in the late morning, as the MS Stockholm headed out to sea, all aboard would see the Empire State Building in the background.

Colonel Milanov and Helmars Rudzitis made sure no one remained on the Stockholm's afterdeck or on the pier. Then they slinked, cobra like, along the water. All the way to the other end of the pier, on a low gurney, the two men pushed something covered in a dark green tarp. When Milanov and Rudzitis came to some overhanging rocks, they slid this amorphous lump into the shiny, black waters of the harbor. Soon after, a base fiddle case tied to ropes around the bundle kerplunked into the water. Both the case and the tarp covered bundle sank quickly under the jagged ledge. Milanov and Rudzitis had loaded the case with river rocks from the mouth of the Hudson, and it was heavy enough to take down the body of Georgie, the Commie thug. They were confident it would take a long time for authorities to find Georgie's body. So long that what was left of his corpse would not show they had violently beaten him before Milanov stabbed him through his vile heart.

Chapter 30

Two weeks later, St. Vincent's called Harry to say Gillian had been transferred to Bellevue Hospital. Gillian's analyst, Dr. Richter, had said she was well enough to be told of Jānis' death, but he was wrong. By the time Dolores found out about Gillian's transfer to Bellevue, Harry had already been there and raised hell when Dr. Richter claimed Gillian had tried to slash her wrists. Harry figured Gillian probably just fell out of bed, ripping the intravenous needles out of her skin.

When Dolores got to Bellevue she was barred from Gillian's room. Doctor Richter's orders. Dolores could look through a little rectangular window that was so high on the door she had to stand on her toes to see inside. This room was far worse than the one Gillian rented at the Y. One stark toilet and wall to wall padding. Light came through a second window, about ten feet up from the cushioned floor.

Huddled in the far right corner, Gillian wore an untailored, ivory colored white jacket with elongated arms, which were wrapped hideously across her chest. She was obviously drugged. Her hair was unwashed and unkempt.

About to throw up, Dolores leaned against a wall adjacent to the door. "Take her off the drugs," Dolores said. "She'll never get better if you don't."

"Your friend," Dr. Richter said, "has severe physical and mental trauma and can't be trusted not to try to kill herself again."

Now frantic, Dolores looked down both ends of the hallway and insisted that Dr. Richter release Gillian to her custody. "I can take care of her," she said to him.

"Even if you *were* her next of kin," Dr. Richter said, "you couldn't care for her twenty four hours a day." He looked amused at her *naïveté*.

Dolores looked fierce now: "Are you married? If you are, I feel sorry for your wife."

"What does my being married have to do with——."

"Look, you jerk! The man she loved was stabbed to death at some ungodly hour of the morning. I doubt that you have any human feelings because, if you did, you would understand why she's such a mess. If she were crazy she'd have gone right out to get another lover or something."

"You are not competent to decide what's best for her."

"You are not competent to be a human being," Dolores said.

Dr. Richter remained clinical and curt: "Only next of kin ..."

"Is that the only way you could release her to me?"

"To her next of kin," Doctor Richter reiterated.

"She's not dead for Christ sake."

Dr. Richter persisted: "How can we contact her parents?

Dolores looked through the little window at Gillian one more time. "Her father is deceased. I'll see if there's something in her apartment with her mother's address on it," she said to the woodwork. Gillian had not moved. Dolores called out her friend's name again and again until an orderly roughly pushed her out the nearest exit.

Dolores Valencia entered a confessional booth inside the Church of the Transfiguration on the Lower East Side of Manhattan. She had been christened here as a baby and had come here with her mother countless times for holy communion before her high school sweetheart, private Antonio Diaz y Centeno, was blown up by a German grenade in Normandy on D Day, 1944. "Bless me, father, for I have sinned," she directed at the screen that separated her from the confessional priest. "It is five years since my last confession." She paused. "My worst sin is the anger I have held in my heart against God. For a long time."

From the other side of the screen a kindly voice asked: "Why, my child?"

"Because *He* took away the boy I loved, and now they're holding my best friend captive in Bellevue." Dolores told the priest about Antonio's death, about her father's death later in the second World War, about her intense love for Gillian and how worried she was about her friend. "My analyst told me I'm afraid to love a man again." She began to cry. "Because my Tony died," she said. "He thinks I feel safer loving a woman. I don't buy that. I'm not really in love with Gillian. Well, maybe only a little, at first. Fiercely protective, yes. Wanting to help her, yes." Dolores added that she prayed Gillian, and God, would forgive her for any confusion she might have had.

"These are heavy burdens indeed," the priest responded. "Do you believe our Lord Jesus feels your sorrows and forgives you for turning away from Him? And that he wants to take your pain away?"

"I am not sure I believe that."

"It would be better not to add pride to your sins, my child. If you are sincere, if you come with an open heart, He will hear you."

"Okay," Dolores said.

"Very good. '... . May God give you pardon and peace. I absolve you from your sins in the name of the Father, and of the Son, and of the Holy Spirit.' But you must also do penance, as you are well aware."

"What is my penance?"

"Say three Hail Marys, three Our Fathers, and three Acts of Contrition before you leave this church today."

"Father?"

"Yes, my child?"

"I also came to ask you how to do a novena."

"To which Saint will you make your petition?"

"Saint Anthony," Dolores said.

"Your mother can help you," the priest said. "She's been doing novenas for you for years…"

Dolores stood up. "I *knew* the confessional was *no de incógnito*!"

Chapter 31

The gang down at Harry's Bar chipped in to help pay Gillian's hospital bills. The place had been like a morgue since they heard the news about Jānis and Gillian. Instead of bragging about the Yankees, Harry tried to purge himself of his burdens: how he had "bad mouthed the Latvian" and how he should have given Gillian that raise she asked for instead of letting her work those extra hours. Even how he missed the brooding presence of Kārlis, Atis and Pēteris. Harry also kept giving Mabel free wine. Dolores had been going to confession again, after buying enough candles to do a dozen novenas.

Dolores got some clothing and toiletries from Gillian's apartment. She also found Hannah's postal route number on the awful perfumed pink envelope. She read Hannah's letter too. It was innocuous. Some rubbish about what was and was not growing in her garden, how the "cabin" needed repairs and how she did not have money to make them. Dolores waited to hear back from Hannah regarding the telegram she had sent her:

Western Union
To Hannah Rysert (etc. etc.). Stop. Gillian in hospital. Stop. Bellevue. Stop. Serious injuries. Stop. Please come to NYC. Stop. Am wiring funds Western Union. Stop. Dolores Valencia.

On the phone four days later, Dolores told Lorna that she was about to meet Gillian's mother at Penn Station. "It must be a full moon," Dolores said to her mother. You know: It makes you want to go out and get drunk." Though Dolores had eaten breakfast that morning, any soothing effects of the food were eclipsed by the volume of coffee she had drunk with her meal.

"*Cariña*," Lorna said to her daughter. "I will pray for you and for your friend."

At Penn Terminal, Dolores spotted Hannah right away, for Hannah was the only redhead who came out of the gate for the train from St. Louis. Hannah was also the only passenger wearing a pink and black dress. She carried a huge patchwork bag as if it had been awarded to her for patriotic service. With a tentative wave, Dolores went right over to her.

Hannah's high cheekbones and *Patrician* nose showed Dolores that Hannah must once have been lovely. Hannah's intense, green eyes glittered with a glazed vitality. There was some resemblance to Gillian: the wideset eyes and the delicate bones, the shape of her head and the line of her hair. But, like *papier mâché*, Hannah's features had fixed and hardened. This woman let Dolores know that she couldn't put one over on Hannah and that she could break Dolores if she wanted to.

Clearly, Hannah was *self*-absorbed. Like others of her kind, she experienced life in prideful tangents. Such people check off vainglorious lists, sympathize only with their own ailments and know who owes them what, how they can get what they don't already have, and where *they* are moment to moment. Talking about someone else makes their eyes lose focus, and the sound of the person talking about someone else gets lost in the rest of creation that is *not them*.

Dolores tried to ignore the nausea she felt when the smell of Hannah's *poison lily* perfume reached her. With no attempt to hide her insincerity, Dolores thanked Hannah for coming.

"You Dolores? This better be a real emergency." In a low, benumbing drawl she added: "Didn't sleep a wink all night on the train. I cannot spend money on a New York hotel." When Hannah set her cloth satchel-like bag down, the latest edition of *The Plain Truth* slipped out from under her arm. "It says here," she said, referring to the magazine, "'the wickedness in big cities shall not go unpunished'." One could almost like Hannah for looking afraid, except that she was too dangerous, for she lived in a jail of her own making. If *she* wasn't free, she allowed no one else to claim that right. It follows that Hannah even felt pleasure that her daughter had been in a Bellevue padded cell.

Dolores handed Hannah a long white envelope. "Gillian's landlord said you could stay a couple nights in Gillian's apartment," she said. "Here are your tickets back to Missouri," she said. "Let me carry your bag for you."

Stashing the envelope in her bodice, Hannah clutched her bag to her Venusian bosom. "*I'll* do it. We *are* going right to the hospital?"

Dolores led Hannah down the subway stairs, which smelled of urine, spit, and tobacco juice. New York was a Gomorrah, and Hannah Rysert was about to wreak "the Lord's vengeance" upon it and on her own daughter. But if Dolores had felt free to speak her mind in this moment, she would have told Hannah that half the city's people were more joyful than she. That Gillian, herself, had shaken off her own Midwestern gloom since May. Dolores knew Gillian's traumas would ultimately strengthen her, for to the self-searcher compressed experience is a great time saver.

Perhaps Hannah's flirting with Dr. Richter got him to release Gillian. He looked like a woman starved sailor after a long voyage at sea. They spoke the same language, their motives camouflaged under a smooth demeanor. They were experts at playing the game of charisma, in which each pretended to support the other's fondest delusions about himself: the kind of veiled Id that social conventions sanction.

Perhaps Gillian had learned to modify her behavior enough over the past several weeks to convince Dr. Richter she was ready to be discharged: "No, Doctor. I don't hear voices anymore. Yes, I feel a lot better." Maybe Dr. Richter released Gillian on December 17th because it was her birthday. Or maybe Gillian's release was secured by Dolores' countless novenas.

Dolores and Hannah found Gillian in a large open room whose walls were painted just one minty shade away from the color of pea soup. In the ceiling a huge skylight let sunshine flow down from above and fill the entire room. Despite the bags under Gillian's eyes and the weight she had lost, she looked serene in a robin's egg blue wool dress. A light tan on her face suggested staff had let her outside. However, she avoided looking at other poor souls in this room: the disheveled, pale, lost crazies who surrounded her. She was not one of them. When Dolores asked Gillian how she was feeling, Gillian let a vacant smile wander where it would. She didn't seem surprised to see her mother. Hannah looked more petite, and even frailer, than she had when Gillian left St. Louis.

Dolores brushed Gillian's hair. "What a nightmare for you, Darling," she said. "Harry wants you to come back to work when you're feeling better. He says he'll give you a raise even if you work less." For a moment, Dolores touched her knuckles to her mouth. Then she said to Gillian, "I've brought your winter coat." It was a casual gray tweed coat with a leather belt, butterfly sleeves, and big pockets.

Gillian had "gone off" somewhere. Still, she let Dolores apply lipstick for her.

Dr. Richter released Gillian to her mother, and with Dolores they walked outside. Gillian squinted in the bright sunlight. She held the flowers Dolores had given her in her fist the way babies sometimes hold rattles: with the rattle head down. And now Gillian descended the subway stairs like a child with a helium balloon tied to her wrist. Gillian sat between Dolores and Hannah in the subway car. Now she seemed only vaguely aware of her mother.

Gillian seemed to have given up her claim on the sensual aspects of reality. Usually when she rode the subway, Gillian looked at ads for toothpaste and hair coloring while her train zoomed by. Today, when they whizzed by the subway boarding zones, Gillian ignored the ads and the woman across from her, who hugged her bags of street treasures. Instead, Gillian hummed to herself the Latvian tune about two lovers meeting along the banks of the River Daugava.

Hannah, who seemed uncomfortable with her daughter, said, "I am here." Neither Gillian nor Dolores saw the single tear at the corner of Hannah's eye. Whenever the subway train lurched, however, Hannah braced herself to avoid touching Gillian. Every time the subway train rolled through a dark stretch of tunnel, Gillian seemed in danger of disappearing until light emerged again. Gillian's condition reflected the kind of powerlessness that sent people to analysts in the first place.

When Dolores looked at Gillian's numb smile, she felt a remorse so deep that she feared it would never leave her. From now on, no matter where Dolores went, Gillian's future would also determine hers, with or against Dolores' will. When they reached the Christopher Street stop, Dolores lifted Gillian up, moved her toward the doors and guided her up the subway stairs.

The next day, Hannah charged forth like a Valkyrie. Armed with a note from Dr. Richter, she had gone to her daughter's bank to withdraw Gillian's entire savings. She paid Gillian's landlord, who stopped by the day before with a wide grin on his face. Seeing Hannah made him leer. His hand lingered on Hannah's as he accepted the wad of bills.

"I'll want a receipt," Hannah said.

At Gillian's apartment Hannah asked Dolores to help pack "some things" for Gillian to take back with her to Missouri. Hannah handed Dolores Gillian's little black alarm clock from the kitchen countertop. "You owe it to her," she said to Dolores.

Dolores watched Gillian stare into an empty cardboard box. "I owe it to her?" she asked Hannah.

"My daughter wrote me, you know. About how big a hit you made with her last summer. She thinks you are God."

"Nonsense," Dolores said. "She thought Jānis was God."

Hannah's smile was radiant but dark, like fluorescent lamplight on a black velvet painting. "There can only be one God," she preached.

"Yours?" Dolores asked. "Will God send a plague of locusts through that window if I say I don't believe in him?"

"I'm taking my daughter off your hands," Hannah said. She began her duel of power. "Judas …"

Dolores' voice turned icy and dropped several levels. "You don't own Gillian."

"I do now," Hannah said, "because it's plain I'm the one who's taking her back home." She finally looked away. "She's my daughter."

"But you don't love her," Dolores said.

"She's my daughter," Hannah repeated.

"That does not mean you've ever been good for her," Dolores insisted.

Hannah's face contorted: "You think being here was good for her? Look at her! She's sick. Her doctor sent her with *me*."

"Her doctor is a horse's ass," Dolores said. "And you both believe Gillian can't take care of herself. That she doesn't deserve to live the life she wants. That night was the only bad thing in everything good that's happened for her here. Everyone stumbles sometimes when life throws them a curve. We all get tested, but only you judge her. If she does get better in your care, she's probably going to feel you're punishing her for loving someone. Maybe even for loving all of us. If you care anything about her you'll help her see that her being beaten up wasn't punishment that she found love. She needs to realize that *loving* has made her grow."

Hannah now stood by Gillian's kitchen counter and Gillian sat on the loveseat. Dolores took the orange beads down from the kitchen doorway and gave them to Gillian. Gillian was absorbed with something the other two women could not see. She fingered the orange beads that now lay beside her on the loveseat.

"May I take my birdcage too?" Gillian asked.

"*That* won't fit in your suitcase, and it'll just be too much to have with us on the train," Hannah said.

"I have an idea," Dolores said. "Gillian? Do you have a hat box?"

"Hat box?"

Dolores took Gillian's hands and said, "To put the bird cage in."

"In the closet ... by the door."

Hannah's look was full of daggers. "She'll not bring that cage!"

Dolores had already packed the little birdcage in the hat box. "Gillian, you'll carry this. Do you understand what's happening?"

"I'm going home with Mama."

"To your dead Granny's cabin in the Ozarks," Hannah said. "Your doctor thinks it's best."

Looking doubtful, Dolores said, "You're going to get well. I'll write to you, and I hope you'll write to me. After you get well you can come back and live with me."

Gillian became lucid for the moment. "Dolores. Why can't I just stay here with you?"

Dolores fixed her eyes on Hannah but said to Gillian, "Because I'm not your 'next of kin'." The daggers in Dolores' voice apparently had landed somewhere *near* Hannah, who had remained unharmed.

However, in the air there was a suspicion that Gillian no longer belonged in New York. A dire warning swooped across her like the shadow of some tremendous, spiraling bird of prey. The Fates had ordained this. They had said, "That's what you get for growing! We tested you but good. If you survive, it's because we let you."

Hannah's announcement that she was going to lie on the couch and rest up for the train ride back to Missouri was Dolores' hint to leave Gillian's apartment.

Late that afternoon, Dolores entered Harry's Bar. Gathered there were all those who cared about Gillian. After Dolores had explained Gillian's situation, they all agreed that they were afraid they would never see their friend again. Harry came out from behind the bar like he was going to slug somebody. "I don't feel good about this," he said. "If she leaves now she might never be coming back to us." He put his arm around Dolores like a possessive father. "I can't stand losing her," he said.

Dolores relaxed into Harry's shoulder. "Write to her," she said. "She'll need to hear from us."

"They got two of the men who beat her up," Harry said. "Here's the other one." He showed Dolores an FBI Most Wanted poster. "This is the guy. He came in here a couple of times. Talked about betting on the ponies. Goes by 'Georgie'."

Dolores recognized Georgie as the guy with the lizard striped pants outside Village Cigars back in May.

Harry put his hand on one hip. "When the G Men brought this poster in and questioned me, they said he's disappeared. Not even the other two creeps knew where he was, and you know how the Feds can get them to talk. Sodium Pentothal, or some such."

"I'm surprised they can't find him," Dolores said. "Why, I wonder." Then her eyes widened. "What if he's lying low, waiting to finish Gillian off," she said.

"She'll already be back in Missouri, safe I hope," Harry said.

Dolores leaned her forearms on the bar. "Have you seen the Latvians?"

Harry said, "They've gone underground." He confessed he missed them, even though they were often so "irritating." Most of all, he wanted answers only they could give him. However, they had remained true to form. Perhaps even to their national identity. Perhaps they were refusing to take responsibility for having their lives touch those of these Americans. Perhaps they just wanted to keep their mystery. The Latvians certainly had not given Harry, or any of the bar's regulars, a clue about whether Gillian's friends had made a positive impression on them.

After leaving Harry's Bar, Dolores stopped by the Treasure Trove to update a chain smoking Mabel, who stood within the fortress of her precious possessions.

Mabel shook her head. "Such a tender thing," she said. "Too tender for this place. You know a person can't *become* a New Yorker," she said to Dolores. "You got to be born or bred here. Still, she had moxie."

"I hope she still does," Dolores said. "We can't give up on her just because she's going so far away."

"Even if she wants to come back someday," Mabel said, "I'm afraid she won't be able to."

Dolores reached over a pile of Mabel's "stuff" and grasped Mabel's hand. "Me too, Mabel. Me too."

Chapter 32

It was after 6:00 p.m. when The Spirit of St. Louis left Penn Station with Gillian and her mother aboard. At first, the sliding and bumping of the train on its tracks soothed Gillian. Soon, however, the galloping thump-thump-thump of wheels on tracks made her feel as if her waspish mother were jiggling a colicky baby. Gillian turned away from Hannah and pressed the side of her body against the small train window. Silently she said goodbye to New York, to her friends, to her apartment in Greenwich Village.

Enriched by her relationships in New York, Gillian had grasped that, for her, railway depots and subways let her *change trains* for her "journeys of the heart." In New York she had related each new person to one leg of her journey: learning to trust a friend, impressing a boss, winning a lover. There she had also welcomed vivid, spicy eccentrics who warmed her like hot mulled cider. She had moved forward. She had begun to share her once Spartan heart.

But things had turned out badly, and Gillian now wondered if these gifts, the people she loved, had been taken from her because she hadn't deserved them. She thought maybe Hannah's malice had somehow cursed her from afar. Her mother's cruelty had magnetically wrenched Gillian away from everyone she loved. Or maybe it was God's fault: the trouncing finality of "the Lord giveth, and the Lord taketh away."

Initially Gillian had welcomed the tranquilizers and pain killers Dr. Richter prescribed when he released her from Bellevue. Sedation helped her remain in the current room of her invention. Gillian preferred her thoughts to her feelings, anyway, for in her mind she was free to wander, to explore all that could be. In Gillian's imagination she rarely created dire realities. But her emotions were like whetstones for the next time a harsh world wished to sharpen its cruel events to test her.

Each time the drugs wore off a little, Gillian could feel a child's kind of loneliness and a pulling down of the muscles along the sides of her mouth. She could feel her tears. Yet she made no sound, no sobbing. She was weeping, yet she was not. When the narcotic weakened, Gillian could feel what hell it was to be confined in this Pullman car with her mother. Not only Hannah's noxious cologne but also by the rasp of her mother's toxic energy continued to harass her. Being back with Hannah now made Gillian feel like a curled brown leaf that swirled in a gush of muddy water on its way down a storm drain.

A challenge flickered now in Hannah's shiny green eyes. "I see you permed your hair," she said to Gillian, "and your lipstick is too dark." Hannah looked expectant. Perhaps she relished a smack of rebellion from her daughter.

Instead of giving Hannah this pleasure, Gillian merely looked down. To Hannah, but only in her thoughts, Gillian now retorted: You *home dye your hair* outré *orange.* (Gillian learned the word *outré* from Dolores.) *Your eyes look like seaweed*, Gillian added, without speaking. She finally said to Hannah, aloud: "I got my hair cut and permed at a salon to look like Katharine Hepburn's." Gillian thought: *May I never dye my hair orange, even when I'm old.*

Hannah put her hand on her hip. She patted the back of her hair and replied: "I think *I* kind of look like Katharine Hepburn, but *I* have bosoms!" she cackled.

Gillian was glad her mother said little in the dining car, where Hannah read *The Plain Truth* and finished a deluxe dinner. Gillian merely picked at hers. When Gillian asked the porter to get her a pack of Chesterfields, Hannah scowled and shook her head. When Gillian ordered a Tom Collins, which she associated with working at Harry's, her mother said "they" didn't drink and waved the porter away.

Hannah said to Gillian: "There'll be no smoking and no liquor in *my* home!" The many stops and starts had the effect of a telegram:

Arrive Newark. Stop. Depart Newark. Arrive Trenton. Stop. Arrive North Philadelphia. Stop. Paoli, Lancaster, Harrisburg. Stop.

When the Spirit left Harrisburg at 9:20 p.m., Gillian was asleep in the top berth of the sleeper car she shared with her mother. Hannah clutched her handbag and walked toward the lavatory to remove her makeup. "Occupied," the latched sign read. Sighing, she decided to go to the observation car. Two older male passengers smoked cigars and made small talk. Their pot bellies jiggled with the motion of the train. Both appraised Hannah for a moment and then continued their conversation. Hannah found two middle-aged women sitting together and plunked down in a plush, red leather seat across from them. After she had stared at the women for a full two minutes, they noticed and asked her to join them.

"Thank you kindly," Hannah said. She now felt invited to lead with her wounds: "My daughter went crazy in New York and I'm bringing her home. Lord knows I've had enough heartache, with my Mama dying just a few months past and my husband passing before that."

The two sympathetic women nodded. One offered Hannah a peppermint Life Saver candy. The other said, "Where are you from, honey?"

"St. Louis, but we have to live in Poplar Bluff now. In the cabin where my mama died. It's a big change from my house in St. Louis. We were only renting, but when Mama got so sick in Poplar Bluff, of course I had to go to her. Most times she was nice, but sometimes she was downright mean, despite how much I gave up to tend to her."

The Life Saver woman said, "My daughter's like that. All her life we treated her like a princess. I tell you she wanted for nothing. And now? Do you think she'd trouble herself to call us? Oh, she shows up for holidays with her husband and three kids. But otherwise we don't hear from her."

The other woman said, "I thank God my children aren't like that. They live just across town with their families, and we get together all the time."

"You're so lucky," the Lifesaver woman said.

"Yes. You are lucky," Hannah said.

Back in the sleeper car, Gillian lay in the top berth. The train wheels jostled her back and forth. She dreamed of walking toward a chapel in the woods. In front of it was a sign: "Service for Ret. Army Sgt. Chester Rysert. 1:30 PM."

The dreamer Gillian stood behind the Gillian who walked inside the chapel. She sat in the front pew, not far from her father's coffin. To her horror, the corpse's lips moved as if giving her a message: "Come closer." She didn't want to, but her father's words compelled her.

Gillian had to push each leg forward as if she walked through deep water. Against her will, something propelled her toward the coffin. There lay her father. His smile showed a peace he had not enjoyed since before he was sent to war. She touched his hair and said, "I love you, Pop."

Now, still dreaming about her father as he lay in state, Gillian noticed that the second hand of his watch still moved around the dial. This macabre detail startled Gillian. When she looked back where her father should be, Jānis now lay there instead. His hair was perfect. His eyes were open. She wailed "Oh no!"

Hannah's hand clutched Gillian's shoulder. "Stop it! You'll wake up everybody on this train. Here. It's time to take your medicine."

"Okay," Gillian said. She knew the medication would help her escape what she still felt, remembering Jānis' face as he lay in the coffin in her dream. Hannah lifted her up a glass of water, and Gillian gulped down the red pill that would bring her the oblivion she longed for. Then she took the white pill that would soothe the pain in her body.

Their train had reached the Alleghenies, where one mountain split the valley into two ravines. Gillian could feel the train slowing, hear brakes screeching, as they came to the treacherous Horseshoe Curve, which bent around a dam and a lake west of Altoona, Pennsylvania. "What time is it?" she asked her mother.

"Almost midnight."

Gillian knew from the timetable that in eight hours they would reach Indianapolis Union Station. There she could again see *the rose window* that had so captivated her before her train headed outbound to New York in April. The enormous round window high up on the north end of the station's Grand Hall. She figured that even though the late afternoon light emanating from the window would be muted, she still would be able to see the exquisite symmetrical tracery radiate out from the center of this stained glass window. She believed the rose window would heal her. She would memorize every piece of tinted glass and every design that radiated like sunbeams from its center. Then she would carry the designs and colors of the rose window with her to the Ozarks like a huge, blessed medallion.

Chapter 33

INDIANAPOLIS UNION STATION: INBOUND

At breakfast on the Spirit of St. Louis, Gillian took her morning dose of sedative and palliative. The pills further dulled Gillian's impression of the bleak skies so typical of Indiana winter. Her past in New York had also dimmed. She no longer craved a cigarette or a Mai Tai, or anything else that would convey her New York life back to her.

Just before Gillian and Hannah left their train car, their porter pushed a pack of Chesterfield cigarettes into Gillian's hand. "For the road," he said. She slipped the Chesterfields into one pocket of her long gray coat and followed her mother down to the station platform. Icy slush smeared the tracks and train platform outside the station. Since neither woman wore boots, making their way between the round steel guardrails and down the stairs to the terminal was treacherous. Gillian's hat box bounced like a pinball off the metal railings. Even in the concourse, a trick of the light cast shadows over those who arrived and those who waited.

Hannah pointed to the grand hall at the far end. "Wait 'til you see what's down there," Hannah said. "I forgot to tell you about it before."

From a distance Gillian could hear the recorded voice of Perry Como, who sang "Santa Claus Is Coming to Town."

"This way," Hannah said. "It's five days 'til Christmas, and I want to show you something."

The grand hall was packed with people. With her head bowed, Gillian saw the holiday crowds from their necks down: men's collars up, tied, closed by their long woolen neck scarves. Ladies' nylon neck scarves, which looked ineffective against the cold, and their fur stoles, made from little, whole foxes whose glass eyes begged Gillian to rescue them and bring them back to life. Children looked up at the Christmas decorations. To Gillian, they all moved sluggishly, as if they were fathoms down in a bottomless sea. A man smiled at Gillian, tipped his hat, and said, "Merry Christmas." His words sounded muffled and macabre, like a 78 rpm vinyl record played at 33 speed.

Gillian felt desperate to find the rose window, which was obscured by a massive, white figure. "I am fifty four feet tall," it boasted through loud-speakers. "I am made of four hundred blocks of Styrofoam!"

"Here it is!" Hannah said.

Gillian blinked. Before her was "Santa Colossal," the world's largest Santa Claus. Seeing this grotesque blob of Polystyrene foam hit her senses like an avalanche, speeding up the movement of people around her and amplifying every sound. People chattered and said "Ooh!" and "Wow!" as they walked be-tween its ten foot tall boots and peered up at its twelve foot long mustache, while Spike Jones sang "All I Want for Christmas Is My Two Front Teeth." Gil-lian felt sick. She paled.

"Whatta you think?" Hannah asked, while Santa Colossal bragged about how his body was shipped from Beaverton, Michigan, in four railroad cars.

Horrified by this monstrous Santa, Gillian pointed to the top of the grand hall. "I have to get there and see the rose window!" She tried to move away from her mother.

"Yor crazy! It's dark up there. Why on earth—. "

"If I don't see the rose window I'll die!"

However, their train to St. Louis was announced, and Hannah began to drag Gillian by the wrist as if she were a child. Gillian held her hat box under her arm and pressed it close to her body. Just before Gillian and Hannah reached the huge archway, Gillian threw her head back to protest. When she opened her eyes, a huge clock displayed its small hand on the number nine and its large hand on seven. High above that was a *twin* of the rose window that she hadn't noticed when she was outbound to New York. Now its colors, its symmetry, rekindled her memory. Hannah pulled her down the darkened concourse to their gate, Gillian engraved the window's designs in her imagination. She felt she might want to live after all.

Chapter 34

Gillian boarded a Greyhound bus with Hannah outside the St. Louis terminal. It was mid-afternoon. Gillian was subdued. During this final part of their journey, she was unable to appreciate the winter of the hills in the mouth of the Ozarks. Instead, her impressions were awash with the drugs her mother made her take.

The bus seemed to fly through Poplar Bluff, and so Gillian saw little of "The Gateway to the Ozarks." Her medications also obscured the visage of Hannah's leathery faced neighbor, Eban Gunter, "handyman" and hunter. Gillian felt uneasy when Eban helped the two women into the front seat of his dented black 1934 Ford pickup truck. To Gillian, the spare tire of Eban's rusted truck, just in front of the passenger door, looked like a giant black powdered sugar donut.

Hannah pushed Gillian in before her. This made Gillian have to sit in the middle, her thigh touching Eban's. His presence alarmed Gillian. In her mind she heard the word "predator."

Eban pointed at Gillian's hat box. "Do you have to hold that on your lap? Give it here," he said. "I'll toss it back in the cargo bed with your suitcase."

Gillian squeezed the thick string handle of her hat box. "No."

Poplar Bluff, in Butler County, Missouri, is northeast of the Black River and southeast of Lake Wappapello. This part of the Ozark highlands stretches south and west from St. Louis and extends to the Arkansas River. The town is one of the gateways between the Mississippi lowlands and the Ozarks. In the old days, trains that steamed through Poplar Bluff had such names as "Frisco" and "the Blue Bonnet Special." As locals would say, Poplar Bluff is "within spitting distance" of the Mark Twain National Forest. As of December 1949, almost fifteen thousand people inhabited the town.

Outside the town proper, the area was still the "heaven" pioneers in the early 1800s deemed it to be. Swamps and wooded hills offered rich hunting grounds full of quail, rabbits, squirrels, deer, doves, and beavers. Woodsmen hunted these creatures with benign ignorance. They endured the rough elements of everyday existence: stoking up a cold wood stove on winter mornings. Pushing through hip deep snowdrifts to get to the outhouse. Eating cornbread and blackstrap molasses for days while they waited for the next thaw, for backcountry roads to be plowed.

The area's riches lay mostly in the woods, which bore trees of ash, maple, linden, slippery elm, honey locusts, redbud, sumac and scrub oak, dogwood, and hackberry. And "paw-paws." Forests provided hickory nuts, hazel nuts, black walnuts, and persimmons.

To hill people, mushrooms were in a class by themselves. Some grew as big as a fist and felt cold to the touch. There is an expansive local lore about mushrooms. Hill people believed that when they picked mushrooms, they must leave part of the stem in the ground so another mushroom could spring up. If someone was not going to eat a mushroom she had looked at, she must cut it anyway. They knew that once humans looked at a mushroom, it would grow "nary an inch" afterwards. Some hill country expressions included "You can walk for miles and never get nowhere" and "They's rain in the mares' tails."

Hannah's family cabin was outside of town. Like most cabins of that vintage, Hannah's was made of logs and had hardwood floors. She used her sheet iron wood burning stove both for cooking and heating. The cabin had glass windows and was insulated with Celotex. In the back yard, Hannah had a storm cellar, dug out and lined with rocks, to keep vegetables and canned fruits from spoiling or freezing. The indoor plumbing, which Hannah had paid to be installed, rendered her late mother's old outhouse obsolete.

When Hannah opened the cabin door, Gillian was sure she would never emerge again, for she believed that seven months of freedom in New York were all she had deserved. God had punished her for expecting too much. When the cabin door closed behind her, Gillian decided that she would give in to whatever *inside her* made her want to forget, whatever it was that hoped she would care that she had just turned twenty one.

Chapter 35

POPLAR BLUFF, MISSOURI: 1916 – GILLIAN'S MOTHER

Hannah Marie LaFont had been the youngest of seven. When she was barely five, her three sisters began to beat her while her four brothers worked as share-croppers. During the one hundred ninety day, frost free growing season, six days a week (except the Sabbath), Hannah's brothers left at dawn. Each carried a cylindrical lunch pail. Every workday the brothers climbed into the bed of their landowner's barn red farm wagon, pulled by a team of heavy boned draft horses.

Every day Hannah endured her sisters' beatings until swirls of dust from the landowner's wagon rose like egg beaten flour above the washboard road that led to their cabin. The brothers unloaded boxes from the field crops they worked: corn, soybeans, and potatoes. Hannah's mother, Ena, culled root vege-tables for the root cellar. Sometimes the brothers would bring back tomatoes. Or wheat flour, coffee, and sorghum from a market in town. Hannah and her sisters combed the nearby woods for sweet potatoes and beets, blackberry sprouts, dandelion greens, "mouse-ear," and plantain. And blackish greenish, custard like paw-paws. Ena canned tomatoes and other vegetables for the raw winter months to come. When the brothers strode in, coughing and smudged with dirt from head to toe, the sisters got busy laying supper out on the table.

Hannah's father, Henri LaFont, was a rugged, hard drinking vagabond who occasionally returned home just long enough to get Hannah's mother, Ena (neé

O'Brien), pregnant again. Hannah did remember Henri cursing Ena one time in the "Missouri French" of his ancestors, who had settled in Old Mines in the early 1800s. Hannah's sisters could sing phrases from the drinking song: "C'est à boire à boire à boire / c'est à boire qu'il nous faut!" in that dying "paw-paw French."

The last time Hannah saw her father, he was yelling at Ena. Ena had reminded him that she could trace her Irish bloodline all the way back to Brian Boru, "King of all Ireland." Henri then called Ena's people "dirty Irish immigrants." Ena reminded him that his people were habitants (farmers), not aristocrats, and that his grandmother was a half-breed Osage Indian. "At least he's Roman Catholic," Ena sometimes rationalized about Henri, not that any of the family attended mass or went to confession. At the end of 1911, Henri got into a drunken fight in bar near Doniphan along the Eleven Point River and killed a German logger. Henri spent the rest of his life in the Missouri State Penitentiary. Neither Ena nor his children ever went to visit him.

Only the town's elders and Hannah's peers would be able to recall that in 1928, when Hannah was seventeen, she had eloped and moved to St. Louis with retired army Sergeant Chester Rysert. This was a year after a deadly tornado killed more than two hundred and injured almost a thousand in Poplar Bluff. Chester was twelve years Hannah's senior and had only an eighth grade education. He had been honorably discharged because shrapnel ravaged his leg. Hannah's sisters called Chester "Gimpy."

POPLAR BLUFF: LATE DECEMBER 1949

On its way back out the window, the sun had already reached, orange, across Gillian's room and dropped out of the sky. The pale apricot light had dimmed and settled like a smoky veil on her bed. In darkness now, from the doorway, Gillian's room looked small. Her bed lay beneath a window which centered the one outside wall. An old quilt hung over the curtain rod, sheltered her from the cold outside. She had slept through Christmas Eve and Christmas.

Wrapped in heavy blankets, Gillian lay dreaming about unfamiliar people, who flickered but said nothing. Her moist hair stuck to her face. Despite the layered blankets, topped with a patchwork quilt, she shivered. Gillian tried to catch up with the flitting images, possibilities that might be as real as events.

But she failed because, even when awake, she dared not explore them. When reason tried to break through, Gillian ignored it, for she wanted only to stop trying, like a rabbit struggling in a snare.

She murmured. Hollow eyed strangers tried to grab her wrists, but their hands kept slipping off, hard as she fought to connect. And then, when the dream turned, she wanted to escape the strangers, but they clamped upon her, beating, beating, beating her until all she could see was a red glare. She was screaming into her pillow. Like her matted hair, her eyelids felt as if they were anchored to her cheekbones. Another Gillian, ghostlike and concerned, hovered four feet above her. "Wake up!" the floating Gillian shouted. The Gillian in bed tried to move but lay instead like a dead person. "Please wake up," a voice inside her pleaded. "I'll try," Gillian said aloud. The yellow nightgown of the levitating Gillian billowed about like an autumn leaf caught in a whirlwind. Though Gillian felt a hand clamp down hard on her wrist, she still couldn't open her eyes.

Hannah's voice dropped on Gillian like a heavy icicle. "Wake up," she said. With her pale work worn fingers she tugged severely at the top of the sheet. "You were screaming again. There now. Eat something. See? Eat this now." Hannah gazed into her own eyes, reflected in the full-length, oval mirror she had bought at a thrift shop in St. Louis. While tending to Gillian she spent as much time gazing at herself as she did trying to rehabilitate her daughter so that the latter would, hopefully, get out of her life forever this time.

Hannah's vanity made this bedroom mirror her most ardent admirer. Before Gillian left St. Louis, when Hannah could tear her eyes away from her own reflection, her next target was Gillian. In her mother's *face* Gillian could see familiar, multi-layered critiques. Never mind that Hannah also criticized Gillian in words that seemed to wrap around Gillian's throat like the hands of the Boston Strangler. "You're pathetic. Worthless. Just like your father."

Gillian checked her mother's image in the mirror now. She thought, almost out loud: *What* are *you?*

The next morning, just before Noon, Eban Gunter came by Hannah's cabin in his dumpy old pickup and Hannah climbed into the front seat. She was bundled in layers of three thin coats, a long fuchsia and black plaid neck scarf, and black rubber boots. Eban started down the washboard road to the main part of town. "I'm about fit to be tied," Hannah said to him.

"I reckon she's a handful," Eban said, hopefully.

"You don't know the half of it."

Eban smoothly turned right on the washboard road. "What about yor Christmas present?"

"You mean the pretty brooch? She barely looked at it," Hannah said. "I have not seen it in her room, so I reckon she hid it."

"She should be grateful," Eban said, "after all you done for her."

Hannah was bitter. "Why should she start now?" she said. "She's lucky there's indoor plumbing, thanks to me. Honestly, she's a cipher. Why she was born to me I'll never know." Hannah pulled her coat collar higher. "It's amazin' cold," she added.

"Bet you'll be glad to be rid of her," Eban said. "It'll be funny, though, to be yor son-in-law," Eban said. His scratchy laugh turned into coughing spasms. His open mouth revealed teeth yellowed by poor hygiene and decades of cigarette tar. "That don't mean you and me can't still have some, you know, good times. Like before."

"Well, we'll see," Hannah cackled.

"When you reckon she'll be ready to come to my place for good?"

"Not soon enough," Hannah said. "I'm so tired of caring for sick people! First Mama, then my prodigal daughter. Always so defiant, that one. When she was three, I tried to take her hand to cross the street, but she would have none of it. She took off running, and I had to chase her more than a block before she stopped. So unlike my Lettie. Now *she* was an angel. When I held her she would make herself real light. And when I told her not to touch things at the market, she didn't. That must be why God took Lettie from me. You know, for years after that, I stopped reading my Bible. Then, when I came back to Poplar Bluff, all there was to do was socialize with church people. I kinda gave in to it after a while. Now it is the *only* balm I have for my soul."

"You really have had yor share of it," Eban said. He parked in front of J.J. Newbury's five and dime store. Its sign spanned the entire storefront. The non-seraphed, tall red letters outlined in white proclaimed Hannah and Eban were about to come inside a high-end establishment—at least for Poplar Bluff.

"I love their cafeteria," Hannah said. "And, Lordy, it's good to get out of that cabin! What are you hankering for today?"

"It's their roast beef dinner for me," Eban said, "complete with brown bread and molasses. You can have the carrots. I'll keep the potatoes."

"Today I'm gonna order down home chicken pot pie," Hannah said, "with a side of string beans. I don't care if they *are* canned. They cook 'em with yellow onions and fatty chunks of ham. Keeps you warm in winter."

Chapter 36

New Year's Eve had passed Gillian unnoticed. Early one evening, she felt brave enough to look out her bedroom window, which faced west. Shadows had just begun to settle on the landscape. To the south she could see gentle rolling terrain. To the north she could make out the edges of the thick woods that lay behind her mother's cabin. Even while in her dissociative haze, Gillian was aware that it must be unusual for there to be no snow on the ground this time of year. She felt an instinctive need to go into the woods, especially since she could see so little of them from her window.

Soon Hannah would bring Gillian the little red tablet that kept her from feeling *anything*. Somehow she had to avoid taking it. She had to break this cycle of numbness. She had to lift herself up so her mind could begin to dissolve this fugue state.

Gillian pulled off her nightgown and put on dungarees and a white sweater. She had put on one black sock and one navy blue sock that had belonged to Jānis. She could not remember where she put Jānis' other sock. Then she slipped on her white and brown saddle oxfords and her long tweed coat. She opened her bedroom window and squeezed through it. Then she slid down to the ground.

Being outside was not as exhilarating as Gillian had just imagined. She faced the cabin. She clung to its outside wall. She moved north, behind the cabin, towards the woods. It was twilight now, and with the sun almost down, a cold wind rose and stung her face. She looked back at the cabin. Her mother's room was dark. Gillian was hungry, but she knew she must keep going. When she reached the edge of the woods she walked faster. There was no sound but the wind. There was no path but only a sort of faint trail made by ways the trees and brush had decided to grow.

Gillian had no idea where she was going, but she kept moving farther into the woods. A full moon that rose in the east began to make the forest shimmer. Because of the wind, the moonlight spawned weird shapes that seemed to writhe on, and loom up from, the forest floor. But Gillian kept walking. She wished only that she had thought to stuff a yeast roll in her pocket. This made her think of the "Hansel and Gretel" fairy tale, and she smiled a little. Then she realized she didn't want to drop breadcrumbs on the ground because she had rather her mother *didn't* find her. And she knew that if she focused on the mean witch in the gingerbread house—the one who fattened children up and ate them—she would run right back. Back to a prison she might never escape. Suddenly this journey into the woods didn't feel much like freedom. Yet some pressure inside her drove her onward.

Gillian's running through the brush made a lot of noise. Dead leaves swished and crackled, and small dead branches snapped under her shoes. A faint light shone just beyond the northernmost part of the forest. Just as she was about to emerge, someone grabbed her by the wrist. She squealed like a terrified baby animal.

"Shet up!" a man's voice threatened. It was Eban. "I been hearing you come at my place for the past five minutes. What the blazes ere you doing out here?"

Gillian couldn't speak. She trembled from terror as much as from the cold.

"Well, girl? I asked you a question. You come to visit ol' Eban?"

Gillian struggled to get out of Eban's grasp. In the moonlight his face looked ghostly. He had wolf eyes, yellowish and ravenous. "Let me go!" Gillian shrieked.

Eban pulled Gillian along to his cabin. He chuckled. "Yes sir, I do believe I have company for supper tonight. You like squirrel? Don't s'pose you got that in the big city, huh? Come on, Gillie girl. I ain't so bad. Why you come all this way if you ain't gonna be nice?" He yanked Gillian this way and that up a hill to his cabin.

Helpless because of how strong this mountain man's hold on her was, Gillian resisted the severe forward tilt of her upper body. She had no ability to balance. Eban lifted her up and out as if she were a balsa wood glider. She remembered her mother's saying how much wood Eban chopped for her, so she knew struggling would be futile.

"Yor a pretty thang," Eban said. He shoved Gillian onto the floor of his cabin. He slammed and bolted the door. "Now, Gil, come have a drink with me." He brought out a crude clay jug and uncorked it with his teeth. "This stuff is made right here in ol' Poplar Bluff. You know. Because of all the poplar trees here. That is why they call it Poplar Bluff. Betcha you didn't know that, growin' up in St. Louie and all."

Eban wore a red plaid hunting shirt and soiled khaki pants, the knees faded and shiny. "Oh, come on, gal," Eban said. "I know yor a wild one. Yor Mama told me about you. How you lived."

With effort Gillian stood up. "Let me go," she said. "I was just taking a walk."

"Yeah? Well I think you need a man's company."

Gillian thought Eban's eyes looked even more glazed than when they were in the forest.

"Don't you be lookin' at me thata way," Eban said. "Think yor better than me? I been drinkin'. So what? You look like you could use some of this here 'medicine' yourself. Here. Take a swig."

"No," Gillian said. "Please let me go, Eban."

"You just set right down in this here chair and talk for a spell. You are gonna tell me why you was wanderin' around my woods."

"*Your* woods? Aren't they my mother's woods?"

"Hell no! The only piece of ground she owns is what's right under her cabin, girl. You hungry? I already et, so the leftover squirrel's cold, but you would not mind it. I promise. Tastes a lot like chicken."

"I have to go. Mama's probably home by now, and she's gonna be worried."

"*Mad's* more like it. Whoo! What a temper! But listen. Let's talk about us. I know you miss a man's company. I mean, I know you ain't no virgin no more. Once women get a taste of it, they come to need it as much as men. Yor mother—."

"I don't want to hear about you and my mother," Gillian said. "Now let me go." She didn't like the way Eban took big gulps of moonshine while looking at her as if she were a deer he intended to bring down with a single rifle shot. Because she was no longer drugged, all her sensations were at peak. She could feel her acute tension and every bruise. Gillian hoped sympathy for her "mental condition" would get Eban's mind off what he seemed to be intending. "Eban, you know I'm not well," she said.

"Yeah," Eban said. "You do look kinda peak-ed. And I can't reckon the way you talk. But yor mama said I could have you here when yor feelin' better. She wants you married and out of her hair. She reckons after you rest up you will forget about that *fer-in-er* and settle down here." Then he tried to hold Gillian's hand. "That is the best thang," he said.

Gillian knew it would be a mistake to go against Eban, so she let her hand stay limp in his. She could hardly believe it when he unlocked his door.

"If'n you go yonder, due south," he said, you will find yor mama's place. Now don't you forget what I said: You are promised me." With the heel of his hand he pushed Gillian between her shoulder blades, causing sharp pain and knocking the wind out of her. He slapped her on the fanny. He bared his decayed teeth when he said, "Now git!"

Gillian bolted out the door and back to the woods. The moon pulled her; the cold wind blasted her back. A darker, more primitive Gillian now stumbled over rocks in the hill. This Gillian led her through dense brush and over fallen trees, and around hidden areas of damp marsh, and outside the compass of bear paths. This Gillian made her gaze up at the moon while she ran, made her feel how the moon pulled and stroked her like a lover. This pleasure mixed with an odd feeling in Gillian that something extracted her from herself and in her place, in slow motion, an arrow pierced her heart. She finally reached the edge of the woods that lay between Eban's cabin and her mother's.

Just as she got to the clearing behind the cabin, she tripped on a large, jagged rock and fell forward on the hard earth. She lay on her stomach. Her ribs ached and her lungs felt deflated. Her impact with the ground made rough scratches on the right side of her face. She wanted to see why her left hand felt so mangled. During her fall, her hand had become wedged under an exposed, arching tree root. On the ground a few inches above her head a little creature lay, quivering. It was a male cardinal. In the moonlight, he looked pinkish white. One wing was unnaturally bent, and his eyes had only a trace of life in them. *I am so cold*, he imparted. *I am so hungry. Please don't hurt me.*

Gillian lay on the ground and looked at the little bird for a few minutes before she decided what to do. "I know how you feel," she said, "because I feel the same way." When she sat up she felt pain all over her body. She cupped the bird in her hand and said, "You'll be safe and warm with me." She then put him gently under one wide lapel.

She could feel him flutter a little. She smiled, knowing that he rested, protected, on her breast.

Chapter 37

The bamboo birdcage from New York hung in Gillian's room across from Granny's old black rocker. A faded pink towel covered the cage. Much of the time now, Gillian lay asleep under layers of blankets. When she was awake, she did crazy things of which she was unaware. One of these episodes involved paper cutting scissors with bright red handles. She liked to hide them in the nightstand beside her bed. Several times when she complained to Hannah that they were missing, her mother brought them back. Since they were the one thing Gillian had apparently come to count on, she guarded them with the ferocity of a badger.

Hannah came into Gillian's room hugging some issues of *The Saturday Evening Post*. "You can thank the ladies at the Christian Church for donating these to me. Otherwise, it would've cost me fifteen cents each.," she told Gillian. "They may be a tad too homey for you after *Vogue*, but just maybe there's something in them you'll like." Hannah thwacked the magazines down on Gillian's bed. "Here, girl. Now don't go cuttin' things out of them." It was twilight. Hannah turned on the lamp beside Gillian's bed. She glanced at the covered birdcage before ducking back to her kitchen hideout.

The church. That was a good one. Gillian remembered that her mother was far from religious. In fact, baby Letitia's death in St. Louis had put an end to Hannah's holiday based church attendance. Gillian suspected, rather, that her mother's recent alliance with the Christian Church probably had more to do with husband hunting. And maybe a little socializing. Gillian did, however, welcome the diversion of the church ladies' donations of the *Post*, for she had grown tired of sleeping all the time.

She paged through the November 5, 1949, *Post* and stopped to read an article called "Russia's Triple Crisis," by Ellsworth Raymond. She thought, *Ellsworth Raymond has a last name for a first name and a first name for a last name. Ellsworth.* She slipped her index finger in before the first page of the article. She felt it with her thumb. *Ellsworth Raymond,* she said to herself. *A man about five foot seven, white at the temples, wearing a tweedy old coat and brown corduroys. A man who held a pipe in his mouth but seldom lit it. When he kissed his wife, his mouth was wet at the corners.* Exercising her imagination was pleasurable, and the *Post* offered her an agreeable escape from confinement in her mother's cabin.

Gillian threw the November 5th issue on the floor and picked up November 12th. She used the open it anywhere and see what happens method and immediately found a piece called "Nobody Enjoys a Right to Plot the Overthrow of U.S." "God," she whispered. Then she flipped to a full-page ad for the John Hancock Life Insurance Company. Johnny Appleseed took up half the page: "He had a white beard and hair, and tattered too-short trousers. He strode across an aisle of beautifully cropped grass. On either side a grove of cherry trees bloomed pinkish white. Apparently undaunted by the fruit trees already proliferating there, he pulled seeds out of the worn leather bag that flew out from his shoulder. He planted seeds for us to reap." *Planted seeds*, Gillian thought. *That's important.*

Gillian opened the drawer of her nightstand. She felt relief that the red handled scissors were still there. While Hannah was out that morning Gillian had crept out to the kitchen and retrieved them. She liked the cool, metallic pressure of the instrument in her fingers. Its edges were very sharp. She cut out Johnny Appleseed's picture and put it in the drawer.

Gillian next found an ad for Auto-Lite spark plugs. "Which is really Jane Wyman?" it cajoled. There were two photographs at the top of the page. In both versions, "Jane" posed with her red painted nails wrapped around a camera. "Starring in 'The Lady Takes a Sailor', A Warner Brothers Production," read text in a box at the upper right. After she had looked a long time at each photo, she decided Jane Wyman was in the photo on the left. However, since the girl on the right was identified as "Ruth Woods of New York City," Gillian cut out both photos. She left a crooked margin of white space and a few lines from below the photos. *New York City*.

She also cut out a General Mills ad for "How the Lone Ranger rounds up jobs," an IBM ad titled "Releasing the Human Mind" and a picture of Barbara Stanwyck. The Lone Ranger sat astride "Silver" next to a blue sedan. "Who's Behind that Mask? The Lone Ranger, symbol of fair play out where men are men," it ended. On the blue sedan was painted the General Mills logo and a grinning businessman. This IBM ad has a sort of Greek statue head rising out of clouds in a sky colored yellow, indigo and greenish aqua. There hung three little atomic structures and an electron tube for "computing machines." Barbara Stanwyck wore bulbous diamond earrings and a hooded ermine coat. She urged everyone to smoke Chesterfields. The actress looked as if she were ready to advance, carnally, on the photographer, and Gillian longed to have a smoke of this, her favorite cigarette brand.

The December 3rd *Post* contained a real treasure: the story "Espionage Express," by Robinson MacLean. Not to be outdone by Ellsworth Raymond, the author had chosen for his surname both a first and last name. Gillian found this fact extremely important. This story's lurid kicker aroused a strange, pleasant feeling in her. "On a night train to the Soviet border the American captain played a dangerous game with the Russian (female) major...."

Though Gillian didn't perceive why, she identified with the woman in the story's illustration: "Picture a beautiful blonde in a long greenish skirt and calf height brown boots, and a white tunic with red belt and red collar insignias. She sleeps on a red couch, her legs draped across a Russian newspaper— NOCEB. Her heavy, greenish overcoat lies crumpled under her head.

"The handsome American major has just found a wire recorder on a red carpet beside her couch! Behind the major another officer, crouched and smug, holds a cigar in his teeth. Wisps of smoke rise from the brown stub. Behind him a woman stands against the train compartment's door. The top of the page cuts off the crown of her head..."

Gillian added "Espionage Express" to her nightstand collection. Somehow this act of cutting was the important thing. She remembered every clipping in the drawer, and so she had not taken them out again to look at them. She put a lot of energy into *not* thinking about her last days in New York. Whenever she did think of things that real, she could feel her pulse tick harder. She could taste fear, like copper on her tongue.

And so Gillian tried to imagine other things. Sometimes she created a black wall. Sometimes she pictured herself lying in the sun, hearing waves splash against the shore and roar out where empty sailboats cut diagonally across the water. On the horizon there was nothing but the edge between sky and sea. The sky was whitish yellow and the sea a clear turquoise, with no people on the decks of big ships or in cityscapes blurred in the distance. Or in a small aircraft, drifting and buzzing in a cloudless sky. Though the drugs Gillian was still taking made her groggy, she often was afraid to fall asleep because of nightmares. Dreams she had during afternoon naps were worse still, for they threatened to bring her closer to full remembrance of why she was here with her mother.

This afternoon she heard a gunshot in her dream. First there was a crack like the sound of lightning on a hardwood tree. Then the sound expanded and echoed across space. A tall wine glass burst into slivers in slow motion. She felt the kinetic vibrations, the shock of the glass. Then the slivers began to fall, sounding like Chinese wind chimes. Each pinged as it hit somewhere below her field of vision. She heard sounds of scraping and crunching. Out of her body now, she watched another Gillian crawl along the sidewalk. That Gillian tried to escape from men who kicked her and beat her. She cried out.

When Hannah entered Gillian's room, she looked with horror at the scissors in Gillian's right hand and tried to grab them.

Her eyes closed, Gillian moaned. "Please. Stop." She had tucked herself into a tight fetal position. Her right arm protected her chest. She tucked her head and turned it to the side. She gripped the scissors so hard that her knuckles went unsightly white.

Again, Hannah tried to take the scissors away from her daughter.

But Gillian stabbed the air again and again. She cried out after each slicing motion.

Hannah backed away from the bed. She shouted at her daughter. "Girl! Girl!" Then again.

When Gillian finally awoke, pain returned to her sides, nipping like terriers.

"You were screaming again," Hannah said, her voice level. "You tried to kill me with those scissors."

Gillian did not hear her mother. She struggled to open her eyes.

Hannah finally managed to get the scissors out of Gillian's hand. She straightened Gillian's blankets, tugged severely at the top of the sheet. "What was it this time?" she asked. Her voice held no compassion. When Gillian still did not respond, Hannah said, "Open your eyes." The mother had secured the scissors, by the pointed blades, in her fist.

Gillian felt pressure around her shoulders and waist. Hannah had pushed her upwards into a sitting position. The pain, the weight against her bruised rib-cage, made her cry out. Hearing her own cry made Gillian open her eyes.

Hannah arranged Gillian's arms across her stomach and said, "You sleep too much. There. That's better. Look at me."

Gillian felt how uncomfortable her head and neck were, resting just above the headboard. "Yes, Mama," she said. She looked at her mother's hair and decided that it was orange. Orange as fire. Sometimes, as now, when wind blew in through the cabin's cracks just before sundown, when rusty light spattered everything in Gillian's room, she thought her mother's hair looked like cedar tinder igniting.

Hannah's eyes glittered like emeralds. She held up the scissors. "You just tried to kill me," she repeated. "With these." She put the scissors, handles down, in her apron pocket.

"No I didn't! Honest!"

"You did so. I knew all along I couldn't trust you with them. But you made such a fuss."

"What?"

"Girl, you just tried to stab your own mother."

"I don't remember those scissors. They were on the table."

"They were in your hand and you tried to kill me."

Gillian began to cry. "I don't remember. Honest I don't," she said. "They were trying to kill *me*."

"Who?"

"Those men in my dream. They hurt me."

Hannah sat down at the end of Gillian's bed. "Until your nightmares stop, I'm keeping those scissors away from you. And I told you not to cut out the pictures."

"I'm sorry," Gillian said. She wiped her eyes on the border of the top sheet.

"Don't do that. Here's a hankie. That's what they're for."

"Okay," Gillian said right before she fell asleep again.

Chapter 38

Hannah dried her hands on a faded red dish towel and entered Gillian's room. She stared at her daughter without speaking.

Gillian caught Hannah peering into her own eyes in the oval mirror and thought: *Seaweed.* The old quilt that hung over the curtain rod behind Gillian obscured the afternoon light. Granny's old rocking chair reigned over the corner opposite her bed. Its scratched black paint revealed other colors beneath. To Gillian the rocker looked like a rigid person, its hands clutching the ends of its arms.

Gillian looked past her mother to the mirror itself. Hannah had painted its frame garish gold. Unlike Hannah, Gillian rarely looked at herself in the mirror. Not even during those times when she walked alone along the room's perimeters like a caged circus cat, making an obsessive pattern from bed, past nightstand, past window, past mirror, past rocker, past doorway, past bird cage, to bed. When Gillian's eyes finally met her mother's in the mirror, Gillian turned away.

Hannah still looked at herself in the mirror. "Eban's here to visit," she said.

"Eban?"

"Your 'fiancé'."

"What?"

"A month back and still busted all over. And that ignorant mountain man. He doesn't care you were out of your head."

"I didn't do anything."

"You cracked is what you did."

When Gillian's mother spoke, it was as if a concrete wall slid between them. It closed off even the slimmest of blood bond they still shared. Gillian wished Hannah would just disappear. "I'm not thrilled to be here either," she said.

Hannah patted a stale curl at the back of her head. "You almost had worse in that city," she said. "I'm gonna fetch Eban, and you *will* talk to him. He's been awful patient, even with you leading him on."

The cement pressure released when Hannah crossed to the door. Gillian looked up at the bird cage. *Sing to me little bird*, she thought. She imagined the bird fly and chirp, hop along tips of branches and launch itself into flight. The bird made no sound now. Still, Gillian smiled. She dreaded hearing Eban's step at the door. She figured he would shuffle in, hang dogged and hurt. And she knew looking at the wall wouldn't save her for long.

"How ya feelin', Gil?" Eban asked. Timid as a chipmunk, he tiptoed into her room.

Gillian sat half upright, her face averted and her neck aching. That walk in the woods, a momentary lapse, was something that had happened to some other person. Someone who could act. Someone who was trying to help her, even though it hadn't turned out well. Thinking about Eban's trying to touch her induced near frenzy. She couldn't look at him. She tried to calculate how long it had been since he had last stopped by. Maybe four days? Having been dragged into Eban's cabin, she knew it was some distance for him to come on foot.

"Well, well," Eban said. He carried Granny's old rocker closer to Gillian's bed and pointed at the covered birdcage. "You should get rid of that dead bird," he said. "It smells."

Sure that the cardinal was just sleeping, Gillian looked up at the bamboo cage. "You're just being mean," she said to Eban. "I want you to leave. Now!"

Leaning forward from the waist, Eban said, "Your Ma says you won't let her take it out of here." He touched her hand. "Yor better now, huh Gil?" He tried to put his arm around her shoulders.

"Leave me the hell alone!"

Hannah was suddenly there. She pulled Eban, hard, by the arm. "I told you not to touch her."

"I'm her figh-*ahn*-say, ain't I?"

"Ssh. Not here," Hanna replied.

As their voices shifted to halftones in the kitchen, Gillian tore the comforter down from the stout curtain rod. A flush of pale peach light spread through her window and over her bed. The low sun now reached across the furniture and her walls. Then the sky turned slightly gray and melted into twilight. Gillian heard her mother and Eban step outside the cabin and close the door.

With Eban gone, Gillian lay quietly. She had rolled herself up into a tight circle under the covers. "Go away. Both of you," she wailed.

In the background, the whispers of Hannah and Eban faded as they walked away from the cabin together.

Later that night, Gillian opened her eyes and looked around her room. The old rocking chair grasped its own confining arms. This time the rocker didn't move. Other nights it crept toward her, but she awakened in time to stop it. And when Hannah lit the hurricane lamp beside Gillian's bed, the rocker always jumped back to its corner.

Gillian did get that imagining the rocker moved meant she gave in to something she ought not. It was her terror, and it was black. Her fear grew more distinct, very slowly, every day and every night. Its roots twisted around her nerve endings and absorbed her reason, her emotions, her future. This process occurred as kinesthesia too. It drove her out of herself in more and more sustained charges until the shocks merged into one shaft of noxious energy.

Gillian cared less now about what was real than she had the night she returned to her mother's cabin after leaving Eban. Then she had stumbled over rocks in the hill and reached the edge of stretch of woods that lay between Eban's cabin and her mother's. She no longer wished to sustain boundaries she once drew between her dreams and her memories. Even the cardinal had lost its power move her. She assumed her mother fed the bird and gave it water. She looked up at the bird's cage now. "When you get well," she said to the bird, "I'll have to let you go." After that, she forgot about the creature.

Chapter 39

MID-FEBRUARY: 1950

It was dark outside. Gillian wore a white flannel nightgown. She sat up in bed and stared through the doorway, into the yellowish white glare coming from the kitchen's overhead bulb. The wide fan of light reached out to her, connected her to her mother, whom she could hear sewing on her machine. The *click-click-click*, *whirr* soothed her. It was a mother's kind of industry. Doing work for, taking care of, a loved one. In that moment, Gillian felt empathy for her mother because she knew Hannah must be sewing baby clothes to sell, as always. Hannah's baby's death had knocked a big piece out of her heart and had taken with it all warmth. Gillian accepted that she now had to live with what was left. Some other Hannah. Gillian knew she and her mother could never be comfortable together.

The warm light and the sewing machine's comforting action made Gillian suppose she ought to be more grateful to Hannah for the warmth of this cabin. She ought to be thankful that Eban had stocked enough firewood for the whole winter. Instead, she was afraid of being even more of a burden to her mother and she resented feeling she owed Eban. Giving something back to her mother seemed impossible, for Gillian believed she had nothing her mother valued. In short, Gillian could no longer imagine a better life for herself.

Gillian lay on her back and continued to listen to her mother's sewing machine. Now it sounded like the beating wings of a hundred doves. She thought of how the cardinal would need her help for the rest of the winter. The bird would be well by spring. Then she could free him. In the meantime, he was safe with her. He would suffer neither hunger nor fear. He would live a long time. Much better to heal. If the other birds missed him, so what? Months ago, *she* had friends. Now she felt alone.

Gillian was crushed that she had heard nothing from Jānis. She recalled the day Harry hired her when she was afraid she would run out of money. Every night she worked at Harry's Bar, she suspected that Harry didn't needed extra help. Did he hire her because he thought she was pretty? Did he feel *fatherly* towards her? Whatever his motives were, Harry had been extremely kind to her. He had given her something just as precious: acceptance. It was the kind of adoration and forgiveness her Pop had offered.

Harry's affection had helped open her, expanded her sense of self-worth. Yet she hadn't heard from him. Not even a postcard. He surely would have asked Dolores for her Missouri address? Maybe he had been jealous of Jānis. So jealous that he was mad at Gillian and was punishing her. *No*, she thought now. *Don't flatter yourself. Maybe he just doesn't miss you at all.* Maybe his kindness meant nothing. Maybe Gillian had meant nothing to any of them.

Of all her friends in the Village, Dolores had demonstrated clearest that she loved Gillian. If that was real, why hadn't Dolores kept in touch? Why hadn't Dolores stopped Hannah? Gillian thought, *I couldn't take care of myself, why didn't Dolores take care of me? She must be really mad at me not to write.* Still, Gillian recaptured in this moment the closeness between them that sometimes made it seem she would explode with happiness. In those moments, from sheer joy, she had wanted to throw her arms around Dolores and engulf her. All of her.

Gillian loved the way Dolores moved through a room like a graceful jungle cat. Countless times Gillian had watched Dolores' body while Dolores walked. She had stared at Dolores' lips on the edge of a coffee cup, and she had experienced pleasure in this. But this had not meant what Gillian was afraid her friend wanted it to mean. Gillian thought, *Maybe I envied her.* She wondered whether the freedom with which Dolores expressed her sensuality threatened to awaken something forbidden inside Gillian. Maybe fearing this made Gillian hurt her friend. All Dolores had wanted was freely to express all her feelings for Gillian. Dolores had wanted only to be herself. And Gillian had made Dolores feel bad about herself for that.

Like Harry, however, Dolores had written no letters. Gillian was convinced that if Dolores cared about her she would have written. This belief racked Gillian, made her mad, made her cry. Again and again she asked herself, *What does it mean if someone says they love you but when you're gone they forget you?* She couldn't picture Dolores' ongoing life in New York. She could think only of where *she* was: in bed in her mother's cabin. She felt chained, hopeless. *Even one letter*, she thought. That *would make a difference, keep me going until I get well.*

None of the bad things that happened to Gillian had been fair. Even while feeling the pain of those events, she missed those special people now and wanted to be back with them. She was certain, however, that she never would be. Separation from her friends made Gillian wonder if they had been worth this pain she felt now. She could not understand why she had been given these people, only to have them taken way. She intended *not* to think of them, and this took all her willpower.

Instead Gillian thought of snow. The snow outside her window. The beautiful snow that had piled up for a week and that lay now, dry and puffy, two feet above ground level. *How quiet snow is*, she thought. She imagined lying in a snowbank with her eyes closed and flakes of coldness mingling with her eyelashes. She would cross her arms over her breasts and hold her feet tightly together, the way mummies do. Like white crystals, stars would cut through the blacker than black sky. She would happily sink into the snow, let go. With her eyes closed under the blackness, she would begin in pure white, and then sink down with delicious slowness. Down, down, where she would divide into a spectrum of colors and burst and glide and arc like fireworks.

When Gillian phased into dark, liquid violet, an herbal aroma drifted toward her. It was strong. Jānis. He called her name. When she opened her eyes her room was totally dark. She looked straight over the end of her bed and saw him. Not for a moment did she fear she was dreaming, that Jānis wasn't standing there. She knew he had come a long way to be with her. She accepted all that was happening.

Jānis looked wonderful. The colors of his skin and clothing shone as if an opalescent light projected through him. These glowing colors were true, and the white light radiated through, and on, the colors. Around his body, and in the background, a sort of rust colored cloud of particles shimmered like sequins.

These looked molecular, energy charged. They flickered from rust to orange, then back to rust. The source of Jānis light seemed to be outside his body. That his feet did not touch the floor was no problem for Gillian.

Jānis made no sound when he came toward her. When he sat beside her on the bed she could smell his skin. He took her hands in his and said, "It is all right now." She was sure Jānis was real, but she was afraid he would disappear if she spoke to him. She had felt the same awe as when, in New York, after days of separation, they met again. Though he was not exactly smiling, his face gave her the impression of a quiet joy. The relaxed muscles of his jaws made his face look softer than she had ever seen it. Something in his manner told her to sit still now and just listen to him. This was hard for her because her insides were doing barrel loops.

Gillian nodded. She would have nodded anyway.

"You are getting stronger," he said. "Let go of your suffering now." He held her hands perfectly still. His touch was warm and light. "When you embrace your freedom, you can make your own choices."

Gillian wanted only to kiss Jānis. She did not feel she was free at all. Not here in her mother's home. She glided her fingers along the inside of Jānis' wrist. "Why do we have to talk? It's been so long."

"Because you must get well now," Jānis said. "You must try harder to get better. You do have all you need."

"I *am* trying," she said, but she knew Jānis was right.

"You do not want to be here," he said. "If you do not leave soon, your mother's trap will kill you. It is time to be *all you*. Do you understand?"

"Tell me, Jānis. Where could I go? They've all forgotten me."

"You are worth saving," Jānis said, "but you cannot do this if you do not believe you are of value." He closed his eyes as if recalling something from long before now. "I left my saber to you. It is safe in New York. You must go back if you want it."

"Your saber? Why?"

"Because the widow gets a soldier's saber. Atis, Kārlis and Pēteris were mad that I asked they do this if something happened to me." He pressed Gillian's hands harder to keep them still.

"But you're here!"

Jānis smiled and shook his head. "Your mother has hidden letters from your friends." He looked toward Gillian's bedroom doorway.

Gillian put her head on his shoulder. "Jānis?" Now she smelled a heavy herbal aroma and felt softness, like snow.

He stroked her hair. His voice sounded more distant now. "These letters will be your sword and your shield. When you read them, remember how we have known each other, how we are together like this tonight."

"I *will* remember," Gillian said. Her eyes held the same expression as on the last night with Jānis in front of 144 Waverly Place.

Jānis seemed not to hear Gillian. "Remember," he said. "Once you have tasted the waters of the River Daugava, you will drink no other."

She caressed Jānis' cheek. "I will love you like no other," she said.

As if he hadn't heard Gillian, Jānis said: "I mean that we go on. That you, here, in this room have so many other lives that you could not count them. But we must fight in this world again and again until at last we are free of it. And we must never stop looking for what is real within and beyond the world. You do know there is something living in you that is not the same as your body?"

Gillian could hardly keep her eyes open. "Yes, Jānis," she said.

Jānis turned away as if he had heard something, and then he looked directly into Gillian's eyes. "You wanted to know what absinthe does when you drink it," he said, his hand gentle, motionless on her head. "Absinthe makes you see yourself in two places at once. Absinthe makes you feel your *self* is lifting out through the top of your head. It makes you feel happy and light. But you pay a price. Absinthe also destroys your brain and your body. You ache and disintegrate, but to open to your feelings is the only way to see what is highest. You must realize while you are flying that after you reach the ecstasy you might fall back down again. You must decide if soaring now is worth the crashing later. They are two sides of the same coin, and you must keep choosing. If what happens is an accident, then you are always a victim. Do you understand what I say?"

Her eyes closed, Gillian hugged Jānis tighter. "To choose to suffer pain again," she said with little conviction.

"This means being brave … and honest." Jānis pulled Gillian gently away from his body so they faced one another. "To be honest," he said, "is to know why you do things. You will try to fool yourself, but you must face yourself. Only then will you be free to make a choice worthy of you. Only then, no matter what you decide, will it be a moral choice. When you meet your darker self like this, it can never again have power over you."

Gillian's eyes kept closing. "My darker self."

"The part of you," Jānis said, "that might not be 'good'. The part that you try to keep under control. The one who gets impatient and mad. But that self is also the most alive part of the you. It *loves*, and it is fierce and dark. Like a wolf your other self holds on to its prey."

Gillian tried not to fall asleep. She propped her head on her hand. "I don't feel like a predator," she said.

"Then let go of what is already gone."

As happy as she was to be with Jānis, Gillian felt very sleepy.

She lay back on her pillow, and Jānis stood over her. He caressed her cheek. "You will remember what I have said tonight. You will survive because you can see what most people cannot. You know what you see is real. Trust your instincts, my dearest Love."

She could not resist sleeping now.

"Gillian," he said.

Jānis had said her name. It was enough for a million years. Gillian wanted to keep seeing, touching him, but she couldn't keep her eyes open. She could still feel him there. "Come to bed," she said to him. She felt him kiss her on the eyes, and she smiled. *A fine time to sleep*, she thought. But he would be lying beside her in the morning. They would make love and talk for hours. She settled into her snowdrift. She hadn't imagined snow could be this warm, like her own pillow, or that the sound of snowfall could be like hundreds of tiny cymbals brushing gently together like paper thin glass wind chimes. Jānis' spice scent faded. Blackness was comforting, like velvet. Even the stars had folded back on themselves and disappeared. There was only darkness And snow. A feeling of snow.

Chapter 40

When Gillian awoke the next morning, she lay on her side. She expected to see Jānis when she opened her eyes. But when she reached her hand out, she felt only the cold sheet. She was sure she had not been dreaming the previous night. Jānis was as real as life, still imparting information to her with his frustrating earnestness. She smiled at that. She smiled at herself for having wanted only to touch him as always. She was impelled to gain knowledge about Jānis by feeling her skin dissolve into his and, therefore, to become him. However, she still avoided discovering who she was. Did Jānis know this? Did he realize that Gillian's touching him helped her *feel* what his words meant?

The many strands of Gillian's adventures in New York continued to resurrect and uncoil as she continued to explore the seeming paradox of feelings versus words. On the playground that last night together, Jānis had said, "Bad and good can sometimes be two sides of the same coin." All along, he had shown her his feelings for her in his touch. He had withheld the words of love she longed most to hear. Yet, he insisted she learn the story of his country, the magic of absinthe, and the caliber of the one whom he loved most: his twin, Mātiss.

Gillian wondered how much she had missed because she had been so dense. She was sure *he* had missed nothing. He knew how alike they were or he would not have kept prodding her to comprehend what he meant. Last night he had said, "You have almost *earned* your freedom. You must face yourself. You must try harder."

Gillian knew he was right: She hadn't been trying hard enough. In a way, it had been easier here, in the Ozarks, to hide from herself. But Jānis' coming to her last night meant he hadn't given up on her. In New York, Jānis must have known that, to protect herself, Gillian half-created those colors that so captivated her. This did not mean the colors couldn't still reveal important truths. It meant that she had to work to interpret them now.

Dolores, too, had proven Gillian was worthy of love and that Gillian had immense potential for giving. Dolores had encouraged Gillian to share this love with her. Even when Gillian hoarded her feelings, Dolores still cared about her, which made Gillian better appreciate what kind of person Dolores must be. This revelation helped Gillian move forward through her own suffering. To bring her close to believing in a Creator, but not yet in the God of the scriptures. It no longer mattered to Gillian that she hadn't heard from Dolores these past months. She could *feel* Dolores' affection. Nobody could take that away. It also didn't matter if Jānis had been with her the previous night or if she had only imagined this, for what he had said could also have come from within her.

Either way, she knew only the power of Jānis' *love* could have conveyed him to her: Gillian knew Jānis was right when he told her, "You must *earn* your freedom." She could acknowledge that it had been easier here in the Ozarks to let go of her own hard won identity.

As a result of Gillian's unfolding awareness in the Ozark Mountains, she knew she had taken advantage neither of the speed nor the accuracy of Jānis' perceptions about who she was. Jānis' recent presence had made her discover that she hated herself. That if she looked too deeply into her own mirror she would see jet black at the core of her being. Like her mother's. This terror had made her ignore signs to the contrary—most especially the reality that Jānis chose her to be his lover. His incorruptible standards reflected her own worthiness back to her. Now she perfectly understood. New York had been all about finding who she was. Now she could fully embrace Jānis' love for her.

As she leaned against the headboard, Gillian thought about how, in many ways, we care about people because of what they reflect of *us*. On the other hand, people love each other in spite of their differences because no one is completely whole, at least not at first. *When people care for each other and spend time together*, she thought, *they become another* person *together: friend, lover, mentor. They create a third being—WE—which is an extension of each that blends to create a whole other unit. What people become in this union is more powerful than any separate person can ever be.*

Because Gillian did not believe in the God of the Bible, these ideas were as close as she could come to believing a person's spirit could survive death. She had seen this in Dolores' eyes when they last talked, when Gillian had finally accepted she loved Dolores fiercely. And she knew Dolores loved her beyond what each of them had to lose or gain day to day. And she had felt this at moments of sexual climax with Jānis when she could feel life flash in every cell of her body.

A cold draft pushed through cracks in the shrunken grouting of Gillian's window. She had started to notice details. When she pulled back the thick curtain to admit morning light through her window, she saw a little framed photo of Granny on the nightstand beside her bed. Funny. She hadn't been aware of it before, and she wondered why her mother had left it there. Because Hannah needed distance between herself and Granny? Because this had been Granny's bedroom and so Hannah had put dead Granny back in here by installing her photograph on the nightstand? Or so that Granny would stare at Gillian all day and even throughout the night? Because nothing in this picture invited Gillian in, she turned her Granny's photo over and placed it facedown on her nightstand.

Gillian was tempted to stay under her warm covers and think about *things* a while longer, but she made herself get up. She pulled on dungarees and a bulky old brown sweater. She put on her soft deerskin moccasins and walked to the kitchen. In the corner that abutted a small parlor stood a bedraggled, runty pine tree nailed to a cross of two little boards. Why had Hannah still not taken it down? There was not much variety in the colors of the faded antique ornaments. Candle-shaped bubblers were clipped to the scrawny branches. Gillian would have been cheered if the bubblers had been lit, for these were her favorite kind of Christmas lights.

Hannah was scanning the women's pages of the *St. Louis Dispatch*, which she had spread over the rough-hewn kitchen table. "Decide to get up for a change?" she asked Gillian without looking at her. "Coffee maybe needs warmed up,. It's on the stove," she added. "Says here they've had a foot of snow up in St. Louie the last two days. We got off lucky, I guess."

At first, Gillian hesitated to confront Hannah about the letters Jānis had urged her to read. She lit the stove and looked directly at Hannah. This act was rare for her. After Gillian asked her mother if any mail had come for her, she watched Hannah's face for a break in its perpetual mask. Hannah turned almost imperceptibly to her right and leaned toward the old trunk that also served as a window seat. Gillian watched her mother calculate whether to lie and marveled at how much time it took her to do this. *She must be getting old*, Gillian thought.

"Don't you think I'd tell you if you got mail?" Hannah said. There it was. The imperious, blatant lying that had always worked on Gillian before.

Gillian found a mug that looked as if it belonged in an all-night diner and poured herself some hot coffee. "I know I haven't been myself," she said. She waited to see if her mother had noted her understatement.

Hannah stood up, her hand curved at the base of her spine. "You are yourself now I s'pose?" She reordered the newspaper sections and went to the stove for more coffee.

"Please answer me."

"All right," Hannah said. "There's letters. I s'pose you would've found them anyway. Or did you already?" She gave her daughter a glittery appraisal, her eyes mostly white because she was looking sideways. "Did you?"

"I just had a feeling."

"You had a feeling you could fly when you were three. You saw angels in the bushes out front. Remember? You could've used more common sense instead of so much 'feeling'."

"It's another kind of intelligence," Gillian said as she sat down at the table. Gillian felt her cheeks tightening. "Where did you hide them?"

Hannah sat down across from Gillian, looked away. "You've been in no shape to read them."

"How do you know they would upset me, unless you read them yourself?" Deception flickered in Hannah's eyes. "Oh really. It's bad enough that you kept them from me. It's worse that you read them! Why shouldn't I see them?"

"You don't remember what happened," Hannah said. Her coffee cup made rings on the table. "You've made me put up with a lot since you got here. You went wild when I tried to take that smelly bird out of your room. I feared you'd take those scissors to me. Or to yourself."

"Bull!" Gillian said.

"If you don't know why you did it, you're still not ready to read those letters," Hannah said.

"It's too bad you didn't hide those letters out of motherly concern. You didn't trust me, like always."

"But because I am your mother, your friend Dolores wired *me*. I was the one who had to pay your bills, which I of course took out of your New York savings."

"I don't care about the money. Give me the letters," Gillian said. It was the first time in Gillian's life that she believed Hannah would do what she asked, because not until this moment did Gillian realize she had this much power.

Hannah's green eyes closed slightly and flicked catlike. "If you think I'm gonna pick up the pieces again for you, you got another think coming. Always acting like you were somebody else's girl. Always believing you know better than me. You never appreciated nothing I did for you. This is the last time—."

"I only needed you to love me," Gillian said, her voice level.

"And all *you* had to do," Hannah said, "was to be lovable."

When rage overtook her like an all-consuming forest fire, that was it for Gillian. She had to fight an escalating urge to strike Hannah with her open hand to wipe that haughty smile off her face. Not quite ready to cut the ties between them, Gillian said, with power surging simplicity: "Give me the letters. Now."

Hannah smiled again, made a mock bow, and went over to the trunk. She dug around in some gift wrappings, photographs, and news clippings inside the trunk. She lifted out a parcel of envelopes held together by a red rubber band and brought them to the table. "Here," she said. She slapped the letters down on the wet coffee rings. "I'll just be goin' into town. So I won't be here when you go nuts reading them."

The letters trembled in Gillian's hand. She watched Hannah put on her black coat and pink and black scarf, which clashed with her orange hair. Hannah also put on black rubber boots and methodically buckled each latch.

Gillian removed the rubber band from the letters.

Hannah grabbed a paper bag full of her sewn things and said, "I won't be back until supper time, but you'll have your hot meal, like always."

Gillian didn't wait for the cabin door to close before she looked through the letters. Except for one Christmas card from Harry, they all bore Dolores' handwriting. Silly that Hannah had kept these from her. On the front of Harry's card was a cartoon drawing of three reindeer and Santa, who waved from his sleigh. At the top, four pointed, overblown stars punctured a surreal blue sky. Harry had written: *Best Wishes for a Very, Merry Christmas*. He had added, "I'm having a stiff eggnog for you this Christmas. Miss you honey. XXOO, Harry."

Now she looked at Dolores' letters, which Hannah had conveniently kept in chronological order. Dolores had written the first one on pale blue stationery.

Tues., Dec. 20
Dear Gillian,

I still can't believe any of it happened. I hope I'm not being too pushy but I feel I should talk about it, though it doesn't make any sense to me. At St. Vincent's you said three men beat you up. It doesn't tally unless it has something to do with Jānis. I tried to contact the Latvians, but Harry said they haven't been back since that awful night. He promised he'd try to find them too. Atis might be the best one to talk to. Easier. I don't know if it would do much good to find out why that horrible thing happened to you. At least knowing why might make you feel better. I'd like to know for myself.

I remember when I first went to see you at the hospital. Your eyelids were black and blue, and you kept saying the same things over and over. You didn't hear me when I talked to you. The woman who first shared your room asked to be moved because you kept waking her up with your screams. And they said they transferred you to Bellevue because you tried to kill yourself, but I don't believe it.

I know how you must feel about being stuck there with your mother, but trust me. It's the only way they'd let you out of that place. And I'm sorry I acted like such a moron when your mother came here to get you. I couldn't help it. When I saw you in that ward, I didn't know what else to do. If she hadn't come, God knows how long they would've kept you there.

It took you about two weeks to stabilize. I brought you a dozen pink roses on the 17th, but you didn't seem to realize it was your birthday. Your doctor said it would be best to get you out of the City and he thought you would recover faster in the Hills with your mother. I pray he was right.

Thinking about you being in the Ozarks makes me think Bowery bums are lucky. At least they only have to walk a few blocks to find a liquor store! They have companions of the vine and sounds of the city to listen to. I've been hounding the man in the information booth at Penn Station. Every few days I stop there to ask him for alternative train schedules to St. Louis. It has gotten to the point where he dashes out for lunch when he sees me coming.

When you feel up to it, would you write and tell me how you're doing? Harry asked me to say hello for him and to let you know you can come back and work at the bar whenever you want.

Much love, Dolores

Gillian didn't stop to digest the letter's contents because she subliminally knew these things already and because she was hungry to read more. Dolores had written the second letter on plain white paper and enclosed it in a white envelope. By Dolores' handwriting, it looked as if she had written it in haste.

Mon., Dec. 26
Dear Gillian,

I wonder if you got my last letter. If you did get it, please know I'm sorry if I opened my big mouth too much. Are you all right? I've been thinking about you so hard 'cause I'm worried. The other night I dreamed you were mad at me. I don't even know where we were in the dream. Maybe in a restaurant here. You yelled at me to mind my own business, and then you walked away from me. I hope you're not mad.

I worked in gift wrapping at Macy's on weekends before Christmas for extra money. We kept long hours there for herds (oops! hoards) of Christmas shoppers. Doing the actual wrapping was fun, but some of those rich women drove me crazy! They're the worst complainers, whether it's about a tiny, unintentional crimp in a bow or wrapping paper that "just doesn't look like" whomever they bought the gift for. With the red hot sales going on, Macy's played Christmas carols in the background while shoppers tore off each other's hair and jewelry. It's supposed to be "peace on Earth," right? I thought if I heard "Rudolph, the Red Nosed Reindeer" one more time, I would convert to Judaism!

Even if I had converted, I would still have sent this Christmas present. It might not be your favorite color but I bought it because it looks soothing. Anyway, Lorna says, "Don't buy clothes that look like vegetables." I think that's a good rule of thumb. If you don't like it, don't tell me. Paying the return postage would break me. Ha!

Well, I'm going to get back to my book now. I'm reading a best-seller for a change. Irving Stone's The Passionate Journey. Men see things so oddly. It's like they're a totally different species. Maybe it's women who are a different species?

I've decided I'm going to keep writing you even if you don't write back, so if you're mad at me you can at least say so in a letter. I'm glad Poplar Bluff has a post office. Thinking of you a lot!

Always, Dolores

The third letter was dated January 16. Dolores had meticulously printed Gillian's address on the envelope.

Gillian Dear,

I have some news. I stopped in at Harry's and he told me Mabel Levitsky wanted to see me, so I went over to The Treasure Trove and she said she has something for you. You won't believe this, but it's Janis' sword! The Latvians brought it to her last week and said it had been Janis' wish ("command" they said) that you have it if anything happened to him. She said they did this most ceremoniously. (You know how they are.) For some reason, Janis asked that Mabel keep it for you. She kept muttering about why he did this when she "had never said a civil word to him." I told her Janis must have trusted her, and she said he was always "such an odd duck" but that she would keep it for you.

Gillian, when she asked about you and talked about what happened to you, tears came to her eyes but she said it was her cigarette smoke. (She'd kill me if she knew I was telling you this.) She's a lonely old woman who's got only her husband. She said that because he lost his legs in the war, he has to use a wheelchair. So he smokes cigars and watches TV (morning, noon and nighttime) in their flat. They live just beyond the curtain in Mabel's store. (Remember that funny little man we saw go through there?) In the evenings Mabel can get over to Harry's "for respite". See how much I got out of her just because she's keeping Janis' sword for you?

Your package should've gotten there two weeks ago. Please tell me if you have it so I'll know if I should scream at Mr. Molark down at the P.O. He assured me you would get it by X-mas.

How's the food there? I hope you're getting fat so you'll look like me. I've been eating beau coups des rum cherries. Barton's bonbonniere chocolate assortments. You'd recognize me by my all over pinkish tinge!

Gillian, I haven't forgotten anything. I'm just trying not to be morbid. It would do you no good. You know you can depend on me for anything. You know I love you and that you're welcome to come back to New York and stay with me if you want to. Take good care of yourself. Please write to me.

Love, Dolores

Jānis' saber. It was just as he had said. Gillian laughed at the picture she had in her mind of a voluminous Dolores, stuffing chocolates into her bulging cheeks. She absorbed Dolores' words with pleasure. Her lost friend had returned.

The final letter lay unopened on the table, its envelope wet from her mother's coffee cup rings. She wiped the envelope across the front page of the *Dispatch* until it was almost dry, and then she pulled the letter out. A black and white photo slipped into her hand. In it, Dolores faced the camera directly, her chin cupped in her left hand. Gillian took in her friend's face with greed as she rediscovered the strong jawline and apple half cheeks, and her full mouth, pulled into a smile as ambiguous and closed as that of the Mona Lisa. And those soft, soft doe eyes that invited affection. Dolores had let her dark hair grow longer, down to her nape. This made her natural curls look more relaxed. Gillian could tell by the cut of Dolores' blouse that it must be the lavender one. Gillian could perceive herself in her friend's face, for Dolores looked like Gillian felt.

In this last letter, Dolores' handwriting was neat and entirely uniform, as if she had recopied it from a draft. This alarmed Gillian. Indeed, the pages shook in her hands.

Jan. 26, 1950
Dear Gillian,

How do you like the pic? It's undoubtedly the real me, without the corniness. I couldn't let just anyone see this, but I trust you to keep this part of me safe from public scrutiny.

I made some stiff New Year's resolutions this year. (God! Look at all the S words!) Anyway, one of my resolutions is to be more sober. I mean, to cut out the constant "glib" and act more adult. I say "act" because it's hard to break your old routines, even if underneath them you are capable of being mellow. You'll say I'm too young to be mellow, but almost 23 is moving right up there. Inching closer to those irrevocable 30s, and by then a person should have pulled her stray parts together or she's a goner. What I'm feeling right now has something to do with being a grownup, and I've been buying slinkier type clothing. Leotard tops, etc., that make me feel not merely feminine but womanly. I've been taking a ballet class too, and I feel positive that once my muscles stop screaming with pain, I'll be a lithe and graceful creature. (Have you tried 5th position? Excruciating! But, then, so is my dance instructor's face.)

I guess I've been putting off telling you some things that will be important because I know they'll also be painful. In fact, I've written this letter three times already, with and without trying to be funny. I can't find the right way to word this or to make it softer for you, but I knew you'd want the truth, so here it is. Do you remember that ugly man we saw coming out of Village Cigars last summer? He was one of the three men who beat you up. The Latvians told Mabel they were thugs, hired by Communists in government positions to scare you out of New York. Evidently, if they had thought you knew anything important, they'd have killed you too. All you did, Sweetheart, was to fall in love with someone who did know. The situation was so touchy it didn't even make the papers. The authorities treated the whole thing as if it were just another anonymous crime.

After the ruffians were locked up, Karlis came to Mabel one night in Harry's Bar. He is the one who finally told her what happened. He said the Feds had investigated. They questioned you in the hospital. Do you remember? (It's odd that they didn't come to see me.) Some of what Karlis told Mabel makes sense, but I can't make heads or tails out of the rest. He said Janis was "a freedom fighter," underground, against the Bolsheviks. (Communists here.) That's the reason for what happened to him. And Gillian, that's why you saw so little of him toward the end. Karlis said Janis was afraid you were in danger because of him, and Janis tried to stay away from you but couldn't always. I feel guilty because of the way I treated him, but we knew so little about what he was going through.

Anyway, here's something Karlis said that I don't understand. He said that "absinthe" was their code word, but he wouldn't tell me what it meant.

Gillian had to stop reading. Here was the story, sudden and clear, of her last days in New York. She felt her throat clinch. She observed from above the Gillian lying in the hospital bed. She could see her body only from the chest down, its length exaggerated. It was as if she were looking at someone else who gaped past the rounded, white metal bedstead and across the room to a sterile, blank wall beyond. Gillian reached out her hand. It was puffy with wound gauze. Her wrist ached and throbbed. She had to let it down again. Because of the curtain that divided her room, she had no idea whether she was alone. She half dozed, and wakened, like this again and again.

A nun stood beside Gillian and inserted something into her left arm with a long tube attached and looped above Gillian's shoulder to a yellowish bag suspended above her head. She had neither thought nor felt much at first. As the days went on, however, she could feel pain more intensely. She wondered why she was there. She recalled that Dolores came in one day looking worried and drained. Dolores didn't talk much. Didn't touch her but only stared, tears in her eyes. Brought flowers. Said, "Everything's gonna be all right." Gillian asked to stay with Dolores.

"You can't," Dolores had said.

In recurring nightmares, Gillian relived the beating a dozen different ways. Once, Jānis' face appeared instead of the ugly man's. Jānis kept slapping her, saying "You're a fool." Black rays floated out from his eyes like flakes of smoked glass.

In one awful dream, Gillian stood up after the men had left. Her chest gaped opened. In this dream, blood poured out of her lungs. Her intestines swelled and throbbed out of her breached abdomen. Then she heard someone screaming, screaming. When she woke up, she realized she was screaming. Nurses ran into her room and asked her to be quiet, but she couldn't stop screaming even then. They said she called for Jānis. They said tomorrow some men would come to ask questions. She told the nurses she had nothing to say to the Feds.

But the men came in anyway. Two of them in black suits. They carried valises and stood at the foot of her bed. They looked at her bandages as if the gauze covered a thing, a sort of curiosity. She knew they liked seeing her that way. When they told her they were "FBI," she said she knew nothing. They continued to question her anyway. One of them spoke the word "absinthe," and then he waited for a long time for her to respond. Since Gillian had no idea what they wanted from her, she just peered down at the crisp white sheets.

When they spoke Jānis' name, she listened with care. But they kept saying, "He was" and "Did he ever tell you" and other things that confused her. Then one of them said, "Before he was stabbed," and Gillian told them to get the hell out of there because she didn't know anything. She didn't even know, she said, where she was or how she got there. The two agents whispered with the nurse in the corner of the room, and when the doctor came in, they left.

Some part of Gillian did realize that Jānis must be dead. However, she did not wholly believe it. She recalled Jānis' going into the darkness again, the way he had done before the three men jumped out of the shadows at her. She again experienced the impulse to go after him. She kept calling to Jānis and seeing fists shoot toward her. She felt every punch in her body. Then everything went black. When she awoke, she was on the floor by her hospital bed. Her falling had torn the intravenous needles out, and blood spurted from an open wound on each wrist. Burly orderlies pulled her upward and held her arms tightly behind her back as she struggled against them.

Next she remembered sitting alone on the floor of a small, cold room. Light entered only through a little window at the top of a tall, heavy door. And there was a window too high on the wall for her to see outside. She was bound in a white straight jacket, that was tied with tapered flaps behind her back. Her hair felt stringy, and her skin was clammy. Her face still hurt from the beating. Occasionally a stranger peered through the window. Orderlies brought in meals, which she didn't eat because she knew the food was dirty.

Gillian had no idea how long she had been there. One day a doctor led her to another room. His office? He asked her how she felt and whether she knew her name. She guessed she did all right because then they moved her to a different room where a lot of weirdos walked around. Some of them tried to talk to her. They made odd movements with their mouths: twitches and repetitive lip pursing. Their eyes looked wild, terrified. She mostly sat in one chair while the crazies circled around her. She began to eat again, though with no pleasure.

One day Gillian noticed that the attending nun talked to her in a different way. The nurse began to treat her more like an adult who was in her right mind. Then Gillian's doctor summoned Gillian to his office and said her mother had come to take her home. She said she didn't have a home and she didn't want to go with her mother. The doctor said it was "for the best." He opened the door, He let her mother and Dolores come in and sit down beside her.

Gillian remembered being back in her apartment later that day with her mother and Dolores. Several cardboard boxes stood on the floor. Gillian had sat on her loveseat in her living room. With her fingers she played with the door of the bamboo cage beside her. She slid its door up and down while watching her mother and Dolores. She couldn't remember where she got the cage. Dolores cried and put Gillian's kimono and the orange beads carefully into a small box. But Gillian just remained on her loveseat, fingering the bars of the birdcage. She had a strong feeling, then, that she would never see Dolores, or Harry, or the Latvians again. She tried not to think about Jānis.

On the train back to Missouri, Gillian had willed herself not to remember any of this for the rest of her life. She believed that none of her relationships in New York had been worth this. There was no point in striving for anything else, ever. She had said nothing to her mother on the train. Hannah kept ranting about what a burden Gillian was, about what a mess she had made of her "great" life in New York City, about what a fool Gillian had always been, about how Gillian would never amount to anything and how lucky Gillian was to have been "rescued" from the hospital, where she otherwise might have remained forever.

Gillian had merely listened to the rhythmic clanks of the train wheels on the tracks, which sounded like far away drumbeats. She could not see much scenery because the sky was gray and vaporous. When a porter offered Gillian hot chocolate, she had waved him away. She propped her face on her arm, which she had raised up on the back of her seat against the white cotton towel on her headrest. Gillian continued to look at the fog and the droplets that slid across the train window. She thought about how slowly those beads of water moved, compared with how fast their train was going. She let fade away the train's droning and clanking in her ears. She let go of feeling the train car and floor and seat vibrating. Then she fell asleep.

Gillian could remember her arrival with Hannah in Poplar Bluff and riding in Eban's beat up truck. When Hannah had opened the door to Granny's cabin, Gillian was sure she would be confined there for the rest of her life. She believed that seven months of freedom were all she had deserved. She had been punished for expecting too much. When that door closed behind her, she decided to give in to whatever made her need to forget. She had bowed to whatever it was that lay passive in her, that needed her to stop fighting.

Chapter 41

Dolores' letters in her hand now, Gillian felt the kitchen walls close in with smothering pressure. The stark, remembered events ached in her lungs. The past two months of amnesia had worked like a narcotic. She had refused to accept the truth about Jānis: He was dead. For months she had felt dead too. The cabin became suddenly tiny. Her pain had expanded and she was afraid she would shatter if she did not escape that cabin and fast. She would go to her room to get her coat, sanely. She would take deep breaths to keep herself calm. Holding Dolores' letters for fortitude, she got up from the table and moved back through the kitchen doorway to her bedroom.

As she was about to take her boots from the closet, Gillian smelled the cardinal's death for the first time. Overpowering and sweet, the odor was like bologna turned green after days in the hot sun. The smell immobilized her by his cage. Knowing the bird was dead, she was afraid of what he looked like. She went to her closet and rummaged for a box to put him in. His death smell permeated her clothing. She found a little white box with a lot of cotton and a costume jewelry brooch in it. About the size of a half dollar, the brooch had red and clear rhinestones glued in it. Gillian vaguely recalled her mother's giving her the cheap costume jewelry for Christmas. She threw the brooch back up on the closet shelf. The back of her throat ached because she was determined not to cry. More than anything else, Gillian was scared because she knew the bird must have been dead for some time. Her not realizing this meant she really couldn't be trusted. But with the cardinal dead, there was nothing left to love here.

Afraid to look inside the cardinal's cage, Gillian stopped a few feet short. The bird would be filthy. Tears fell below her chin to her sweater. She felt as if she were swimming and opening her eyes under rank water. She should get a cloth or Kleenex to pick him up with. No. She would put him in the box with her own bare hand. Something had broken his wing and killed him. It was not his fault she hadn't realized it until he had turned ugly like this. With a gentle glide of her fingers, she picked the cardinal up and held him in her palm. The bird didn't look so bad. Just very dry. Especially his open eyes. But death had made his face look mean, like a bitter little old man's face. His beak was slightly open. It was like a sinister laugh, captured forever as in a photograph. "Look what they've done to you," Gillian said. She cried some more as she stroked his neck feathers. He was cold. He was rigid as cardboard.

In the past, Gillian had envied birds their simple lives. They know hunger and then satisfy it, she had thought. They feel sleepy and then nap; they fly when they wish it and breed, and lose, their young. But these are just the birds we can see. She felt keen awareness now that other birds perish behind the scenes, that others suffer injury somewhere in the background and Nature most often obscures this, as if to dignify their journey back to nonexistence. She realized that if such creatures are aware of their impending fate, they cannot tell us. If they are then missed by others of their kind, we never can know this.

*It is we who are **self**-conscious*, Gillian thought now, *and this makes our suffering worse.* If her mind had let her understand more clearly, she might have realized that our much longer blossoming, and the much greater complexity of our existence, guarantees that none of us will emerge unscathed as each travels through her allotted lifetime. And yet, as with a bird's transient life, we also drop suffering into the background, behind our consciousness, as Nature does with its other creatures: beneath bushes, behind trees, in the forest, even at sea. We relate and then disband. We build up and then break down. We recall and then forget. We maintain but rarely thrive. Though we move forward in linear space, we carry with us our many wounds and scars.

Gillian slipped on her boots at the door of the cabin and thought about how oddly practical boots are. She buckled the belt of her coat and buttoned its wide lapels at the neck. She blew her nose before walking outside, onto a dusting of snow. *This is what it's like to be two people at once,* she thought. *One is practical and the other blubbers like a fool.* Then she realized for the first time that she was swinging the bamboo birdcage in her left hand. *You might as well make it a good one while you're at it,* she thought. *This isn't just some movie. This is death. Something beautiful and sweet has suffered a lot, and now it is dead. There is no honor in death.*

She walked toward the woods. She occasionally glanced behind her. This made some of her footprints go sideways like a turkey's. The cold air was sharp and clean in her nostrils. Now the cage felt heavy, but the little white box in her right hand felt lighter than a snowflake. At the edge of the woods behind the cabin, a hawthorn bush bore its long withered fruits. Dead leaves around the bottom of the shrub made the earth look softer than did the frozen, open ground. She began to dig with the heel of her boot. She kicked up snow and underbrush until she hit semi-frozen earth. Gillian knew she would have to find something else to dig with, and so she searched until she found a thick clublike branch with a point on one end. She began jabbing it into the earth under the hawthorn bush. She dug harder, grunting, her voice emerging in cries while her hands gripped the branch and stabbed and stabbed the ground. Tears shot straight out from her eyes now while the dirt broke away in hard little chunks and fell back into the hole she was digging. She slipped down to her knees to scoop the chunks out with her bare hands. It made her nails brown underneath, and the little clods crumbled down the front of her coat as she squatted on her heels.

By the time the hole was deep enough, Gillian had stopped crying. She wiped her nose on her coat sleeve and blew warm air on her hands. Then she put the little white box in the hole, and she pushed and scattered earth over it. She pressed her boot down to pack the dirt and, for several minutes, she looked at the impression her boot sole left. The outline of her footprint was soft. Inside her footprint, with a twig Gillian drew a heart, pierced by an arrow. Inside the heart she scratched GR + JD and wept quietly. She traced her lover's initials with her fingers before putting her gloves back on.

Gillian stood up. With neither anger nor bitterness, she began to pull the cage apart and separated its sides, roof, and floor into sections of three and four bars of bamboo. Her fingers stung. They were dark pink and stiff when she at last clutched all the pieces of the birdcage in her two hands and threw all of them out into the air. With her back to the woods, she watched the bamboo cage bars sail and zig zag in the icy wind. When they fell, they stuck at angles in the snow.

When Gillian turned to walk back to her mother's cabin now, she realized she felt better than she had in a long time.

Chapter 42

MID-MARCH 1950

Gillian stood before the oval mirror in her room. She had stopped just now to take an objective look at herself, for she was sure that changes in her would reflect in her face. She was no longer the wide-eyed young woman who had left Missouri less than a year before, when events seemed to occur at random. Today she peered directly into her own eyes for the first time. She held her head erect. This kept her hair out of her face for a change. She touched her fine cheekbones, which had become more prominent because of her weight loss during the past several months.

Reflected in the mirror, Gillian's hand looked larger than normal. Her fingers were thinner and the veins in her hands more pronounced. She found her veins fascinating, for she was now keenly aware that in their bluish hue something lived, moved, and replenished her. She remembered the texture and sweet pressure of her lover's mouth on hers. She touched her own lips. She relived the way, so many times, she and Jānis had kissed for what seemed hours. The way it had filled her, yet had left her hungry too.

When she resumed the chore of cleaning out her closet, she found a glossy red gift box from Macy's. It lay on top of a medium sized, sealed cardboard box on the closet floor. The red box seemed familiar, but she could not remember what was inside. Now she lifted off layers of white tissue paper and found the pale peach colored cashmere sweater Dolores had sent her for

Christmas. She pressed the sweater against her cheek and felt its rich softness on her skin. It was a slipover with a round collar and four mother of pearl buttons on the front. The enclosed card said,

X-mas, 1949
Dear Gillian,
   Something to go with your eyes and your beautiful skin. I'm jealous of how good I know you'll look in this.

   Love, Dolores
   P.S. Lorna helped me pick this out for you.

As Gillian's friend had promised, the sweater *was* soothing. It helped fortify her to open the other box, which she sensed contained some of her treasures from New York. She slid the box out of the closet and ripped the tape from across its flaps. There, right on top, was her kimono. Folded within the kimono was the beautiful ebony and mother of pearl cigarette holder from Levitsky's Treasure Trove. She expected suddenly to be flooded with memories, to re-experience the kimono's colors as messages of ineffable beauty and truth. Instead, the kimono's oranges, reds and blacks looked pale. They had not exactly faded; rather, she could not bridge the seeming chasm between her and the colors themselves. When she lifted the curtain of orange beads from the box and onto her lap, she felt nothing from them. She feared that her growth would require her to forego the luxury of feeling. To let go of the past … Did this mean she must give up its highest sensations? Or had her perception of the beads changed because the beads held no innate power after all?

   Gillian's time in the Village had conveyed her light years beyond her starting point in St. Louis. For seven precious months in New York, she had dared to believe she could be loved. No longer fearing disappointment, she had stopped holding herself back. In New York Gillian had learned to view life as an adventure. Even hilarity, absent in her childhood, came to her as if by magic. In her thoughts, revelations arose and enhanced her unfolding self-knowledge.

   When Gillian took *Trilby* from the box she finally understood why she had not been able to finish the book in New York. She couldn't participate in it because she had expected the words to make magic *for* her. Trilby's suffering had made Gillian stop reading after the first chapter. Left Bank Paris, 1890s. Greenwich Village, 1940s. Artists and foreigners ... so many, including Gillian, searching for *the* path to their destiny. They were all, perhaps, characters in this book but also real people in her life a few months ago. Her own life ...

Hannah stood in the doorway of Gillian's room. "I felt a draft," she said. "Why did you open that window?"

"You can close it," Gillian said as she took her alarm clock out of the box. "I was airing out my room." Her mother took a sidelong glance where the bamboo birdcage used to hang.

Hannah pulled the old black rocker to the center of the room and sat down. She faced her daughter and fiddled with the *faux* gold hoop in her left earlobe. "Well, I'm glad you finally got rid of that, that *thing*," she said. "And now seems like a good time to talk about whether you plan to stay or go."

Gillian wound the little alarm clock a little too tight while it ratcheted and clicked. "What time is it?"

Hannah looked sullen. She crossed her legs and said, "It's about four. Why?"

Gillian set the clock and then cupped it tightly in her hand. "Do you realize," she said, "you haven't called me by my name since I've been here? Except to shout at me about something. In fact, you haven't called me *anything*."

"What?"

"I mean, it's like you haven't acknowledged me."

"You haven't exactly been homey yourself." Hannah grasped the ends of the rocker's arms and said, "Look at you down there, sitting like a child with her toys. Then think about how I should treat you. And, by the way, you never call me your mother."

Gillian weighed the clock in her hand. "That's because you don't act like a mother."

"I guess this has been our little problem for years."

Gillian let down her guard and said, "Let's talk about it some more. Maybe things could change."

"I can never look at you without seeing your father," Hannah said, evenly.

"I didn't make Pop drink! And I didn't make my baby sister die either. You loved Lettie because you thought she was like you."

"She was perfect," Hannah said. "She died because he hated me."

257

"But what about *your* hate?" Gillian pointed at the mirror. "You don't love anyone but yourself."

Hannah stood up. "You—."

"I'm not finished," Gillian said. "And I'm not afraid of you anymore." But she *was* afraid of the way her mother's eyes glowed. "I used to believe it was my fault you didn't love me. That it was only me you didn't love. The truth is: You never loved anybody. And if you come any closer I'll throw this clock right through your face!"

Hannah let her arms back down to her sides. "You ungrateful little bitch. All you ever did was take."

"Oh yes. Take anything you'd give me. And you sure made me pay for it."

"By taking care of you until you were twenty. When you couldn't even get a decent job?"

"You almost won," Gillian said. "You almost kept me from finding love. I helped you do it though. I believed I could never be free of your awful world."

One hand on her hip, Hannah said, "You made it on your own real good. Yeah. You were loved. With fists!"

"You're wrong. I had friends. I found all the love I ever needed."

"When I saw you in that hospital," Hannah said, "your face looked just like I feel about you. You want me to love you. I want to be able to *respect* you."

Gillian fingered the face of her little clock. The effort she made to keep from crying now came from the same source as her anger. It twisted in her stomach. But her voice was soft when she said to her mother, "I feel sorry for you."

"Feel sorry for *yourself.*"

Numbness spread from Gillian's feet up her tense legs. "It was my life," she said through clenched teeth.

"Except you made a fine mess of that too," Hannah said.

Gillian's feelings galvanized. "Let's do keep talking," she said, "because I got a feeling that when we're finished, you're never gonna be able to hurt me again."

Hannah came nearer and stood in front of the oval mirror. "You would not do nothing to me," she said, her hands opening, closing.

"No? But I'll tell you what I want to do." She waited to see if her mother would strike her.

Hannah chose this moment to look at her own reflection in the mirror. Gazing, as always, into her own eyes she said, "I could have had him, you know."

"Who?"

Now Hannah's eyes fixed on her daughter's. "Your boyfriend."

Gillian couldn't believe what her mother had just said. Though Hannah's lips moved, the sound that roared in Gillian's head drowned out whatever words her mother spoke now. Some sap like primal energy shot up through Gillian's feet to the top of her head like molten silver. For a time, she was aware only of how her head throbbed. Then she felt the alarm clock burn, heavy, in her hand. Her mother's face contorted, and Gillian felt her own rage building almost beyond her control. In this split second she made a righteous decision. Supported by all she knew was right, Gillian hurled the clock like a grenade at her mother's reflection in the mirror.

The image of Hannah's face blew apart from the center outward, shattered into jagged pieces that flew out from the mirror's frame. Slivers landed and shone on the floor of her room, just beyond the farthest strand of her orange beads.

Hannah's face went as white as a ringed, hazy moon.

How small Hannah looked to Gillian now. Laughing until tears streamed down her cheeks, she said, "I know one thing I've learned. I didn't inherit it, this violence inside."

"... that you got from your father," Hannah murmured.

"Bull!" Gillian shouted. She wiped her wet cheeks on the backs of her hands.

Hannah backed away a little and pointed at the shards of mirror glass on the floor. "That is what's inside you."

"No," Gillian said. "I found out in New York that I'm quite a person. I found out that my world is much better than yours. And the funny thing is, I met people in New York also belong in my world. I learned that pain is supposed to make us grow. Some of us must *earn* who we are, but we shouldn't have to earn love the same way. Knowing this, I feel sorry for you."

"Save it," Hannah said as she walked away.

"And you *will* give me the rest of my friends' letters," Gillian said. She followed her mother as far as the threshold of her room. Shortly after, she heard the muffled click that meant Hannah's bedroom door had closed.

Chapter 43

Gillian wore the cashmere sweater Dolores had mailed to her. She sat at her mother's kitchen table. She held a blue ink fountain pen above a tablet of lined yellow paper. While writing this first letter to Dolores, Gillian felt exhilarated. Her thoughts were about to move through her fingers to pages that would travel more than a thousand miles and come to life again when Dolores read them. This letter was Gillian's act of commitment.

April 7, 1950
Dear Dolores,

I am wearing the peach sweater as I write this to you. I think of you holding this letter and scolding me for not writing back to you sooner. (You've always been so hard on me!) But I have excuses, like always. First, you know I've been a real mess. It's been scary, and I'm so stubborn. I feel like I've been groping my way along some road through a black fog & missing all the signs that could have helped me find my way. I did it to myself. But I feel much better now. Honest!

Reading your letters helped me a lot, though I didn't see them until a few weeks ago. (My mother hid them from me. All of them. First I believed she was protecting me. Now I know she was trying to keep your love from me.) I treasure each and every one of them because they show how much you care. And how well you know me. It's still so hard, though, to think of New York. And especially Janis. I believe he did love me. And I know he tried to help me understand the most important things. Like, I'm not dumb. In fact, I know I'm very smart. Maybe that's been my problem all along. See how cocky I've become?

I am not sure I have a home anymore. I don't want to stay here anyway. I know you'll say I can have a home with you, but wherever my new home will be, I'll have to make it for myself eventually. You know what I mean. It's just so clear that I don't know how to love people right. I mean, not for the right reasons. Someday I'm going to be a great person. Someday I'm going to be able to see things clearly right off, instead of messing around and getting myself massacred (sp.?). There should be other ways of learning too, though I know things probably won't get much easier.

But I am much stronger now! You'll see that right away when we're together again. We'll drink champagne (not beer! Ha!) and probably cry, and laugh a lot too. By then maybe I can look you right in your eyes and tell you how much you mean to me. Maybe you can even teach me how to be an odalisque. Maybe I can get a job as a high fashion seamstress. Will you please keep holding on to me until then?

Love, Gillian

Gillian stamped the envelope but left it unsealed because she wanted to read it again before the postman, Homer Beals, came by. Earlier that morning, when Eban had pulled up in his pickup truck to give Hannah a lift to town, neither Eban nor Hannah had spoken. Gillian knew she and her mother both recognized, and accepted, a lifetime of losses. Naming this broke their only tie, for blood alone could not convey their hearts to each other. The finality of Hannah's loss would never again be Gillian's, for Gillian had found herself. And freedom.

When Gillian stepped down from the cabin step, something new in the Spring air made her senses seem to skate on tiny, clean edges. She could feel sap stir in the veins of tree trunks she touched. After creeping its slow thaw, the icy edge of wind had abruptly fallen away, had invited a warmth that she perceived as aroma. Mild fragrances hovered in the woods beneath the smell of hickory smoke rising from small chimneys. The feeling of ascending tree sap found her again and again, out of the forest, and drew her eyes to color: purple crocuses, three of them, sprouted through a patch of snow. Their stalks were as sturdy as summer vegetables. Purple pioneers, spring's first low trumpets in the born again sun.

Gillian also witnessed trees reaching up to an achingly blue sky. She could feel the tips of their branches tingle where leaf buds were about to form. *Now they will be free again*, she thought. *The sun will free them all.* These yellow rays of sunlight were like lines pushing out from the sun she had seen on the Latvian crest at Marija's flat. They meant death was not an ending, because the sun would always make things new again. And this sun above her now was only a reflection of the real one, the one of heat and light that was inside every living thing. The sun that can never be extinguished.

Gillian emerged from the woods and headed over bumpy terrain to the road. After she had climbed a steep embankment, she stood on the road as she waited for Homer's dinged up postal truck. She watched melting ice trickle through quartz pebbles at the side of the road and selected an opaque, round stone shaped like a small egg. She warmed the stone in her hand. She decided to keep it for luck. From one of her big coat pockets she pulled the cigarette holder from Levitsky's Treasure Trove and inserted a cigarette from the pack of Chesterfields the kind porter had given her months before. In her other pocket, she found the box of kitchen matches she swiped on her way out the door of her mother's cabin. Lighting one of the cigarettes reminded her of the good times she had in the Village. The cigarette tasted stale, but inhaling the smoke satisfied her craving.

The three purple crocuses she had seen moments before, the perfection of triangles, shot through her awareness. A few months ago, she had been one of three. Two other people's lives had touched hers in a symmetry of pain. Jānis was gone, but the triangle still held together because what he had given her would remain alive in her. Dolores, too, leaned securely at Gillian's side. The *quality* of Dolores' fondness also maintained Gillian's life. Someday, soon perhaps, they would be able to give to each other again.

Gillian had a talent for growth and courage enough to sustain that growth. By the sheer grace of her being, she had conquered impressive odds. Leaving St. Louis those many months ago had been a plunge into the abyss. Having had so little knowledge about what her new life in New York would be, she still threw herself headlong into it.

Gillian held her unsealed letter to Dolores as if it were a sacred relic, pulled the pale yellow lined paper out of its envelope and unfolded it. Its pages trembled in her hand like butterfly wings for, like Spring, the letter was both an ending and a beginning. She stood by the road and read her letter one more time, aloud.

Chapter 44

HARRY'S BAR: LATE APRIL 1950

Gillian did go back to New York. Having learned from Jānis how to be mysterious, she sent a cryptic telegram to Dolores on April 26th:

Dolores. Stop. Will see you at Harry's in AM on April 28th. Stop. Don't go to Penn Sta. Stop. Don't stop loving Gillian. Stop.

In Harry's bar at 9:00 a.m. Dolores, Kārlis, Atis, and Mabel drank Mai Tais while they waited for Gillian. Pēteris was late. Even Joe Capetti, laundromat owner, and his wife Louisa were there. Both looked a bit out of place but excited. They sat at a table just inside the green door, which Harry had risked leaving open for Gillian. Only devotion could have inspired Gillian's friends to be at Harry's that early. Harry had posted a sign that his bar was closed. Mabel Levitsky had also closed her shop. The Latvians looked happy. They wore their native tunics and explained that their attire had something to do with their pagan "rites of spring". In this spirit, Harry had agreed to wear a crown of flowers on his balding head.

The purple and yellow crêpe paper ribbons that Atis had hung from the ceiling looked like radioactive seaweed. Kārlis lifted his glass and said: "Purple and yellow are royal colors. Spiritual too."

"Yeah, yeah." Mabel said.

Harry offered that when he looked at the crêpe paper, "some kind of combustion of the eyes" happened. Even in this heat, Harry refused to unbutton his white dress shirt or to roll up his sleeves. He said he didn't want to "look like a slob" when Gillian walked in. Never mind that his shirt was drenched with sweat from his neck to his navel.

Mabel peered deeply into her almost empty glass and muttered: "Prit-ty, pritty colors." Behind Mabel, on black a royal blue velvet cloth, lay Jānis' sheathed saber, which Mabel pondered between chugs of her Mai Tai. It was a Latvian officer's saber. The black, seasoned leather scabbard was plain, and a little strap was affixed with two delicate bronze loops to make a handle. However, the saber's hilt was backed with a metal cross guard, cast with an ornate Latvian coat of arms. Thin, black leather strips were wound tightly around the handgrip of the saber.

Dolores pleaded: "When Gillian gets here, let's not be morbid, okay?" Even to Dolores, her "okay" sounded like Yiddish. "She might be kind of shaky from her trip," she added.

Like cartoon buzzards, Gillian's friends peered at the green door of Harry's Bar all morning. Conversation was tepid. They all just kept drinking and were plastered by Noon.

Ever the stoic, Kārlis leaned against the bar. "Doh-loh-rees," Kārlis said, "let me speak about my duty in this matter. I am the right hand of Jānis. You see the saber of Jānis?" He patted the top of his trouser zipper and added, "After Jānis died, this too becomes his saber."

"Yes," Atis said. "In Latvia there is a custom. The righthand man goes to the dead man's woman to give her his 'saber'. It is Kārlis' right!"

Red faced, Mabel shouted: "All sabers will remain sheathed or I'll chop them off myself!"

Everyone laughed except Dolores, who tried not to smile. "You guys never change," she said.

Kārlis hugged Dolores and said: "Do not worry. I won't take duty literal." Then Kārlis lifted up Jānis' saber and Harry hid it in his office.

"You think Gillian will be okay?" Dolores asked Kārlis.

Just then a taxi driver appeared and dumped one string-tied cardboard box and one ratty cloth suitcase just inside the door. Dolores clung to the top of a chair. Mabel looked dazed but hopeful. Kārlis and Atis staged themselves at their "American home" table. They giggled together like children.

"Everyone stay where you are!" Harry commanded. "I want Gillian to feel like it's just the way it was before she left."

Then Gillian appeared in the doorway. She carried her long gray coat over one arm and brushed back her damp bangs. "Hi," she said shyly. "Here I am."

At that, except for Mabel, they all rushed over to smother Gillian with affection. In the process, Gillian dropped her coat on the floor. Her friends brought her to one of the bar stools. After Harry stopped hugging Gillian, he handed her a pitcher of Mai Tais ... but he begged her not to drink it all.

Gillian downed her first Mai Tai with the gusto of a backwoodsman. Radiant with her friends' welcome, she bent down at Mabel's chair. "Seeing you there sure makes me feel good," she said.

Mabel's guard was down. The corners of her mouth crept up. "I been praying for you every day," she said. She gave Gillian a little peck on the cheek.

"I always felt your heart of gold," Gillian said to Mabel.

Mabel turned quickly away. "Now, now," she said.

Gillian felt like a princess at her first grand ball. "Let me look at all of you," she said. She took Dolores' hand and Harry's at the same time. She focused on Dolores, who was crying. Then she embraced her friend and whispered: "Thank you for all you did for me."

"Welcome home, Dear," Dolores said. She still held Gillian's hand. "I can't let go of you," she added.

Atis dabbed his moist eyes with a cocktail napkin and merely said, "Oh, Gee-lee-ann."

"Where's Pēteris?" Gillian asked.

"Maybe he has a headache?" Kārlis said, smiling. "But he said to tell how much he looks forward to—."

Gillian interrupted: "How're are things going with him and Lilija?"

Kārlis and Atis looked at each other. "Oh," Kārlis said. "Peteris and *Dārta* are now together."

"How *did* you break free from Hillbilly Land?" Dolores asked. "Any trouble with *Brunhild* about your leaving?"

"You mean my mother," Gillian answered. It was a statement.

Dolores persisted: "Where did you get the train money? Is that stuff by the door all you brought with you?"

Gillian left Dolores' questions unanswered. She had learned from Jānis that leaving questions unanswered heightened *longing to know*. She turned to everyone else in Harry's Bar: "I have presents for all of you. Now don't look down on them just because they came from Missouri. I slaved at Connie Shop long hours to pay for them."

Dolores lifted one eyebrow. "'Connie Shop'?"

"Don't be a snob," Gillian said. "They sell Marquise, Jacqueline, Connie Natural Poise clothing, the latest Paris fashion … and Buster Brown Shoes." Her laughter was bounteous.

Dolores teased Gillian: "In Poplar Bluff?"

"In Poplar Bluff," Gillian said. She then retrieved the wrapped cardboard box from beside the green door and put it on the bar top.

Kārlis whispered something to Atis, and Kārlis went back with Harry to his office without Gillian's noticing.

"How *are* you?" Dolores insisted. "I *can* see that you look self-contained. And more gorgeous than ever."

"I'm back here with you all. What does that tell you?"

"You sound like Jānis," Dolores said, "and I'll need to ponder that."

"That you're pretty gutsy," Mabel retorted from her Mai Tai haze.

"That I'm free now," Gillian answered.

Dolores smiled. "It tells me that you love us," she said, "and you finally accept that we love you."

"I would have gone through hell just to see you again," Gillian said. "In fact, I *have* been 'round the bend' a few times since I left."

"You're the same," Mabel said, "and yet you're not."

Kārlis hurried out of Harry's office. He held something behind his back. He whispered to Dolores, "Tell her to keep her eyes closed."

"Yes, Kārlis," Dolores said.

Atis kissed the top of Gillian's head. "I brought these for you." It was a bottle of champagne and eleven daffodils.

Behind his back, Kārlis held Jānis' saber, which was pointed at the floor.

"You can have your job back if you want," Harry said to Gillian. He handed her a blue envelope that smelled of Mennen Skin Bracer. "Here's two weeks' pay in advance and a little extra to get you back on your feet."

Gillian pressed the envelope against her cheek.

Mabel gave Gillian a gift certificate, "good for *any* item in Levitsky's Treasure Trove." Her careful hand lettering now bore booze stains from the morning's celebration. "Even the 1945 Bernina sewing machine," Mabel added. "*You* know: the portable zigzag one."

Gillian felt so excited that she could hardly breathe. *A Bernina*, she thought. *The zigzag with a free arm.* "My *future* ... here I come!" she shouted. She hugged an embarrassed but happy Mabel.

From behind the bar, Dolores pulled out a white gift box from Gimbel's. "Here, my friend," she said. "Maybe this will help you remember me on *my* birthday next year."

Gillian opened the box and held up the pale yellow dress and white sandals that Dolores had bought her. They were the latest in summer wear. "Boy, do I need clothes!" Gillian said. "I had to leave so much behind."

"But I still have a lot of your things, including clothing," Dolores said. "For your information, your stuff has been taking up half my flat. I'm holding them for ransom."

"My Degas? My loveseat?" Gillian asked.

Dolores nodded. "Made my flat look a little like Levitsky's Treasure Trove. No offense, Mabel."

Embracing her friend, Gillian whispered: "I owe you a thousand apologies," she said, "and I have so much to share with you." Her expression held a question that showed no confusion. In fact, the look in Gillian's eyes made Dolores do a double take.

Just then, Pēteris and Dārta showed up. They looked like siblings, as lovers often do. They were disheveled and rather flushed. "Hey!" Pēteris shouted. He pointed at Gillian. "Here is the girl!" He looked miraculously healthy. He did not cough once. "I mean ... woman"

"Haah-ee," Dārta said. "Too bad about Jānis. Oops ... *mana kļūda žēl.*" She hid her face in Pēteris' shoulder. Her sandy blonde hair was braided with red ribbons. She wore a sweet white, puffy dress embroidered with rosy pink flowers.

Pēteris consoled Dārta and actually smiled. "I will hug you," Pēteris said to Gillian. "There. Now let us dance, Dārta."

"I hope you *oyslenders* ain't gonna sing too," Mabel said. As if to prepare for the worst, Mabel put one hand over the ear closest to the group.

Harry put quarters in the jukebox and punched some buttons.

"But I want you to open the gifts I brought you," Gillian protested.

"We've been waiting for you all morning, young lady," Harry said, "and now we're gonna dance."

The easygoing "*C'est Si Bon*," with Yves Montand and Bob Costella's Orchestra, began to play. When the tune's chorus started, everyone in the bar joined in with accents that revealed the boroughs, or countries, of their upbringing. Dolores, of course, trilled the Parisian "r's" and intoned the French nasals with perfection:

> *C'est si bon*
> *De partir n'importe où,*
> *Bras-dessus, bras-dessous,*
> *En chantant des chansons.*

"See? Yves Montand sings about singing songs," Atis said. "We want to sing."

Now Mabel held her forehead. "I just knew it," she murmured.

"Oh, come on, Mabel," Harry said. "You haven't cracked your shell since you were what? Seventeen?"

Mabel smiley-scowled. "So you knew me when I was seventeen."

"I can tell," Harry said gently. He went over to Mabel, took her loosely in his arms and tried to dance with her.

Mabel moved like an iron girder being guided by a crane across a construction site. "Take it easy, Pal," she said. "I ain't gone this fast since I ran down the aisle at my wedding."

Joe and Louisa Capetti got up from their table and began to dance. When Joe twirled Louisa in a little circle, she laughed with delight. "It's been a long time, lover boy," she said to her husband.

Pēteris and Dārta were in their own world. Dancing together as one, they looked like they had smoked something besides cigarettes.

Atis picked Dolores up from her bar stool as if she were a ham sandwich. However, he turned out to be a smooth dancer, at least for someone who *waltzed* to the voice of Rosemary Clooney singing "If I Knew You Were Coming I'd Have Baked a Cake." Dolores stepped on Atis' shoe only once, and that was when Atis made Dolores turn so quickly that she almost collided with the jukebox.

Kārlis chose this odd moment to give Gillian Jānis' saber. From the background of this noise and laughter and drunkenness, Kārlis had walked quietly up to her. He said something audible only to Gillian while Atis whirled Dolores around the floor. "We sent Jānis Dieviņš home," he said.

Gillian stiffened. Kārlis presented Jānis' sheathed saber to her. She was surprised at how plain it was. Though the saber was lightweight, she lifted it out of its pencil thin scabbard like Arthur pulling Excalibur out of the stone. Kārlis looked bedazzled. When he kissed Gillian's hand, she noticed something in his eyes she had not previously seen: adoration. And then he pressed something into her hand. It was the photo booth picture, from Coney Island, of Gillian and Jānis laughing. Kārlis had mounted it in a tiny silver frame.

Kārlis' eyes grew moist when he said: "Jānis Dieviņš would want you to remember him this way"

Before Gillian could respond, Atis rushed over to the jukebox and unplugged it. He had nearly dropped Dolores on the floor. Then, puffing from exertion, Atis got a shot glass from behind the bar, poured whiskey into it and gave it to Gillian. "Drink it!" he commanded. "Drink it down."

Now Dolores was at Gillian's side. "You know you want to," she said to her friend.

After Gillian quaffed the whiskey in one gulp, the Latvians shouted "Break it! Break it! Break it!" Dārta whispered it, Pēteris and Atis bellowed it, and Kārlis sang it like a love song.

A small crowd of passersby had begun to gather outside the green door of Harry's Bar. High from the springtime warmth and what they were witnessing, they could no longer bear Harry's "Closed for Private Party" sign. All rushed in, demanding liquor and a chance to join the party.

Mabel and Harry encouraged Gillian to break the glass. "*Mazel tov!*" Mabel shouted.

The party crashers joined the *mêlée*: "Break it! Break it! Break it!" they shouted while Dolores waited to see what Gillian would do.

One of the "intruders" plugged the jukebox back in. It seemed to cough and, after a pause filled with static, began to play last year's tune: "So in Love." The Latvians formed a little tableau and the bar became quiet, except for the jukebox.

At first, longing for Jānis, Gillian let herself miss him. Then she smiled at Pēteris and said: "It's your turn to be in love."

"Hey!" one of the crowd yelled. "Get that mush off the box!"

"Shut up, punks," Harry said, and Patti Page sang on.

"Don't snap your cap, man," one of the outsiders said to Harry.

Gillian grasped Jānis' saber handle in one hand and gripped the shot glass in the other.

"Break it, break it," Kārlis sang.

"Do it! Do it!" everyone shouted.

"You know you want to," Dolores said, with an inviting twinkle of *esprit*.

Then Gillian let the shot glass drop to the floor and stomped down on it in one clean, hard motion.